GRAY
WOLF

A NOVEL OF THE WEST

TWO BLANKETS · VOLUME TWO

GRAY WOLF

A NOVEL OF THE WEST

R.L. ADARE

TIREE
PRESS

an imprint of
THE OGHMA PRESS

OGHMA

CREATIVE MEDIA

Bentonville, Arkansas • Los Angeles, California
www.oghmacreative.com

Library of Congress Cataloging-in-Publication Data

Names: Adare, R.L, author.
Title: Gray Wolf/R.L. Adare | Two Blankets #2
Description: First Edition. | Bentonville: Tiree, 2019.
Identifiers: LCCN: 2019942407 | ISBN: 978-1-63373-527-9 (hardcover) |
ISBN: 978-1-63373-528-6 (trade paperback) | ISBN: 978-1-63373-529-3 (eBook)
Subjects: | BISAC: FICTION/Thrillers/Historical | FICTION/Westerns |
FICTION/Historical
LC record available at: https://lccn.loc.gov/2019942407

Tiree Press trade paperback edition May, 2022

Jacket art by Venessa Cerasale
Jacket & Interior Design by Casey W. Cowan
Editing by Dennis Doty

Published by Tiree Press, an imprint of The Oghma Press, a subsidiary of The Oghma Book Group.

This novel is dedicated to those forgotten girls and women whose strength and valor helped make the old West into what it is today.

ACKNOWLEDGEMENTS

M Y ETERNAL THANKS for this novel go out to my two supportive beta readers, Kathy Ann Trueman and Kerri O'Donnell, PhD without whose assistance this book would never have been written in its present form. I also want to thank my editor, Dennis W. Doty whose skill shaped this book. As well, immense thanks to Oghma Creative Media, Casey W. Cowan, its CEO and guiding light, and Venessa Cerasale who painted the cover. Thank you all.

GLOSSARY

NEZ PERCE

Nch'i-wána: The great river, The Columbia River.

Nimi'ipuu: The Real People, the Nez Perce.

CHINOOK JARGON OR TRADE LANGUAGE

busi: pudendum.

camas: a starchy bulb eaten by many different tribes and the white pioneers, creates gaseous condition when undercooked.

cultus: weak, useless, small, frequently used in the negative as in cultus whiteman, useless white man, but used also as a positive as in cultus potlatch, a free gift.

dentalium: shell used as jewelry as well as used as a money trade item.

mamook: to do, but also an obscenity for copulate as in "to do someone."

mistshimus: slave.

nika: mine.

potlatch: gift, gift giving ceremony.

quamash: synonym for camas, a bulb eaten for its starch, leads to gas when undercooked.

tatoosh: breasts.

tenino: vulva, pudenda.

Tyee: local clan leader of Chinook, they had no overall chief.

whiteman(s): used as a referent to Caucasians.

Wimahl: the Columbia River, the great river.

wootlat: penis.

GRAY WOLF

A NOVEL OF THE WEST

MARSHALL'S VICTORY

CHAPTER I
APRIL AND MAY, 1856

S O, YOU FINALLY decided to come back and take care of your husband? Lately, you spend more time with your clan than you do with me." Marshall threw down his work on the counter upon Two Blankets'ss entry into the longhouse.

"When you married me, husband Marshall, you became Chinook. I thought, at the time, you meant it. The *Tyee* did, as well. Now, all know it was just an act to get what you wanted, this trading post."

Marshall laughed. "Well, it sure took you Indians long enough to figure that out. I thought the Chinook were supposed to be such mighty traders. No one could get the best of them. You ain't so hot now, are you?"

"You have lost the Bent Creek trade. That has to hurt a bit."

"It did a little, in the beginning, but it's more than made up for by the steamer trade. You see how every steamer stops here." Marshall's voice got louder. "That's bound to get stronger when they find out I warned the U.S. Cavalry about the massacre coming up at the Cascades."

"I would be a bit quieter bragging on that score, honored husband Marshall. You are only one whiteman in a Chinook village of ninety or so."

"I ain't afraid of them savages." He took down his Mississippi Rifle from where it hung and took the several steps to the doorway. He pushed open the flap with the rifle barrel and peeked outside. "Ain't none of those thieves about."

"Mayhap you just cannot see them, mayhap they are not there. Caution is still the better course, in this savage's opinion."

"I ain't no fucking coward. Only thing they respect is this," Marshall slapped his musket.

The next day the *Belle* came steaming upriver. She blew her whistle twice as she approached. Two Blankets was feeding the chickens and picking up eggs. She looked up.

Marshall, working nearby, stopped and said, "You will see, presently, what kind of trader I am."

The others in the Bent Creek Clan heard the whistle as well. To Two Blankets surprise, they all ran with weapons in hand for their canoes. First one then another pushed out into the water and began paddling upriver toward Marshall Johnston's Landing. Soon there were eight or ten canoes, including the *Tyee's*, all sixty feet of it, in a line in front of Marshall's makeshift dock.

"They can't do that. They can't stop the steamboat from landing here."

"It is still their land, husband Marshall," Two Blankets said, "I believe they can."

"We'll see about this."

Marshall got his rifle from the longhouse and ran down to his own canoe. He paddled out to confront the Bent Creek Clan. The line of Chinook canoes opened to allow him to pass. The captain came down to the main deck.

The *Tyee* stood in the bow of his canoe and spoke, "This is Bent Creek Clan land and ours to decide who may stop here. Until June twenty-fifth of this year, it is our decision. This piece of paper, this treaty says so. Your government says so."

"That ain't right," said Marshall. "I got cargo on board."

The *Tyee* handed the captain a piece of paper. He read it over carefully and then read it again. He passed it back.

"He is correct, Mr. Johnston. This paper guarantees the sovereignty of the Chinook Nation over their land until they move by June 25, 1856. They cannot stop traffic from going through their lands on legitimate business elsewhere, but I got no legitimate business anywhere on this land."

"But what about my cargo? My trade?"

"You may take what you can in your canoe. That's between you and the Bent Creek Chinook. You can leave written instructions with my purser when we come back downriver on what to do with your cargo when we get back to Portland. You will have to pay shipping both ways."

"You can't deliver, and I got to pay shipping? And storage when it gets back to Portland?"

"Ain't no free rides in this country. You should know that, Mr. Johnston."

"All right. Give me my newspapers and my whiskey. I may have to take a ride into Portland on your downriver trip. I can't believe you are treating me this way after I risked everything to warn you and the U.S. Cavalry about the massacre."

Heads turned among the natives, and faces took on an implacable look of dislike upon this mention. Many may have heard of Marshall's involvement before. Hearing it secondhand, and hearing the man openly talking about it, were two different things to their minds.

"You are always welcome on the *Belle,* Mr. Johnston. I'd thank you if you'd pipe down on the massacre talk. The *Mary* had three men injured in that event. We don't want to repeat it." Two men brought a bundle of newspapers and two cases of whiskey. "Sign here for the delivery, Mr. Johnston." Marshall signed then got back into his canoe and paddled slowly through the gap in the Bent Creek canoes.

"Goddamn weasel captain. After all I done for him," Marshall said on his return. "Now, I gotta go into Portland to see my factor and shippers about storing my goods there, maybe go to the bank to see about getting a loan to tide me over until June twenty-fifth when I don't have to deal with you people no longer. I already can't make the payments on the steam-powered sawmill. Was depending on trade to tide me over."

"Come inside, please, husband Marshall, I will prepare you some eggs for breakfast."

"Ain't we got anything else? I'm sick of eggs for breakfast and dinner every day," Marshall said as he followed her into the longhouse, lugging the two cases of whiskey pints.

"We are out of bacon and potatoes, but we have lots of eggs," she said cheerfully. "Or, I'm sure I could get some salmon from the Bent Creek Clan."

Marshall pulled the cork from the whiskey bottle and spit it out. "No, make it eggs." He took a long swig. "Leastwise, I still got whiskey."

"I will fix you eight eggs since we don't have anything else. You must keep up your strength, husband."

When he finally finished eating the last egg on his plate, he said, "I see another egg I'm going to puke."

"No more eggs until dinner, husband Marshall. Now I must go and do our share of work for the clan. I will be back in time to cook for you this evening." She took off her whiteman's dress and donned her cape.

At Stinging Nettle's she sat down and began immediately to work. After a bit Stinging Nettle said, "Let us cease a bit in our labors and have tea, *Nika.*" Stinging Nettle got up and returned with a stone bowl with herbs within. She took hot rocks from the fire and dropped them in followed by water. The water steamed when it hit the stones. Two Blankets watched the steam form above the tea, to be whisked away by the morning breeze. When it had steeped for a few minutes, Stinging Nettle dipped a carved wooden ladle into the pot and poured a cup for Two Blankets and herself.

Two Blankets sipped her tea. The peppermint taste she was familiar with. "What is the other herb in this tea Stinging Nettle? I like it, but I do not recognize it."

"The whitemans call it anise. It has medicinal value, including treatment for the bleeding cramps, for digestive issues, and for cough. I like it for just the taste. I got some at last year's trading at The Dalles."

"I like it. I have learned so much from you."

"Ah, well, then pay for your bargain, *Nika.* How is your husband, Marshall, taking all this?" She waved her hand at the canoes pulled up on the beach.

"I should never gossip about a true Bent Creek Clan member, I hope you know that. When husband Marshall asks, I try to tell him the general feeling in the clan."

"I understand, *Nika.* But we all know how you feel about your husband."

"Yes, husband Marshall is not clan and not a true husband to me. And he is no warrior. He was upset when the steamboat was not allowed to land his cargo."

Stinging Nettle wafted the odor of the tea under her nose and breathed it in. "Indeed. Go on."

"Perhaps you already knew he reported on the warriors from the Bent Creek Clan going to support the attack. He has been loud enough about it."

"Yes, I had heard something about that."

"He is upset that he does not get the warrior's song for that in his newspapers and such. He says he must go to Portland to see his factors, I do not know this word, factors."

"Ah. I think in whiteman's language it means business agent. But one who sometimes gets a share of the business for the work he does, especially financial assistance."

"Oh, all right. Well, these factors need to be talked with in person. He has to see about storing his cargo if the boats cannot deliver it and may have to see a banker about extending his loan. Again, I don't know what this means."

"The whitemans have a way of making things complicated. It would be like our *Tyee* seeking help from another *Tyee* if we did not have enough food to last the winter. This other *Tyee* might give us the food, trusting our *Tyee* to make payment later in trade. Now the trade terms would favor the other *Tyee* because ours had to ask."

"That would be a difficult position to bargain from."

"Yes," Stinging Nettle said. "All the elements of strength go to the other *Tyee*."

"And he would demand a hard bargain in return?"

"Yes, maybe two salmon for every salmon given. Now, imagine if we had another bad year, how hard it would be for our *Tyee* to go and say he could not pay, that he needed more time? Perhaps even that he needed more salmon to get through a second winter?"

"How horrible," Two Blankets said.

"I can think of only one time that it happened. A *Tyee* had to go and serve the other for two years to pay him back. The *Tyee* was a broken man when he returned to his clan, but he did it to protect his word and his honor."

"I have heard how the whitemans count money as honor," Two Blankets said. "If you do not pay, they come and take everything a man has."

"Yes, I can quite understand the thing they call money as a substitute for goods. We use the dentalium shells in much the same way. It is said that among certain tribes you can buy a horse for a five-foot string of dentalium shells."

"Truly?" Two Blankets had grown so used to the wealthy title born and their dentalium shell chokers she hadn't realized how much wealth they were wearing upon their bodies.

"Yes, truly. That may be where the shells are rarer than they are here, and perhaps a horse is cheaper. But the principle remains."

"That may be, Stinging Nettle, but the whitemans count money as honor."

"It is somewhat different, but have you not heard it said, 'We have a wise and honorable *Tyee*. He has many *dentalia?* Look how rich he is.'"

"I have heard something like."

"So, we also count wealth as a sign of honor."

"Mayhap, but our *Tyee* also bargains fairly and honors his word, even when it costs him dearly."

"That is true. I only point out similarities. The whitemans carry their trades into the area we would consider war and think little of it. That line is not so distinct for them."

Two Blankets mulled over this thought. "Even in war, they know no limits, Stinging Nettle. The *Nimi'ipuu,* my original tribe, has been at war with those the whitemans call the Blackfeet for a very long time. Lifetimes perhaps. Yet we do not seek to wipe them out completely and take their territory."

Stinging Nettle put her cup down. "Truly? Because you will not or because you cannot?"

Two Blankets began to answer and then stopped to ponder Stinging Nettle's question. "You mean if we had *cultus* whiteman's weapons and they did not?"

"Now you are thinking."

"Perhaps then we would kill them all or make war slaves of them and adopt the children and women into our tribe."

"It might be so. Do you know where the *Nimi'ipuu* came from originally?"

"Always they have ranged the same lands," Two Blankets said automatically.

"Our stories say different. They say the *Nimi'ipuu* came from the lands the whitemans call Canada. Many tens of lifetimes of summers ago they came down and pushed out the tribes that occupied the land they call their own. Now, no one remembers the names of those other tribes."

"I never thought in those terms, in tens of lifetimes."

"Even the Chinook who have lived on the *Wimahl* for these many tens of lifetimes were not the first to live here. We were not the original people here. Only the ancients, like Bone Rattler, speak of such things, but when she speaks there is truth to it."

"That may be, Stinging Nettle. I still hold that the whitemans are different. We live in balance with the earth. They only see it as something to make money from."

"It is true they do not have the same reverence for the earth as we do. Perhaps this is a lesson we have learned that they have not. Remember the day of the Great Hunt?"

"Yes, I do. We killed many animals in that hunt."

"We did. And we used every part of each animal we killed that day. We apologized to the spirits as well. It is told in the very ancient stories that Bone Rattler knows, stories that go back before the Chinook and the *Nimi'ip-uu* were here, that there were once huge creatures that roamed this place, creatures three or four times as tall as the largest buffalo."

"I have heard such but only as tales to frighten children."

"Once, the tales say, they existed here in numbers as many as the buffalo. The people at that time would have huge great hunts and burn the prairie. They would run the animals off cliffs in hundreds. Then they would take only the prime parts of the meat to eat and smoke for winter."

"Why would they do such a foolish thing?" Two Blankets was appalled at such waste and more so because she thought she already knew the answer.

"Because, so the tales say, they thought there would always be more. They could not imagine a time when the buffalo was the largest creature they could hunt."

"What happened to these creatures?"

"They are gone from the earth. But I once saw a set of tusks at The Dalles. Someone had dug them up. They were easily three times the arm span of the tallest warrior and curved up to points. The tales say the creatures carried these like the elk wears his antlers but in front of him. I do not know, but I can vouch for their size and that no creature today is large enough to carry such horns."

They were silent for a time. This was a great piece of knowledge to digest. "So, you are saying, Stinging Nettle, that the way we honor each animal killed now—" Two Blankets was unable to complete the thought.

"The way we honor the small animals we work very hard to kill now, and use every part as we should was learned, and learned very painfully, after we had killed the great beasts of the time through our greed."

"That is a sad thought, Stinging Nettle, and a little heartening as well. Perhaps the whitemans will learn this lesson as well."

"Mayhap they will, Two Blankets. They have the chance to learn. But I suspect it will be many lifetimes after you and I have passed from this earth before they do—if they learn it at all."

Two Blankets returned to Marshall Johnston's Landing in the midafternoon.

"So, you are goddamned back I see," Marshall began his usual complaint about the time she spent with the clan.

"Yes, husband Marshall, I have returned. I have done our share for the clan for this day. I will prepare eggs for your lunch."

"Christ, eggs again. Yeah, go on about it."

"I will do eight eggs again. You will need your strength for the trip downriver." She turned the ashes out and exposed the coals in the fire pit.

"Just scramble them. I'm sick of eggs over easy."

"Scramble?"

"Yeah, just stir them together, whites and yolks and cook them all together."

Two Blankets got a bowl down from her cooking shelf and cracked eggs into it. "So, I stir them together," she beat them a bit with a fork and showed Marshall.

"Yes. It is amazing you don't know nothing about cooking. Now, just pour them into the pan, and watch you don't burn them."

"Will you bring back bacon from Portland? I did like that bacon."

"I'll bring back supplies for a month or so. I will go crazy if I have to live on eggs."

"I like this frying pan. The *Nimi'ipuu* and the Chinook don't have anything like it. It is so heavy."

"It's cast iron, and every pioneer woman has one. You have lived primitive for far too long. Them's done. Pull them off the fire."

Two Blankets dumped the pan of eggs onto a plate and handed it to Marshall. She took the pan out to wash it in the creek. It still surprised her how much the whitemans had, and how they still wanted more. She didn't particularly like chicken eggs, but she was grateful for the constant food source.

When she returned to the longhouse, Marshall was gathering up his supplies for the trip downriver. "I will be gone a couple of days, depending on the bank. When I get back, I expect you to be here."

"Please excuse me, husband Marshall, I must apologize. My bleeding time approaches so I may be in the moon cycle hut when you return."

"Goddammit."

She turned to him. "The steamboat is not here yet. And I am very apologetic about the requirements of my cycle. Perhaps, I might please you a little before you go? It will be a long wait for me, as well."

He was near their sleeping furs packing up his good pants and coat as she approached. She let her cape drop to the ground and moved with a cougar's hunting grace toward him.

"Well, I do have to get ready to travel, but—"

Two Blankets unlaced his rough trousers, and they dropped around his ankles. His drawers followed. She gave him a little push, and he sat back, surprised at how his wife could take control and make him ache for her.

"Lean back and rest, husband Marshall." She knelt between his knees. "Your wife knows how to handle this wild animal." Two Blankets took him into her mouth. She did not want to catch a child from Marshall, and he seemed to like this just fine. As she worked him with her lips and tongue, she thought, soon he would be gone for a few days and then she would be in the moon cycle hut. A good ten days, if she was lucky, of relative peace. It was only a few minutes of work for her, much like collecting eggs or feeding the chickens. It was certainly not as difficult as tanning a hide. He began writhing on the sleeping furs, and she kept up her pace. At just the right moment when she felt the surge within him, she lifted her head and caught his seed in an old rag.

He lay back panting, "Goddamn you are good at that, Two Blankets. Best I have ever had."

She smiled. A few minutes every few days, and he was content. He was a dangerous man when provoked but easy to control otherwise.

Late that afternoon they heard the steamboat whistle, and Marshall hurried down to his canoe. The tribe rushed their canoes into the water as well, but the *Belle* made no attempt at a landing. She just slowed and waited for Marshall to paddle out. With the help of two other men, he hoisted his canoe on deck, and the *Belle* steamed downriver.

Two Blankets removed her whiteman's dress and threw her cape on over her shoulders. She realized that it no longer, and had not for a very long time, bothered her at all going about virtually naked. When she first had come to the tribe, it felt odd to not wear any clothes at all. Now it seemed normal to her, and somehow freeing, to walk in the open air and feel the sun on her breasts and loins.

She walked up to the longhouse and entered this familiar and comfortable place. The people she saw here were friends and, more importantly, were fellow members of the clan. In all, the Bent Creek Clan came first. Before rank, be one title born, round-head, or even *mistshimus*, before property so important to the Chinook, before individual pride and honor, came the clan. The survival of the clan meant the survival of the individual. More than survival was at stake. It was as if the clan were a living thing and the individuals, its legs and arms, hands and fingers.

To that end, the *Tyee* signaled Two Blankets forward. "Sit with me."

"Yes, *Tyee*." She sat, and he beckoned her to move forward. She slid forward, and he beckoned again. She moved until they were almost knee to knee.

"I wish to speak privately with you, *mistshimus* Two Blankets."

The shock must have shown on her face. "Yes, *Tyee*. My apologies. I am not used to hearing the name that Marshall calls me come from your lips."

"Yes, I forgot myself as well." His eyes crinkled a bit into a smiling look. "Mayhap it is the times, or I am just getting old, but sometimes what used to seem so important to me now seems unimportant." He paused a moment. The smoke and cooking salmon smell permeated everything, as it should. The conversations as the meal was prepared were light and laughing, as they should be. For one moment all was as it should be. "How is Marshall Johnston taking the clan's not allowing the steamboat to land?"

"*Tyee*, discussions of my husband Marshall's life make me uncomfortable."

"I understand your dilemma, but as the Bent Creek Clan and its well-being are involved, I must insist."

"Yes, *Tyee*, of course, I will attempt to answer." She drew upon all her strength. Even though Marshall did not act like he was clan, in fact, did not even pretend to, she still felt it a betrayal. "My husband, Marshall, is very angry. He hates the tribe Chinook and the Bent Creek Clan. Your actions, when you would not allow the steamship to land, put him in some sort of difficult position with his suppliers, his factor, and his bank. Not all of this do I understand, but I get the impression from him that he does not have enough of the whiteman's money to survive their demands. He goes to Portland to try to arrange a bargain with these people, and it seems his trade position is weak."

"Ah, it is as I suspected. Go on."

"Still, he expects to win the battle with the Bent Creek Clan, and I think he plans on using the *Tyee's* longhouse, as well as others, as his new trading post. When he bought the sawmill, he also bought twenty hands of windows. He plans on making this a little town when you finally must leave. But for now, he is in a difficult position."

"Thank you, *mistshimus* Two Blankets."

Again, he had used her name. After five years of having basically no name of her own, hearing her name from the *Tyee* was very disturbing.

"I am sorry to disturb you, Two Blankets. I am too old to change my habits very much, and the Bent Creek Clan and the Chinook have existed for ten hundred years honoring the same system. Of late, though, I have begun to question. I cannot change it, or not very much. Perhaps it is just the sadness that I feel from having to make this move. I do not know. Sometimes I wish things were different and we could have just adopted you into the clan, as the *Nimi'ipuu* do. Then you could have married Standing Bear."

Her heart suddenly beat very hard, and she choked it down.

"But I am not that strong, and such a change would not be accepted by the clan."

With tears in her eyes, she looked at him. "I understand, *Tyee* Running Blade, and honor you for saying to me what you have said."

"I have come to value you, and that is a strange thing for an old *Tyee* to say. I would never have thought such a thing possible before, but you have honor and worth as a person. Your sacrifice for the clan brings you much honor. That is as much as I can give you, Two Blankets."

On impulse, and knowing her impulses had caused her to be beaten before, she leaned forward and kissed the *Tyee* on the forehead. "You have given me a great gift which I cannot return, *Tyee*."

For a moment the *Tyee* seemed taken aback. He said, "Perhaps you can, Two Blankets. The clan is so small now that we cannot afford to treat the *mistshimus* as non-persons any longer. This I do believe. What is one thing I could do to begin the process of bringing them closer to personhood? It must be something important to them that the other elder title born would not object to extremely."

Two Blankets bowed her head and pondered this for a minute. Many things passed through her mind. Adoption into the regular ranks of the tribe? No, too extreme. The right to wear clothing or have property? No, still it ran too much against clan custom. Finally, she straightened up and delivered her answer, "Please forgive this *mistshimus* if she offends, but you have asked a direct question, and I will give a truthful response."

The *Tyee* nodded to her. "Please continue."

"Give them the right to earn a name as their own property. I believe they and I would value that above all else."

"Ah, I would not have thought of that, and it is not so great a thing that

I would end my life as a pauper for commanding. Thank you. You may go, Two Blankets."

"I will retire to my husband Marshall's longhouse then."

"Two Blankets?" he asked.

She turned back to him.

"I will send Standing Bear to join you. You have sacrificed your happiness for the clan. I can sacrifice my pride for a few nights."

"Thank you, *Tyee* Running Blade. It is difficult for me, but I am determined on my path."

ONE NIGHT OF LOVE

CHAPTER 2
MAY, 1856

O N HER WAY back to Marshall's longhouse she passed the midden pile and then stopped at the stream that flowed full into the *Nch'i-wána*. She tossed off her cape onto a nearby rock and sat to take off her moccasins. Slowly she waded into the stream, which ran deep in its center, and felt the chilly waters wash away the scents of the day. Not just the familiar smells of the *Tyee's* longhouse, but also the sour smell of Marshall's sweat still upon her body.

Mayhap is it just an illusion, but I swear I still smell him upon me.

She was waist deep when she squatted down and submerged herself completely. Her hair swirled about in the current, green with the sediment and leaves of the spring run. She held her breath and listened to the burble of the creek. Finally, she released a lung full of air and watched as the bubbles of air rose to the surface, glistening in the late afternoon sunlight. She stood abruptly and shook herself. She felt a new cleanliness in body.

When she had picked her way back to Johnston's Landing, carrying her moccasins and cape, she glanced around. On this side of the creek, there was still the influence of the Bent Creek Clan. That was not erased yet. Yet it seemed to be more a whiteman's camp, with its sawmill and corral for the penned-up animals, and its kitchen garden. This side was always Johnston's Landing to Two Blankets.

This is the choice I have made. I made it. It was not forced upon me.

She opened the door flap to the longhouse and entered. For some reason, she always looked around before entering completely, as if searching for some enemy. She realized that this was something she did not do when entering Stinging Nettle's or the *Tyee's* longhouse. Those, she always assumed were filled with friends, or at least allies.

She sat before the firepit and blew the banked coals back into life. Her hair had grown long since she married.

One benefit of marriage to husband Marshall. I don't have to keep my hair short like the other mistshimus.

As she combed out her hair, she pondered the question that always arose.

Two Blankets knew the dangers of meeting with Standing Bear like this. Not a danger from the Bent Creek Clan. Almost all of them knew, and if they did not approve of the secret meeting of a *mistshimus* with a title born, neither did they consider it more than gist for idle gossip. The *Tyee* obviously knew. He had taken some pains to make it known this time. If he had no problem with it, then they did not either. Nor was she concerned that Marshall would find out. If he did find out, no doubt, it would be an explosive discovery. Unless he came back early and discovered them, there was little chance he would find out from the tribe. Marshall had no allies there. If he were more aware, perhaps, he would get the gist of chuckles as he passed, but he was a blind and deaf man in Two Blankets's opinion.

No, the danger to Two Blankets did not come from outside. It came from within herself. Each time she met with Standing Bear, it became more difficult to tear herself away when they must. They always knew that this might be the last time they would be thus together. Despite this, she could not resist the opportunity of meeting one last time, even if the pain on parting should be that much greater.

She bent and stirred the little fire. It was May, and the weather did not demand a fire for heat any longer, but the flickering light warmed her in other ways. Now, all she could do was wait and hope. The fear was there.

What if Standing Bear does not come? What if he does not want me anymore?

Then the whole decision she had made to stay with Marshall for the good of the Bent Creek Clan would be for naught. She could go with the clan and try to get used to the idea that Standing Bear had gone on or found someone else.

There was no end to this circle of thought. Either Standing Bear would come, or he would not.

She set herself on that point of thought and waited. It was darkening outside. She could see that through the cracks surrounding the door flap. He would not come until full dark.

If he comes at all. Why do I keep returning to that thought? She, of course, knew the answer to this question. It was the only question that really meant anything to her. It was the quandary that kept her awake when she should be sleeping and disturbed her thoughts when conscious.

She felt a scratching on her ear. She slapped at it as if it were a bug. It was no bug. Tiny sharp claws pawed at her ear. How long since she had thought of White Mouse?

Too long, came the chittered answer in mouse speak.

"I am sorry."

Yes, you are, said White Mouse

"What?" she asked, a feeling of insult washing over her.

Sorry. You, sorry creature. You wait. Yes. The Standing Bear either come or not come. It simple.

Two Blankets ran her hand along her ear through the strands of black hair. There was no mouse there, but Two Blankets knew that White Mouse did not occupy this reality. Her world was much closer to the spirit world of the dead than this one.

"Thank you, White Mouse. I will not forget."

Likely you will, White Mouse said, *but I will be here to remind.*

Two Blankets sat before the fire and calmed her mind. Too many thoughts intruded. She listened to the sounds about her. The flame of the little fire crackled. A fly buzzed in the longhouse somewhere near the door. The evening sounds throughout the village began to replace the normal day sounds of voice and laughter and work. Over it all and through it all passed always, day and night, the rush of the *Nch'i-wána.* It, too, had a personality. Sometimes it was angry and tearing. Presently, it had the hurried sound of late spring, of the buildup of the snowmelt rushing to the sea. The waters that rushed by just this second were pushed upon by waters behind with great urgency. If she let them, they would carry all thought and never even notice she was there. So, she allowed all thought to escape her and be drawn out the door, like a tributary stream into the great *Nch'i-wána*. Soon, the waters that flowed through her were no longer marked by the leaves and bark and sediment of thought. They ran clear like snowmelt, a hard, icy-blue that scoured her clean. For the moment, she was at peace.

A scratch at the door flap startled her back to this world and this time.

"Two Blankets?" Standing Bear's voice called.

She rose. He was standing at the entrance. "Standing Bear. Do you come in?"

Standing Bear looked uncomfortable. "No. We will not dirty what we have in this place again. You come out." He let the door flap drop.

Hurrying, she put her moccasins on and the old rabbit skin Bent Creek Clan cape. She banked the small fire in the subdued light and exited through the door flap.

"Come. I have made a place for us." Standing Bear led the way back along the creek toward the wood. About a quarter mile up, where the canyon widened a bit, he turned off on a rabbit trail. Two Blankets followed. A dozen paces in, and they came upon a grassy open space surrounded by brush and trees. He stopped. It was almost pitch dark here, but Two Blankets felt his sleeping furs upon the ground.

"I made a place for us. I could not stand holding you in his longhouse." He sounded wistful and plaintive.

Two Blankets hugged him tight. She spoke into his chest, "This shall be the longhouse of the warrior Standing Bear and the secret woman who loves him."

The first time was all passion. Two Blankets knew it would be. They had only just touched, and they fell back upon the sleeping furs together in a tangle of limbs. There was no sweetness to this lovemaking, not this first time. This was the pure animal need of two persons forced to live apart and take what few minutes they could together. She did not mind it thus. The passion rose in her with her blood. He took her almost violently, yet it was not violence toward her. It was a fierce taking that rejected all elements of culture and mores. Each primitive thrust by Standing Bear was met by an equal need from Two Blankets. When he pulled back to drive into her again, she trapped his hips, wrapping her legs about him and crossing her ankles behind. They did not think. They did not worry about the other. Neither of them did. Only this moment could they feel, and this moment would end all too soon. Two Blankets sensed the surge building in him and an answer in herself. She knew her answer would not be of the same explosive quality as his. She had not had the time, nor the stroking to reach that place, but she had the passion to be filled, and she was filled. He cried out, and she bit upon his shoulder.

If only, if only.

White Mouse chittered, *Take what seed you can, for the winter is long.*

He fell to the side panting. Two Blankets lay in the crook of his arm with her head upon his chest. She heard it then in his breath. There was a catch to it, and she looked up to his face. A single tear ran down his right cheek above her, and she reached up to touch it with her fingertips.

"You are as sad as I am," she said.

"Yes. Sometimes I feel I will break like the river ice in the spring. I feel the water surging beneath me, and there is nothing I can do."

"My sweet warrior, Standing Bear, there is nothing we can do."

The night sounds danced around them, first coming from one direction then another, overlaid by the creek nearest and then the *Nch'i-wána*, farther away but omnipotent in its power, the skitters of the night seed hunters, like the mouse and vole, and the quieter but more potent sounds of the predators that sought them out. Always this cycle of life, but in the village, as close as it was, one lost track of this.

Two Blankets ran her hand down Standing Bear's thigh. "So, is it only to be this one time tonight, my warrior? Is your strength sapped?"

"So," he said rolling up half above her, "you mock your warrior now?"

"Well, your *wootlat* is only half interested," she said giving his penis a hard squeeze.

"Only in consideration of your delicate self, little Two Blankets."

She pushed him down onto his back. "My delicate self, warrior Standing Bear?"

She climbed on top of him. "Oh, it seems your *wootlat* maybe has something left after all." She rose up and pressed the tip against her furrow, rubbing it against her place of need. "At least it is good for something."

She lay his hardened *wootlat* back upon his belly and stroked herself against it. When he moved to take control, she pushed him back with a "Rest, my tired warrior. Rest." She moved upon him then in complete abandon. Grinding her open self upon him, stroking up her own passion. She was not long in feeling the surge building in her own body. Standing Bear ran one hand over her breasts and tight nipples, the other gripping hard upon her buttocks. The bowstring twisted between the sensation in her breasts and her root need. It turned upon itself, and each twist of it tautened the connection. When she knew she was close, so close, she took him within her all at once and laughed at his groan of surprise. She rode him now like a wild Appaloosa *Nimi'ipuu* horse. The horse had spirit and rose to meet her. She twisted and ground down upon his *wootlat*. Her wave passed over her first, and she threw back her head, looking at the wheeling stars above. He was not far behind, only a dozen strokes, and he came up and held her in his arms.

"Tonight, you are mine, Two Blankets, solely mine."

"I will be yours, Standing Bear, even if the *Nch'i-wána* should always stand between us." She rolled on her side, and Standing Bear pulled her up against him wrapping her in his arms. They fell asleep like that, body to body and heart to heart.

A few hours later, in the dark before the dawn, she felt him stir. Half asleep, she lifted her left leg, and he slipped his *wootlat* between her *busi*. He let it lay there, and she rocked against it for a bit. Then she arched her back and let him into her *skutch*, the secret place of pleasure. They lay like that for some time in a half-doze, barely moving. Just a slight rocking motion was all that belied the fact that they were not asleep. It was not lust as it was the first time when they could not wait to climb into each other. Nor was it the mutually satisfying passion of the second time where both recognized the others needs and desires. This was different in a much more profound way. True, his hard *wootlat* was inside her and slid, oh, so slowly, in and out as she rocked her hips. His motions were so slight that she could almost fall back asleep to the pleasant, filled feeling.

They lay like this for perhaps an hour or more, just a pleasant joining of lovers in no hurry. The sky began to lighten, and Two Blankets snuggled deep into his embrace.

I know I cannot stop time any more than I can halt the flow of the Nch'i-wána, but when he holds me like this and fills me, I feel as if I can, if even for only a moment.

White Mouse whispered her chitter into Two Blankets ear, *It is good. It is good.*

"Yes, White Mouse. It is good."

Though the wheel of the sun could not be stopped, they could slow it and feel the union of peaceful love spread and hope to sustain it. Eventually, the sky signaled the predawn hour and Standing Bear pulled out of Two Blankets. He was still hard, but they both knew there was rightness about his action. Two Blankets pulled on her moccasins and cape, and he gathered up his sleeping furs. Silently, to preserve the sensation as long as possible, they walked back down the creek. At the base of the creek, Two Blankets hesitated and leaned back against him. He held her for a short time. Then she straightened and walked resolutely to the longhouse of Marshall Johnston.

About mid-day, a steamboat came upriver. The Bent Creek Clan scrambled for their canoes and paddled up to Johnston's Landing, but it did not stop. They paddled back, laughing and maybe a bit downcast that there was no confrontation.

So, if that is the last steamboat for today, that means Marshall will be gone until tomorrow or longer. That thought brought an inner smile. *Mayhap, Standing Bear and I can have another night together.*

Late in the afternoon as she went about her chores at the Landing, a cramp hit and almost doubled her over. She ran into the hut and got a moon cycle pad from her personal stores and dabbed up the blood on her leg.

"No, no, no," she said. "Why today? Why not tomorrow?" There was no arguing with the human body. It had its own time and rhythms. She would sadly miss Standing Bear, but it also meant she would likely miss her husband's return, as well. Small consolation that, but it was something. She glanced around the longhouse, and everything was in order, so she headed for the moon cycle hut.

The village had a different feel to it of late. True, everyone went about the usual tasks necessary to the continued existence of a village of ninety people. That had to continue. They were preparing for the spring run of salmon when they must send a contingent to Celilo Falls to fish and dry the salmon. Others gathered spring herbs and plants from the forest. There was also the considerable preparation underway for the move to Warm Springs on the Deschutes River in little more than a month. Personal items were packed into large baskets. One load of dried hides had already been sent up-river, and the Bent Creek Clan was not happy with the preparations there. Very few of the promised houses had been built, and each of them only had limited storage available. No warehouse or common building had been prepared to hold all the communal supplies that this tribe needed to survive. It was as if the U.S. Government expected them to live off government hand-outs until they could get crops planted, which no one knew how to grow.

It is a sad time, but that is not my problem. My problem is what Marshall is going to be like once the tribe, and its limiting authority on his behavior, is gone. She couldn't stop it, and she couldn't change it. All Two Blankets could do was wait for it and deal with it as best as she was able. For the hundredth time, she questioned her decision to remain and came to the same conclusion. She must.

She entered the moon cycle hut and saw that Bears-Many-Children was there. A familiar, if not always friendly, face. "Greetings to you, Bears-Many-Children."

"Greetings to you, *mistshimus,*" she said. She stopped a moment. "Let me begin again. The *Tyee* Running Blade has discussed with us allowing *mistshimus* to earn a name. I know what you have done and sacrificed for the Bent Creek Clan. We are so used to not thinking of *mistshimus* as people, but I am also coming to see that you suffer for the clan, too. If anyone has earned a name, it is you."

"It is not necessary, Bears-Many-Children, if you do not want. I have long since accepted my status here and respect your customs."

"Silence, *mistshimus*," Bears-Many-Children said. "Allow me to get this out. I greet you, *mistshimus* Two Blankets."

"Thank you, second wife of *Tyee* Running Blade. It means much to one such as I, coming from a title born as you are."

"Two Blankets. Two Blankets. When I think about it, I wonder why names were property in the first place. It is not so hard."

"I did bring some of the tea from Stinging Nettle that helps you if you would like me to prepare it."

"That would be kind of you—Two Blankets—thank you. I am still not used to it. There is so much upheaval with the move to Warm Springs. I fear nothing will remain of our old life—or of us."

Two Blankets stirred the coals into life, and a flicker of firelight rose up. She pushed some rocks near the coals to heat and sprinkled some of the herbs into a steep-walled stone bowl.

"I know it is wrong of me to speak so of my husband, but I think, in a hundred years, it is the Chinook that will still be remembered, and Marshall Johnston will be forgotten." She poured water into the stone bowl and added the hot rocks.

"Normally, it is considered wrong to speak so of your husband." Two Blankets looked down, a feeling of some shame overcoming her. "But, Two Blankets," Bears-Many-Children waited for Two Blankets to look up, "in this case I believe you can be forgiven. Marshall Johnston has refused to be a member of the Bent Creek Clan. He is no Chinook."

Two Blankets looked away while she stirred the steaming tea. "Thank you, Bears-Many-Children."

"Forgive my asking into your marriage life, but I do not quite understand why you are choosing to stay with your husband. Surely, you know you can step away from a bad marriage. Even a *mistshimus* has that right."

Two Blankets poured the tea and took a cup to Bears-Many-Children. She sipped it with appreciation. "I must remember to thank Stinging Nettle for this. Or does she even know that you still provide it to me?"

"She did not order me to prepare the herbs, but she knows I take them for you."

"In that case, I thank you, Two Blankets." She smiled. "It gets easier with practice, and there is something right about it. So, why do you stay?"

"I fear I may be violating a trust by answering, Bears-Many-Children."

"Are you talking about that business with Standing Bear? I don't know anyone who does not know something of that."

"Do they also know of the *Tyee*'s involvement?" Two Blankets hoped even this might not be going too far.

"I know, as his second wife. You may trust that anything you tell me will not go beyond the *Tyee* Running Blade and myself."

"Then I will say it to you and hope I do not hurt anyone." In fact, Two Blankets already felt the pressure of such a secret was too much to bear alone. "I love Standing Bear, and I believe he also loves me."

"That much is obvious by how he moons about and looks at you when he thinks no one will see."

Two Blankets looked down when she felt the rush of blood to her face. "That gladdens my heart, and it also makes me sad." She took a little sip of her own tea. "The only reason the *Tyee* has allowed us to continue as we have is because he knows I will not be leaving with you."

"Ah, yes, that makes sense."

"So, yes, I could choose to come to Warm Springs with the rest of the Bent Creek Clan. You do not know how dearly I want to. Once I wanted nothing more than to return to my own tribe, the *Nimi'ipuu*."

Bears-Many-Children laughed in a guttural way. "I remember those days very well, Two Blankets. You were quite a trial for me, and an insult to my standing in the clan."

"I apologize deeply and truly for that, Bears-Many-Children."

"That is last year's salmon."

"Still, I do apologize. I once wanted to just return to the *Nimi'ipuu*, to my family, to a life I was familiar with. But I was afraid I could not find them for they change their summer camp quite often. I also believed the *Tyee* would kill me if I did not succeed."

"I am certain he would have," Bears-Many-Children nodded.

"For four years I thought of little else but could think of no way to accomplish that goal. Then I became a woman and shortly after that mated with Standing Bear. I was punished and married to Marshall Johnston. At first, I thought it might work, but he resists all the things the clan holds dear, and I found I held them dear myself. I realized then that I had become a Bent Creek Clan member. He is a mean man. I don't mean he beats me, because he does not. His thoughts are mean. He has no feeling for clan or tribe. And I think he does plan on getting all the Bent Creek Clan land for himself once you are gone."

Bears-Many-Children drank the rest of the tea to the dregs. "Come, Two Blankets, sit on my pallet."

Two Blankets drained her tea as well and sat next to Bears-Many-Children's suddenly very comforting presence.

"The thought of staying with this man truly fills me with dread. Until now, I could bear it because the clan was always there. When you have departed, I will be truly alone with him. And I cannot bear the thought of having his child. I would be permanently trapped with him and would always think of him when I viewed our child. It would not be fair to the child either."

Bears-Many-Children put an arm tentatively around her shoulders.

"In my darkest moments, I think of the river rushing by. I could throw myself into it, and soon my problems would be taken up by the *Nch'i-wána*. But I still want to live."

"And you do not go with us to Warm Spring because ...." she let the question hang but was sure she knew she already knew the answer. This girl, this *mistshimus* Two Blankets, had borne her burden too long alone.

"Because if I go to Warm Springs with the Bent Creek Clan—with *my* clan now—I would not be able to stay away from Standing Bear. And worse, I fear he would not be able to stay away from me. He would disgrace himself and dishonor the *Tyee* and the clan, my clan. He is the *Tyee's* only son now, and he must marry a title born. I know title born can take *mistshimus* to their furs, but they cannot love them, not as Standing Bear and I do. That is the reason I do not go with you to Warm Springs though my whole self desires it. To honor our love is to protect it, by honoring those we love—not just Standing Bear but the family of Standing Bear, the *Tyee* who has treated me fairly and the Bent Creek Clan that I now love as my own." She spat out the last words with a sob and let Bears-Many-Children's embrace enclose her as she cried.

"What a hard life the *Wimahl* has chosen for you, Two Blankets, truly."

PREPARATION FOR THE GREAT MOVE

CHAPTER 3
JUNE, 1856

EACH WEEK, THERE was another large canoe or two loaded and headed for Warm Springs. Even though it was not very far, perhaps a hundred miles or less as the crow flies when he has not been eating fermented berries, it was still a considerable undertaking. Marshall took some pleasure in this as he counted down the days.

"Twenty-five more goddamn days and these goddamned Chinook will be gone. Then we will have a little civilization around this place," he said.

"Have you no care for my feelings, husband Marshall? These are my people after all."

"No, I don't give a fig's fuck about your people. Them bastards practically destroyed me. They cost me in storage. I had to rent warehouse space in Portland for the goods that the steamboats refused to deliver. I still say, if we had shot a couple of them, they would have backed off. But that damn Indian licking captain refused. Coward." He spat on the ground. "Look there. There goes another steamboat, just passing us by. Do you know how long I worked on getting them to stop here regular-like?"

Two Blankets looked up. The sternwheeler was passing on the far side of the channel. She also saw that the Bent Creek Clan noticed the steamboat, but when they saw it wasn't going to stop, went on about their tasks. Some joking was evident. Though Two Blankets could not hear the words, she heard the laughter and saw a couple of clan members pointing upriver toward them—toward Marshall. *No one has been anything but kind to me, especially after my last week in the moon cycle hut.*

She had emerged to find one of the storage huts partially disassembled, the long, thick cedar planks stacked on the beach. The planks had adorned and protected the storage longhouse for generations, silvering with the weather but none the worse for wear. They were not just boards. They were heritage. A history of many lives was written onto those planks in smoke and the oily skin of those who had passed before. Apparently, Marshall had not noticed, since the longhouse roofs reached almost to the ground and this hut presented its flank to Marshall's Landing. The hides that had once been stacked in the rafters were piled high in a large canoe.

"Yes, husband Marshall. I do know. So, did your trip to Portland go well?"

Marshall Johnston's face reddened. "Those bastards. They don't know in Portland what it's like out here. What we must deal with. They all act like we was still back east in Chicago or Boston." He took a swig of his whiskey. Two Blankets noticed that he was rarely without a bottle nowadays. "All they care about is assets and liabilities. Damn tight-ass accountants, every one of them. So, you really want to know what it was like for me in Portland?"

"Yes, I do. I am interested in your business, husband Marshall. Make it simple so I can understand." She had to be cautious playing Marshall, because although he was not clever, he was cunning.

"The warehouse wants a guarantee of payment before they will store my goods any longer. Even though I always paid pretty much on time before. The factors—that's the agents for the suppliers—all want to see a statement of assets and liabilities. They don't care about potential profit. I don't got title to this land yet. I won't have that until your friends leave, then I have a promise that I'll get a thousand acres of this land. The whole village, the forest behind and the prairie on top. My claim to that is based on you being my wife, you being Bent Creek Clan and all. But I can't get a rightful deed to the land because it still belongs to the Bent Creek Clan. So, I still got to put up with their shit. So, I owe too much, too many liabilities and too few assets. Damn clan wouldn't let me saw cedar logs into planks. Otherwise, I could count those as assets. I still got a big debt for the portable sawmill. So, the warehouse is on my ass. My suppliers and the factors are on my ass. So, I went to the bank to get an extension of my credit."

Two Blankets touched his arm. "You were trading from the small position?"

Marshall began to reply in anger then stopped himself. "Trading from the small position. Without leverage. Ha. Yes, Two Blankets, you understand in your primitive way exactly what it was like."

"Thank you, husband Marshall."

"I went to talk with the bank fellers. You'd think they would understand that making big money requires a little risk on their part. They loaned that feller, Francis Chenoweth, thousands to build his little mule and cart railway on the Washington side of the Cascades. Thousands of good dollars for four miles. Now, they're talking doing the same for Col. Joseph S. Ruckle and Harrison Olmstead on the Oregon side. Two wooden railways, one on each side of the river. And the steamboats running for one or the other in competition."

"That seems like a lot of money," Two Blankets said.

"Damn right it is. So, I went to the bank to explain how I just needed a bridge loan for a month or two. At that time, I would own all this land and timber and buildings, everything. You want to know what they said?" Marshall took a deep draw on his bottle.

"Yes, I want to know how you handled those bank fellers."

"The bank feller, Mr. Shales, said, 'It's all well and good that you will be granted that land after June twenty-fifth, but what assets do you have now to cover a loan?' That little man, with his little wax mustache, in his suit and his soft hands. I said I was going to own it all in another month. He said, 'Do you have a deed or a letter of intent to grant a deed?' and I said they can't write one until June twenty-five. It ain't territorial land until then."

"That sounds very frustrating, husband Marshall, and unfair, if the territorial governor promised."

"That's what I said. I was in the territorial governor's office, and he promised me, and we shook hands on the deal. But the little bastard at the bank would not budge. He said to get the loan, I would have to take on a partner. After I spent two years here building up my trade, I was going to have to take a partner. So, I finally said, all right how much of a partnership. That there banker sat there, added some figures for a few minutes. Pulled on that damn sissy-boy mustache a few times and finally said, 'Ten percent partnership will get you a bridge loan for two months.' I was furious. Ten percent for two months? I asked. And he sat back in his chair and said, 'Yes. You can try elsewhere, but I expect this will be the best you'll get.' I knew I was beat. Who would this partner be? I asked. He leaned forward and said he would do it himself. That little weasel."

"Did you have to agree, then?"

"No other choice. We shook hands, and he drew up the papers."

"Will you be able to make it work?"

Marshall got a crafty look on his face. "Come on inside, and I'll show you. That man ain't been out here to see this place."

They went back inside, and Marshall pulled out a large sheaf of papers, the most prominent of which was a detailed map of the village and the area around it.

"That is a picture of the village. There is the *Nch'i-wána."* She put her finger on the map. "And there is our longhouse, Marshall's Landing. Here is the creek running up toward the prairie. But what are all these marks, running through the village, crossing the creek and going up alongside it."

"This here is a map of the town of Marshall's Landing. That there is a road running through the village and a bridge across the creek. A proper road that I can push up the creek to the plateau above."

"I can see it now, husband Marshall. How amazing."

"You think that is amazing, take a look at this." He pulled out another set of pages and put them down, weighing down the curling edges with whiskey bottles.

"I recognize these. That is Stinging Nettle's longhouse. She has one of the bigger ones. And that looks a little like the *Tyee's* longhouse, but with a square door. And are those windows?"

"Exactly, Two Blankets. I figure we take the longhouses, there's at least four major ones and build proper doors. Put in framed glass windows, and we have a building. The cedar is good for another hundred years, and the *Tyee's* longhouse is a good sixty to eighty feet long. See this sketch. We partition off a part in the back for our living quarters. Put down a proper floor and have a section along one wall for a bar and the rest for shelves and storage for the store. Same for the other buildings."

"Wouldn't this take a lot of planks?"

"That's why I bought the sawmill. With that and the forest behind the village, there's all the lumber we need—cedar, fir, and spruce. We are going to be very rich. So that little son of a bitch can have his ten percent of the trading post. This idea of mine is a lot bigger than just a trading post." He began rolling up his maps. "A whole lot bigger. This here is going to be a town, my town, Johnston's Landing."

———

ONE EVENT OF note took place about a week after this. The Bent Creek Clan assembled in the *Tyee*'s longhouse. It was late in the afternoon, and Marshall would want his supper soon, but Two Blankets was curious, so she followed the others in. She looked up to the elder's seating, and they seemed to be aware, but everyone else was as mystified as she was. *Tyee* Running Blade stood, and the clan quieted down immediately.

"As all of us know, we recently lost Fire Stick in an honorable action of war against the whitemans at the Cascades. Many others died that day and on the days following in the fighting, and several were hanged by the U.S. Government. Though they were warriors engaged in war, they were convicted of treason, though the U.S. Government says the natives are a separate nation. As a separate nation, they cannot commit treason. Of those hanged in this trial were Chief Chenoweth and several others who were not involved in the fight at all. But this is how the whitemans make their justice. We are all saddened by these events and give honor to those dead of other tribes and clans."

There was disturbed talk among some, but most just waited for the *Tyee* to continue.

"The immediate period of mourning is over for Fire Stick's wives, Sweet-Pollen-Flower and Fox Tail. It is the time for them to be remarried so that they have a warrior to provide for them and for the child."

Many of those attending nodded. This was common custom.

"Normally the wives of a fallen warrior would be taken in marriage by the warrior's younger brother. If no younger brother is available, then by his older brother. In this case, Fire Stick has no brothers in the clan. Both his older brothers, as well as the rest of his family were killed when the whiteman's disease killed so many. He had no family except the Bent Creek Clan."

Drifting Smoke stood to speak and waited for a gesture from the *Tyee*. "I could take Sweet-Pollen-Flower and the child. Or I could take Fox Tail. But I cannot take and support both. My household could not support two more wives and a child."

"This is the problem we face when our numbers are so small," the *Tyee* said. "We have not enough title born warriors to care for our own."

Fox Tail stood to speak. His skull so recently shaven in grief was stubbled black. The *Tyee* signaled him to continue. "You all know me. I am Fox Tail. Though I am now a Two Spirits, I was once regarded as a competent warrior and hunter. I am better at the women's tasks that now occupy me, but I am still good with the bow and knife and fishing spear."

The clan nodded in general agreement. They had seen the Two Spirits' competence with weapons as a warrior, and her tanning skills knew few equals since she had taken up women's tasks.

"I love Sweet-Pollen-Flower, and we both love her child. We have discussed this for many nights, and we would like to remain a family. I would serve as her warrior when needed and warm her sleeping furs. Any clan woman may take any man to bed with, and we both agree she would be free to do so. Any child she had would be loved and cared for. We are both in agreement on this. We would like to remain married, a trial marriage if you wish. At the end of a reasonable period, say a year, if the arrangement is not satisfactory to the clan I will withdraw, and Sweet-Pollen-Flower could then marry Drifting Smoke."

Fox Tail sat down and was embraced by Sweet-Pollen-Flower. All could see they did truly love each other, but this request was unprecedented.

The *Tyee* said, "Sweet-Pollen-Flower, this is your wish as well?"

She stood. "Yes, *Tyee,* it is. Fox Tail was beloved by both Fire Stick and me. And our child has bonded with Fox Tail as well. I believe Fox Tail can provide for us."

The *Tyee* gestured, and she sat down. The clan elders gathered close to *Tyee* Running Blade and talked in whispers and many gestures. In ten minutes, they were done, and the *Tyee* stood again.

"None of us have any memory of a precedent for this situation. Not even Bone Rattler can think of one. All of us can think of several difficulties to such an arrangement."

Fox Tail held Sweet-Pollen-Flower's hand. Both looked to Two Blankets like they were preparing for bad news. The *Tyee* and the elders of the clan did not like situations where there was no precedent, and they were very conservative in their approach. What worked for a thousand years, worked. There was precedent for everything, even for unlikely events such as a person stealing from the dead.

"This, though, is the year for unprecedented events. Never, has the clan been so threatened, even during the years of the whiteman's sickness. We have never been forced from our lands. We will allow this trial marriage between the Two Spirits, Fox Tail, and the clan woman, Sweet-Pollen-Flower."

Fox Tail and Sweet-Pollen-Flower embraced each other.

"But not for a year. In three full moons, we will meet again and make a final determination. So, it is up to you, Two Spirits Fox Tail and clan woman Sweet-Pollen-Flower, to make this work. In three moons we will be settled in Warm Springs, and we will make a permanent decision.

"On June twenty-one, of this year, three days after the full moon, we will meet for the last time in this place, our home, to celebrate the longest day of the year. Two days later, the steamboat will dock here and take us and our remaining possessions aboard for our trip upriver. We will take Fire Stick's death canoe before that and raise him in the new place. That is all I have to say."

The *Tyee* sat down, visibly tired, but resigned in a way Two Blankets had not seen before. He caught her eye and gestured her forward. She got up and began to sit at a respectful distance. He motioned that he wanted her closer.

"Come close, Two Blankets. I would speak with you."

She sat down by his side. It still felt strange to sit next to the *Tyee*. "*Tyee* Running Blade, how can the *mistshimus* Two Blankets serve you?"

"I would know of Marshall Johnston's plans if you have any news."

"I do know of much, *Tyee*, and will gladly relate the news I have. Husband Marshall plans to get a deed to the whole of the village of the Bent Creek Clan, including the forest behind and some of the plateau above. A thousand acres, although I do not know what an acre is. He says the territorial governor has promised him this deed. He plans to make this whole place a town, Johnston's Landing, with everything a whiteman's town has. It will be no trading post. I saw plans for a road from your longhouse to the creek, a bridge across the creek, and a road up to the prairie. He will make lumber from the forest and put windows and a door and a floor in your longhouse. A bar and shelves, and a wall where we sit now. He will go to Portland, I believe, for the deed and for men to do this thing. I am sorry."

The *Tyee* waved off her apology. "Do you know when he plans to make the trip to Portland?"

"I do not. I can try to find out. I believe he must wait until the twenty-fifth to get the deed though."

"Find out, if you can. For our plans, it would be good if he were gone that last week, from the twenty-first to the twenty-third. I know these whiteman's dates mean little to you but find out if you can. And mind you, Two Blankets, he will be very angry when he returns. Protect yourself."

"I will, *Tyee*. I must go to my husband."

Two Blankets hurried back to her husband, Marshall. He would be angry this day if he had to wait any longer for his supper, and the meeting at the *Tyee's* longhouse had run much later than expected. When she entered the longhouse, Marshall was absorbed in his plans. Every once in a while, he would laugh and make a note on the plan papers or in his accounting book.

Two Blankets began cooking, preparing his favorite foods—venison steak roasted over the flames, fried potatoes and gravy. Soon, she had everything frying and began tidying up the longhouse.

"Damn, that smells good, wife," Marshall said a half-hour later. "I sure am hungry. I could almost eat salmon, I'm that hungry."

Two Blankets dished out his meal into a metal plate and brought it to him. "You are still working on your plans?"

"Yes. I hope there ain't no delay in getting the clan out of here. I want to get that deed and get started."

"That is what the clan meeting was about. There is a big longest day celebration on the twenty-first and the steamboat to take them to Warm Springs is coming on the twenty-third. They have to be there by the twenty-fifth and are not planning any resistance."

"Goddamn, that's perfect. If I leave on the twenty-first, that's a Saturday, on the downriver steamer to Portland, then I'd take the Willamette steamship up to Salem. I could get my land grant deed from George Law Curry, the territorial governor, on Wednesday, the twenty-fifth. That'd give me a few days to round up a small crew, and I could be back here on the twenty-sixth or the twenty-seventh, latest. I don't even want to look at those flatheads one more day than I have to." He started writing the dates and his plans into his notebook.

FIRE BURNS

CHAPTER 4
JUNE 21 TO JUNE 22, 1856

ON JUNE 21, 1856, Marshall boarded the *Belle* bound downriver, and there was no blockade of natives forcing him to take his canoe out. "You see, Two Blankets, they know they are beaten. They have finally given up the senseless obstruction, and my plans can go ahead. Full steam ahead. I will be back about the twenty-sixth with title and deed in hand and a crew to get started working."

"I am glad for you, husband Marshall." She gave him a kiss, and he boarded. The steamer backed away from the landing with a great huffing and belch of smoke. The sidewheels churned the river water white, turning both in reverse. The starboard wheel stopped and thrashed water in forward, the port continuing in reverse until the *Belle* was lined up with the current. With two short blasts of its whistle and a release of white steam, she headed downriver with black smoke from her wood-burning boilers drifting off ahead of her on the late-morning downstream breeze.

Two Blankets wanted to hurry through the Bent Creek Clan village, but she slowed her step. This could be one of the last times she saw it, and more importantly felt it in its entirety, as it had functioned for perhaps a thousand years. There was something to that, the continuity of a people's existence on the land and the river, the *Nch'i-wána,* that could not be argued. Some feeling existed in the soil and the trees that had been permeated by the Bent Creek Clan living here for generations beyond her ability to count, a living that was not parasitic like the whitemans, where they took from the land until it would give no more. No, the Bent Creek Clan gave of their lives and of their dead to the land. Unlike the whitemans, they recognized the clan must take custodianship of the land. Then, and only then would the land support and care for them. Only in this way had they survived and thrived here for so long. That time was coming, day by day, to an end.

She walked past the midden pile and thought this the perfect example. True, the natives were not the perfect custodians. They produced trash and sometimes, up at Celilo Falls, waste in abundance. However, it was all organic, and time and nature would break down their leavings in just a matter of a few years until all that was left here would be a deep mound of soil. She walked up toward the forest verge, and here were examples. Yes, the Bent Creek Clan did take a cedar if a new canoe was being built or new planks were needed for a longhouse, but the number taken was less than the number that the god of the forest replaced. As long as that balance remained, there would be no sign that the Bent Creek Clan had been here. This was far different from Marshall Johnston's plans to strip the forest to build his town, just as the town at The Dalles was built, or the settlement that Fire Stick and the other rebels had burned at the Cascades.

The whitemans had a vision of what they thought the world could be and it conflicted directly with the native people's. Their vision was winning, and the native people's vision and the land were losing.

She turned past the *Tyee's* longhouse with its doorway cut into the *totem*. When she passed through that hole in the *totem*, it always felt like she was entering a different world. Her objective was Stinging Nettle's longhouse, once the house of her enemy, now the house of her friend. Approaching it, the thought of all the days she had spent here grinding herbs, making infusions, and just talking to Stinging Nettle passed through her mind. She tried to fix them into her memory, to burn them in so she would never forget them. Knowing the memories would fade, as all did, she still tried. Suddenly a memory flashed to the forefront of her mind, one she had not thought of for a very long time.

It was an image of the *mistshimus Nika*, Stinging Nettle's *mistshimus*, on the portage up the *Nch'i-wána*. *Mistshimus Nika* had been babbling as was her wont. Two Blankets remembered that her incessant babbling had been irritating. She wished for that irritation now. *Mistshimus Nika* turned to her beneath the canoe they were carrying to say something inane and never finished her sentence. Her foot slipped off the edge, and then all that held her was the infernal tie that Stinging Nettle had insisted upon to prevent Two Blankets's attempt to escape. She remembered so clearly, as if she could see it with her eyes open, the look upon *mistshimus Nika*'s face. First surprise at having fallen down the decline. The look of relief and hope as the strip of leather brought her up short. Her eyes impossibly wide as she watched Stinging Nettle's knife come down to cut the life-saving strip of leather. They were losing the canoe and possibly Two Blankets as well. She knew her life was not as valuable as a canoe. Lastly, her quiet voice as she declared *mistshimus* to *mistshimus*, "Live for me."

The tears misted her eyes as her mind passed through this remembrance. Life was fleeting, that was something important to always keep in her mind. And *mistshimus Nika*'s last words, "Live for me." She had once sworn never to forget those words, and she had almost forgotten them.

I will not forget you, mistshimus Nika, and I won't forget your words. In this way, I honor you and your first friendship to me.

Stinging Nettle was out in front of her longhouse with a stack of baskets, stone pots, wooden bowls, and bundles of herbs of every description. "Ah, here you are, Two Blankets. Help me please and supervise these two *mistshimus* and two round-heads. They are stacking my herbal supplies and other goods on the beach. I will handle the goods coming from the inside if you would take over at the beach. We must get this done in a hurry."

"Yes, Stinging Nettle, of course." Two Blankets wondered what the rush was about. Of course, they needed to be expedient, but something more was afoot. Had Stinging Nettle only this one day to complete her task? Stinging Nettle passed back into her longhouse with a shout at one of the workers.

Two Blankets took up a closed basket of herbs and made her way down to the bank of the *Nch'i-wana*. She remembered collecting this particular herb last year and the trials of getting the herb at just the right stage of development. All her supplies were stacked on the beach. Two Blankets could see why Stinging Nettle needed her here. Everything was stacked, but not neatly. One basket of dried spearmint was leaning precariously against a stone jar of pennyroyal. Pennyroyal wasn't native to the lands of the clan and had to be traded for. Two Blankets righted the leaning pot and set the basket straight and then went about organizing the supplies in better order.

After a couple of hours, the steady stream of herbal supplies trickled off, and Two Blankets headed up to Stinging Nettle's longhouse. What she saw there stopped her in surprise. Workers were dismantling her longhouse. Taking great care, they were removing every plank from the high front of the longhouse and the four long planks along each side. Peeking inside she could see that they were also removing the planks from the rear of the building. The boards were being stacked with care alongside the river side of the longhouse, and the longer planks were sawn, so they were all approximately four or five paces long.

Stinging Nettle turned from her position by the doorway. She smiled at Two Blankets look of surprise but said nothing.

She is waiting for me to understand. Why are they stripping the longhouse? They can't mean to burn the wood. They are taking too much care with it and sawing the planks to a suitable length and stacking them with care. She shut her surprised mouth and pondered this a moment.

"You are taking the village of Bent Creek Clan with you to Warm Springs," she said.

"I knew you would understand," Stinging Nettle said. "We can't take the posts, but the cedar planks and any fine cedar work inside are going. The treaty says we may take our possessions. The cedar that has been on this longhouse for ten generations is the property of the tribe. The posts that support it and the roof can be replaced with fir in Warm Springs, but there is no cedar there. That we will bring with us."

"Are you doing this with all the longhouses?" Two Blankets asked.

"All of the larger ones. The sweat lodge and moon cycle hut, as well. I am sorry about that for your sake, but you can build a new one just for yourself."

"That is all right. Marshall Johnston would probably have decided to use it as a storage shed or barn anyway." Two Blankets tried to imagine her husband Marshall's surprise when he became aware of this new development—surprise, followed quickly by anger at the disruption of his big plans. This brought a smile to her face. She knew it should not. She should respect his plans and his attempts to "improve" the village into the town he planned, Johnston's Landing, but found she could not give him that respect. She had none to give and could manufacture none.

"Mine will be going up by canoe raft tomorrow. That is why we are hurrying," Stinging Nettle said. "Let us have some lunch, and we can talk a bit." She signaled, and a *mistshimus* brought them dried salmon and *camas* cakes. "And some of my peppermint and anise tea. You will miss that when I am no longer here." Stinging Nettle smiled to take some of the sadness from her remark.

"I will miss your tea, Stinging Nettle, but I will miss you, all of you, more." She held back the tears.

"I will miss you, as well, Two Blankets. You challenged me at first, and the Bent Creek Clan, but it has been good for us. I don't envy you the choice you have made, even though I understand it."

"Yes. Let us not allow what may be and what has been to spoil this tea and this moment." They drank their tea in silence, both thinking their private thoughts.

"I do have something for you, Two Blankets," Stinging Nettle said. She fished out two packets and handed them to Two Blankets. "The herbs and seeds for you and Marshall if you should decide to continue using them. That is all the seed that I have. There should be enough there to last well into next year. After that, I do not know where you will get them, for I had to trade for them. Your herbs, you can gather, so there is a three moon's amount there."

"You know I cannot repay this *potlatch,* Stinging Nettle," Two Blankets said seriously.

"This is a *potlatch* between two women, a *cultus potlatch* if you want to call it that. From friend to friend, not a barter."

Two Blankets tucked the packets away. "Thank you, Stinging Nettle."

When they had finished the tea, Two Blankets told of her husband Marshall's plans for the next week or so. "He will be upset when he sees the village." Two Blankets smiled, and Stinging Nettle giggled a bit. "I shouldn't be smiling, but there is nothing I can do about it."

Later that evening, as the sun was beginning to set in a red glow, the whole clan gathered before the *Tyee* Running Blade's longhouse for a feast. The clan celebrated the longest day, and another year of life and survival, the last such celebration the Bent Creek Clan would have of the longest day on their traditional homeland. As such it was particularly poignant for every member. As they ate in their different groups, they told stories of events they remembered. Although each group was somewhat separate, they were also joined together into a larger whole, and occasionally a title born would shout a comment to a round-head. Two Blankets still ate with the *mistshimus*, but the more significant issues diminished her lower caste status. She was just glad to be here among these people.

After the feast had been mostly consumed, Bone Rattler stood and shook her staff. Two Blankets noticed she was painted in the same way when they had raised Fire Stick into the trees. "Six warriors and I will go this night and retrieve the canoe of Fire Stick. We will honor him and say to the dead there that we take him to a new place and raise him there. This is the longest day and is an appropriate day for such a task, the longest day and suitable to our task of leaving this place on the sacred *Wimahl* to venture forth on a new journey to another land. We shall look upon this not as a defeat but as a new beginning for the Bent Creek Clan. The whitemans think to crush us by moving us to this new place, but I say this. Once we were not here. I know most of you are not aware of this, but the Chinook people have not always occupied this land along this river, the sacred *Wimahl*. Once we lived elsewhere, and we came to this place and made it our home tens of lifespans ago. As we have not always been here, now, we will go elsewhere. One day, perhaps a child will ask his grandfather, 'Is it true we have not always lived in this place, this Warm Springs?' And he can say, 'It is true. Once we lived elsewhere, and now, we are here.' This I say to you. Once we lived elsewhere. Now, we will live elsewhere again. We will make it ours as the Bent Creek Clan of Chinook do. This is all I have to say." She shook her staff with the bones dangling and walked from the great fire, followed by six warriors similarly painted.

The moon had risen and was just three days past full. It cast a stark light upon the Bent Creek Clan. The stars penetrated the black blanket that covered the earth, and the *Tyee* rose. He took up a torch beside him, and other elders did the same. Without speaking, they began a procession toward Stinging Nettle's longhouse. Two Blankets saw that all the planks and Stinging Nettle's supplies had been removed. The elders lined both sides of the longhouse from back to front with Stinging Nettle standing at the left corner and the *Tyee* at the right.

He spoke to the assembled group who looked on in question. "This longhouse, which has served Stinging Nettle as healer, and Warm Hands before her, and served each Bent Creek Clan healer for two hands of lifetimes, will go with us to Warm Springs. We are only able to take the cedar planking and crossbeams. The rest we commit to the fires so that it is not used by the whitemans in a way that does not honor those who came before."

With this short commemoration, he touched the torch to the eaves of the longhouse. Stinging Nettle did the same on her side. The roof, dry with the summer heat and shaked in bark, caught fire immediately. The flame started small but licked up to the crest. Soon the whole longhouse was aflame, and all stood back from the heat. The flames were as tall as the cedar that once was sacrificed to build the longhouse, and sparks rose hundreds of feet into the star-pierced blanket above.

Walking back to the feasting area, Two Blankets saw Standing Bear talking to his father. He looked up, and their eyes met for a moment. She knew she could not approach him, could not ask. He continued talking to the *Tyee* for a few minutes. Two Blankets did not know what to do, only that she would not return to the longhouse of her husband this night or perhaps any night she did not have to. She sat back with the other *mistshimus* but a bit apart. They were going, and she was staying. They did not have much to say to each other, but the nearness of their company was comforting.

A hand touched her shoulder, and she started. At once, she knew. It was Standing Bear's hand. She rose quietly and followed him back into the village through the shadows. They walked with silent agreement back to the creek and up along it to their secret place.

"I am sorry I did not bring sleeping furs, Two Blankets. I only have my cape to offer."

Two Blankets looked at him illumined by the bright, almost full moon filtered by the trees. Here stood her warrior, at least for this night. "I do not care about sleeping furs, Standing Bear. I only care for this moment when you are mine. Please, just let us lie together and hold me. I will fix you in my memory so that you last forever."

Standing Bear spread his cape on the soft grass and drew her down with him. His arms wrapped her, his love enclosed her. They did join bodies, and he just held her barely moving. This joy she felt, this joining with him might have to last a lifetime, and now it seemed like it could. Two Blankets knew the memory would fade into a bittersweet past, but she did not care. She already had the best out of life. If this were to be all, then she would make it enough.

The next morning, on June twenty-second, they both rose as one. There was no time, and this was no moment for regrets or goodbyes. To say good-bye would be to interrupt and negate the memory, and Two Blankets wanted to keep the sensation of being held in Standing Bear's arms fresh as long as possible. It was the hour before dawn when the wood had not awakened yet, but soon it would be full of the sounds of daylight. The world took as much notice of the passing of the Bent Creek Clan as it would of the fall of a tree or the death of an elk.

Passing through the village Two Blankets could see the plume of smoke still rising from the burning embers of Stinging Nettle's longhouse. Three of the supporting timbers still stuck up out of the smoldering remains of the roof like an ancient skeleton. Otherwise, all was gone. They went to the *Tyee*'s hut for the morning meal and a gathering of the tribe. Everyone wanted to be close in this time of sadness and uncertainty. There was strength there, not in numbers but in closeness and continuity.

Two Blankets took a bowl of porridge from the communal pot and sat to eat. Stinging Nettle passed by and, though she did not say anything, laid a hand on her shoulder as if sharing strength and their inner bond. Two Blankets leaned her head over to feel Stinging Nettle's knuckles on her cheek for just a moment. Stinging Nettle had her own problems to deal with, and Two Blankets did not want to take from her. Just long enough to share, then she lifted her head, and Stinging Nettle walked by to take her own morning sustenance.

As the sun began to rise, all went outside. They walked down to the beach, where there was considerable activity. Stinging Nettle was there with her canoe packed tight with supplies and a raft of cedar planks, tightly bound, tied behind it on a tether. Forward of her canoe was the canoe of Fire Stick, the stench of a dead body emanating from it despite the number of herbs packed all around. Before that was Bone Rattler's canoe of eight paddlers. The *Tyee* and Bone Rattler stood on the bank, speaking quietly. There was a young boy there as well. Two Blankets looked at him. He appeared very familiar, a round-head boy about four or four and a half.

He looked at Two Blankets, wide-eyed at all the excitement, and pointed. Bone Rattler stopped her conversation with the *Tyee* and listened intently. She looked to Two Blankets and nodded. Her lips moved, and Two Blankets thought she heard the words "White Mouse" emerge. She moved unconsciously toward the pair.

"See," said the child, Sees-What-No-One-Else-Sees, "she has a white mouse on her shoulder." The boy laughed at the sight.

Bone Rattler leaned in toward Two Blankets, peering at her shoulder, then looked her question at her.

Two Blankets answered only, "Yes."

"Thank you. It is a confirmation. This child sees things even I must work very hard to catch a glimpse of. We shall see if it lasts. Mayhap I have found my apprentice after all these years." She patted the boy on the head and let her hand drop protectively to his shoulders.

The *Tyee* Running Blade said, "Proceed to the Cascades, Bone Rattler. If you can find help there with the portage, then take it. Tell them we take our honored dead to Warm Springs. For most, the honor of serving the spirit world would be enough, but we do not know how far the whitemans greed has infected native peoples. If they insist on coin, pay them with this. If you must, you will have to portage the canoes yourself. May all the spirits bless you on your venture."

"Do not worry on my account. If they do not help us, I will shake my bone stick at them." Bone Rattler cackled at the thought.

Bone Rattler climbed into her canoe, shaking off the assisting hand of a paddler. Her canoe pulled out onto the river, towing the canoe of Fire Stick with the inverted canoe of the raising over him.

Next in line was the canoe of Stinging Nettle. Two Blankets felt her eyes go moist at the thought of losing this friend, perhaps forever.

I do not know what is happening to me. When they beat me, I did not cry. Now, I feel like crying all the time.

She wiped the incipient tears with the back of her hand and sniffed her nose. She merely stood where she was near Stinging Nettle's canoe until she had finished talking with the *Tyee*. Two Blankets saw that Stinging Nettle also received a pouch of coin for the portage.

"Go now, Stinging Nettle. You should reach the Cascades by late this afternoon. Help Bone Rattler if she needs help with her portage then continue with your own. Your supplies are necessary, of course, but it is critical that Fire Stick reach his new raising place. We cannot risk insulting the spirit world. Our Bent Creek Clan needs the spirit world's help if we are to survive."

"You can depend on us. And you will have some cedar planks to begin building the new longhouse as well. I will make sure of it." Stinging Nettle saw Two Blankets standing at the head of her canoe.

"I knew I could. The Bent Creek Clan honors your journey. The rest of the clan will follow your path tomorrow, either by canoe or on the riverboat they send to collect us. Anything you have left behind, be assured we will take care of it." The *Tyee* Running Blade stepped back, his jewelry reflecting the new sun, the bone in his nose gleaming. He looked for this moment, fierce and prideful. Two Blankets knew a little of how much it cost him to look so fierce and determined when she was sure he felt nothing but sadness at leaving his home behind.

"Bent Creek Clan, come, we have much to do today," he said.

As her paddlers eased her canoe into the water and the cedar plank raft behind her canoe stretched out its tether in the downriver current, Stinging Nettle approached Two Blankets.

"My *Nika*," she said and put her arms around Two Blankets. "When you came to me, we were enemies of a sort. I knew I could not break your spirit as I might another *mistshimus*. You had already proved that with Bears-Many-Children and Swimming Salmon. I admit I took a risk with you. If you had run again and been killed, my status would have suffered a significant blow. And I cared little more for you than that. I thought to try kindness on a ten-year-old girl, though the foraging trip where we stopped by your old *Nimi'ipuu* camp was not kind. I intended to shock you. My actions had the results I expected, and I was a little proud of that fact. What I did not expect was that you would have an impact on me, and on clan Bent Creek, as you did. I believe we have been changed more by you than you have by us. For that, I thank you deeply, *Nika*. I shall not forget."

"Stinging Nettle, your original *mistshimus Nika* was my first friend. When she fell from the cliff, she looked at me and said, 'Live for me.' If she had not spoken so, I believe I would have thrown myself into the river. But I accepted it, first as a burden, then as a gift. You have been a true friend and teacher to me. I will not say goodbye. It is too permanent. I can only say good fortune on your journey. And trade well." Two Blankets pulled away to arm's length and smiled.

"Trade well," Stinging Nettle said. "I shall indeed. I suspect we shall see each other again, though I cannot say when or what makes me think so. I have never had a true *mistshimus* friend before. Trade well, *Nika*." She did something completely unexpected. She kissed Two Blankets on the lips. It was not the kiss of lovers, of passion, but the more intimate kiss of two individuals bonded for all time. It lasted but a moment. Stinging Nettle broke it and without another word waded through the shallow water to the head of her canoe. Her paddlers sang out a chant and pulled out into the current. The floating raft of cedar tugged at the tether, and then obediently followed. If there was one thing the Chinook knew, it was the river and its ways. They knew how to tether a load so it would tow well. Two Blankets stood still on the bank, watching the back of her friend as they made their way upstream. She knew Stinging Nettle would not turn around to look at what she left behind. That was not her nature, yet she still wished to look upon her face one more time. Soon they were but a small creature stroking along the river like a water bug, and she turned away to attend to her own tasks.

She saw that crews were stripping the planks from Bone Rattler's small longhouse, the *Tyee*'s longhouse, the cooking house, the salmon and meat drying shed, and the longhouse dedicated to tanning, even the sweat lodges. The planks were removed with care and sawn into that same three to four pace length before being bound up tightly in bundles that two could carry. These were in turn tied into larger groups on the beach. Finally, they would be bound into one large boat-shaped raft. Bone Rattler's longhouse was almost finished. Five buildings altogether were being stripped, as well as the sweat lodges. Two Blankets looked upriver. No one was bothering with the two longhouses that her husband Marshall Johnston had contracted for. Such was the nature of a Bent Creek Clan bargain. The Chinook remembered the letter as well as the spirit of the deal. If they were crossed, their honor in trade made it almost impossible that they would violate their end of the bargain. The smallest missed word could spell disaster for the other party if they felt he had violated the spirit of the deal.

Such it would be with the Marshall Johnston bargain. Two Blankets had no doubt that if he had honored the word as well as the spirit of his bargain, the results would be entirely different. As it was, when he returned, he would find he received exactly what he had bargained for and no more.

This made her smile as she took her place binding up the planks on the *Tyee*'s longhouse.

It may be true that he will get a deed for this land when the Bent Creek Clan is departed on the twenty-fifth, but he will not get what he expected. I still do not understand how the whitemans can divide up the land and give pieces of paper that give one man more than he needs and prevent others, who have greater need from having any land to live on and care for. But his deed will be worth far less than he thinks.

Even the *Tyee* worked at tearing down his longhouse. With his longhouse, there was not only the planking on the sides, which were some ninety feet long, and the front and rear, which were some thirty-five feet, but there were also carved timbers from within that workers were attempting to remove without collapsing the structure.

Two Blankets moved to the moon cycle hut. She knew she would have to rebuild it, but perhaps she could salvage some part of it. The sweat lodge was covered with reed mats which were coated with clay. She managed to remove enough of these to build herself a smaller sweat lodge later. Some of the bent sapling frame she removed, as well. With a nod of permission from the *Tyee*, she removed these to the edge of the forest and hid them beneath branches.

It was hard work. One might say back-breaking, except the Bent Creek Clan did not think that way. It was merely an arduous task that everyone fell to until it was done. Afterward, they tiredly, but steadfastly, moved on to the next task. It was their way.

As evening came on, a great meal was prepared in the outdoor fire pit. Everyone sat and enjoyed the meal and congratulated the cooks. It was strange to see a people happy to have performed the difficult work of the last two days when such work represented the tearing down of the Bent Creek Clan's heritage. At that moment, Two Blankets was proud to belong to the clan.

After the meal had mostly been consumed, the *Tyee* stood up to speak. "Bent Creek Clan of the tribe of Chinook, never have I seen such an effort on the part of any clan. When times are rich, we become absorbed in the bargain and the trade. That is right. That is how we Chinook became the greatest traders our world has ever seen. But it is at times like these, days that are not generous with the salmon runs when I am most proud to be a Bent Creek Clan member. For that reminder, I thank you." He waited a minute for his appreciation to take effect. They were proud of the work they had done, true. But the fact that the *Tyee* was proud of them made them more aware that they were part of a whole that worked together.

"We must work late tonight. The canoes must be ready to leave as the first rays of brother sun touch the *Wimahl* tomorrow. Sometime in mid-morning, a steamship will come to take those of us remaining on board, as well as all our personal belongings. If you are assigned to a canoe, any belongings you do not take with you need to be stacked on the beach. The U.S. Government will send some of their warriors, I am sure, to be certain that we comply with our side of the bargain. They do not know that if we intended not to comply, we would not have signed. No Chinook, at the stake of his honor, goes back on a bargain he has made. But they do not know us so they will send soldiers. We will do as they bid us, but we will insist they comply with their side of the bargain. That includes transporting all of our personal property."

Great Bear stood to speak. The *Tyee* recognized him. "Why do we not insist they carry our canoes and the planks from our longhouses, then?"

"The question has arisen among the elder's discussions. We do not think they would recognize the boards that made up our longhouses as property. To them, a board is just a board, and they are willing to provide us with a sawmill at Warm Springs. As to the canoes, I do not think they even thought of that. But this is a whiteman's trade. That is why we are taking them upriver ourselves."

Great Bear sat down.

"When we are finished stripping the planks, we will burn what is left. It is unfortunate the *totem,* that stands in front of this longhouse and has stood so since the time of my grandfather's grandfather, cannot come with us. But it cannot. Perhaps it will burn. Perhaps it will watch over this Bent Creek land awhile longer. Let us go to work."

Within three more hours, they had stripped and bound everything together from the longhouses. The raft, shaped somewhat like an ungainly boat, floated, waiting for the dawn. The *Tyee's* canoe was tethered to it and awaited only the paddlers to make it go. All the possessions save a sleeping rug for each were bundled and stacked on the beach waiting to be loaded.

The torches were lit, and clan members lit the smaller huts on fire first. The moon cycle hut was lit ablaze, and Two Blankets remembered the time she had spent there with Bears-Many-Children. A time spent, to begin with, in hostility, as Two Blankets had been the cause of embarrassment and a significant loss of status for Bears-Many-Children. Later they had become, if not friends, for friendship with a *mistshimus* was yet an unknown and impossible concept for Bears-Many-Children, at least friendly in their relationship.

The men's sweat lodge was set alight, and Two Blankets remembered the grand bargain that was started there when Marshall Johnston had first come to the village seeking a wife. Little had he known then that he was dealing with a master trader in the *Tyee*.

The tanning hut and the cooking and smoking huts followed in quick succession. Each of these held special memories for Two Blankets. It was not that her memories and their roots were disembodied and rose with the smoke and flame and sparks into the sky. When the cooking hut went up, she remembered Bone Knife and her pride in her cutting skills when Two Blankets was only ten years old. She was not allowed a knife because a knife was exclusive property. She was only allowed to gut the salmon with her hands.

Why, oh why did that irritate me so much at the time, and now, I remember it fondly? Either my memory is faulty, or I have changed my perception.

Of course, she also remembered how angry she was at the time over being abducted. When the tanning hut was set ablaze, she recalled the scraping and the stink of the brain tanning, but most of all she thought of Fox Tail. One of her original abductors turned Two Spirits. She could only wish—honestly wish—Fox Tail and Sweet-Pollen-Flower well in their new home as husband and wife.

Bone Rattler's longhouse followed, and as it went up, she thought of the ancient woman and her stories and the little boy saying, "She has a white mouse on her shoulder."

It was becoming increasingly hot and uncomfortable as they gathered in front of the *Tyee* Running Blade's longhouse. He stood at the right-hand corner of the longhouse. She could see it was more than just a building to him. With no speech, he tossed his torch upon the roof, and they all pulled back a safe distance because of the heat. Two Blankets looked over at *Tyee* Running Blade and saw that he had not moved back with the others. He stood like a statue transfixed by the flame. He was no longer fierce. He was no longer proud. His face showed only sadness as tears streamed unstopped from eyes that had looked upon this as a home for all his life. She had only spent six years in this village, and she felt the connection. He had spent a lifetime. All the lifetimes of his forbears running back many hands of lives were spent here. Finally, Swimming Salmon pulled him back. His hair gleamed in the fire from his burning home, the sweat on his body intermixed with his tears reflected the light.

All the Bent Creek Clan pulled back into an open area near the beach. The fires raged all around, although some of the smaller huts were already reduced to smoldering coals and flame-licked posts. Two Blankets curled up in her sleeping furs, knowing she would not see Standing Bear this night but aware she was part of something so significant and so old that her problems flowed like the *Nch'i-wána,* away from her and downriver always.

As she lay there comfortable and almost dozing, she felt a body ease down behind her. She did not turn to him. He snugged his body as close as possible to her backside and wrapped an arm about her, pulling up the sleeping fur. No words were spoken, and none were necessary. Two Blankets could feel his breath upon her neck, and she wriggled back against him. She could truly sleep, in total peace for the moment with the river.

DEPARTURE

CHAPTER 5
JUNE 23, 1856

O N JUNE TWENTY-THIRD, all were awake in the village well before the sun cast its rays upon them. Indeed, it was still full dark when Standing Bear nudged her with a plate of food. Two Blankets rolled over to take the plate and to see the remnants of the fire. Most of the smaller buildings had burnt to embers, with an occasional post still standing amid the rising smoke. The *Tyee*'s longhouse was what caught her eye. She seemed not to be the only one whose attention had been captured by the vision.

First, there was still an immense amount of smoke rising and obscuring the stars in a gray-white haze. Several of the posts and roof beams were still standing glowing in the night. Flames flickered, occasionally leaped to five or six U. S. government feet from within the smoky depths as a new piece of fresh wood caught fire. What struck one though was not the skeletal framework, or the smoke roiling, or the flames flickering up. The *totem* that had always stood in place of a doorway and rose above to the full height of the roof beam, still stood. True, it was smoke-blackened, and no doubt charred black to the rear where it had faced the fire, but the front side showed no significant damage. Two Blankets could see the doorway from where she sat eating her porridge. The door flap had been burned away, and, now that there was a little light, she could see some smoke damage where flames had eaten the door flap. Peering in, she saw flames within that looked like they were burning in the gullet of some fantastic spirit beast. The *totem*, which had stood the lifetime of the *Tyee*, and his grandfather's lifetime, still stood and watched over the village of the Bent Creek Clan upon their departure. It seemed to Two Blankets appropriate somehow, and she was pleased to see it. She was confident that her husband, Marshall Johnston, would pull it down, especially now. He would not have such a reminder of his failure staring at him.

She turned to Standing Bear. "I don't want to leave, but I must feed the chickens and other animals. I will be back soon."

"I must go to my father. He may require you as well, to translate when the steamboat comes for us."

She hurried back to Johnston's Landing and checked on the chickens. They had eaten most of the grass and other greens in their pen. She fed them grain and picked up eggs, remembering to post the totals in husband Marshall's ledger book. She had to fudge the numbers a bit as she hadn't collected in three days but thought it would pass. The pigs were ravenous as she fed and watered them, and then she fed and milked the cows. In an hour she was finished, in a cursory fashion, and headed back to the gathering area near the fire pit. Everyone was hurrying but in a purposeful manner. They had time to get ready for this event, and almost all the preparations were made. At the dawn, people gathered on the beach to see the last canoe off, the *Tyee*'s personal canoe. It was a full twenty-five paces long. Already twelve paddlers were in it, and the cedar plank raft-boat bobbed behind it, ready to be off. Standing Bear waited near the bow for his father's words.

"Paddle quickly, my son, and aim to reach the Cascades before nightfall. It will be difficult, but you have our strongest paddlers with you. If you can, try and line it up the rapids. The waters there should still be high enough but not so high as to make it impossible. Engage portagers for the cedar. Here is a purse for their pay. If you can get there before we do, you will get all the portage men, and we will wait. That would be best. I trust your judgment. Go now."

Standing Bear climbed into the canoe, and the paddlers began to paddle upstream. Unlike Stinging Nettle, he did look back and located Two Blankets. There was no waving goodbye and no tears. The Chinook were not like that. They did remember though, and Two Blankets looked at Standing Bear and he at her until they were so distant the canoe and its following raft were just a dark spot on the waters.

She turned and almost ran into *Tyee* Running Blade. It was unlike him to watch someone leave. Perhaps he was only watching his canoe depart. Never in his entire life had it departed this beach without him aboard.

"Excuse me, *Tyee*," Two Blankets said, "I was just watching—"

"There is no need to explain. Soon the whiteman's steamboat will be here to transport us upriver. There will be soldiers. I see you have two options. One is to hide in the woods until we are gone. That way you will not be taken by mistake." He looked at her trying to judge her reaction.

Hiding was not in her nature, though she could see the reason for it. To the whitemans, one native looked much the same as any other of the same sex. Witness the native men rounded up and hanged after the Cascades attack. They didn't much care if they got the right ones, or even if the ones they did get were friendly to them. They hanged them in their anger until the anger burned out.

"And the other option, *Tyee* Running Blade?" she asked.

"Your other option would be to stay and be a translator for me. Your English is better than mine. These soldiers may speak the Chinook Jargon and they may not. I will admit we could use your help, Two Blankets."

She noted he used her name. It was difficult for him, but he still used it. "I would stay and help in any way I can. If you affirm I am wife to Marshall Johnston—I am, how do they say it, Mrs. Two Blankets Johnston, I will be fine. The captain has also seen me many times at Johnston's Landing."

"Thank you. You did not owe me this, either for honor or as part of our bargain. I will take it as a *potlatch* for which I will owe you in return someday."

"If it is *potlatch*, then it is *cultus potlatch*, given freely and without expectation of return."

"Nevertheless. You will need to meet these whitemans in your whiteman's clothes. I give you leave to go and change into those clothes for this meeting."

"I will go and make ready my appearance. Except for my skin, I will be a whiteman's wife."

The *Tyee* Running Blade did something which totally surprised her. He gripped both her shoulders in his strong hands and pulled her close enough to kiss once on the forehead. "I will not forget you, Two Blankets, daughter of my heart," he said and turned away to attend to the list of tasks still remaining.

Two Blankets returned to Marshall Johnston's longhouse to dress in her whiteman's clothes. She had three dresses to choose from, and she picked the fanciest. It had a little lace at the neckline and long sleeves with lace at the cuffs. It even had what Marshall had called a pleated waist, though she was unsure of what that meant. To her, it was a garment that covered her from neck to ankles.

She shrugged off her cape and drew the dress down over her body. It felt strange and constricted to be so covered, especially on such a beautiful day. The sleeves pulled when she made any extreme movements. Next, she braided up her hair and coiled the braids on top of her head as Marshall said some whiteman's women did. Finally, she dug out a bonnet and slipped it over her hair and tied it in place under her chin.

How can whiteman's women stand to dress like this? I can't move. I can't stoop down without the dress pulling on one spot or another. My hair feels like it is pulling my scalp, and then they put this hat thing on top of it all.

In truth, she felt like the cake that Marshall had shown her a picture of in one of his newspapers, complete with all three layers. She looked at the petticoat and decided she could do without that.

Enough constriction is enough.

Two Blankets walked back up to the beach where everyone had gathered their goods and supplies. Everyone turned and stared at her as if she were a whiteman.

I suppose that is the idea, but dressed like this, I feel humiliated.

She ducked her head in shame as if that would make the looks go away. She couldn't see the looks anymore, but she could still hear the voices muttering.

"Two Blankets," the *Tyee* said.

"Yes, *Tyee*. I have done as asked."

"Come to me." Turning to the crowd gathered about he said, "Do not mock Two Blankets. She is dressed as she is expressly at my desire. Honor her instead for this service she performs for the Bent Creek Clan."

Surprisingly, that was all it took. Conversation returned to the activity of the day, and the clan was congenial to her once again. Two Blankets knew they had also not missed the *Tyee* calling her by name.

"I do feel ridiculous dressed like this," she said.

"The whitemans are a strange people," the *Tyee* said. "Perhaps it is because of their odd white skin that they cover their whole bodies thus. I do not know."

Someone shouted, and soon several were pointing downriver.

Just emerging from a bend in the river the steamboat came puffing up-river, side wheels churning the water. They had all seen enough steamboats that the sight was not unusual to them any longer, but Two Blankets doubted any had ever ridden on one. Few, if any, had even boarded one. The side-wheeler could not pull alongside the bank, her draft was too deep, but she could nose in close enough to the bank to lay down boarding planks. As soon as she did an officer and ten soldiers crossed to the shore. The soldiers lined up smartly on shore with weapons on their shoulders at a command from their sergeant. The officer approached the *Tyee*.

He was an extremely short man with a long body and short legs and such long arms they looked to reach his knees. Strangely, he appeared to have no neck at all, but he had the crisp, attentive look of an officer on the rise. Penetrating eyes that brooked no disruption to his plans gazed upon the *Tyee* with a cold disregard for who he was dealing with. To this officer, the *Tyee* was just another Indian to be checked off in his ledger, and then he could move on to more important tasks suited to his abilities.

"Second Lieutenant Phil Sheridan of the United States Army, 4th Infantry, sir. You are the chief here?" he said in English.

The *Tyee* said, "You Sheridan of army? You no speak Chinook Jargon?"

"No, I don't speak Chinook Jargon. You chief?"

The *Tyee* turned to Two Blankets. "He doesn't speak the Chinook Trade Jargon. He wants to know if you are the chief."

"Ah, too bad. Ten tens of a thousand people, native and whitemans alike, speak the Trade Jargon from California to the big island on the north coast. We get an officer who does not. Explain I am *Tyee* of this clan and introduce yourself."

"Sir, Lieutenant Sheridan," Two Blankets began in English. The Lieutenant turned to her. "I am Mrs. Marshall Johnston, wife of the trader, Mr. Marshall Johnston. I speak some English. This is *Tyee* Running Blade, head of the Bent Creek Clan of Chinook."

"Mrs. Johnston. Could you ask the—*Tyee*, is it?—if the people could cover their private parts for the journey? My people are not used to such a display of immodesty."

"*Tyee*, whiteman Sheridan would like you to ask the clan to wear some clothes," she said in Chinook Jargon. "He is afraid the whitemans will embarrass themselves around us."

The *Tyee* looked down at his dangling *wootlat*, perplexed. He said in a stern voice in Chinook to the clan, "Everyone, put on a loincloth or skirt to cover your *wootlat* or *busi*. The whitemans are afraid of our *wootlats*, and the woman's *busi* make their *wootlats* stand up. This embarrasses them. Round-heads provide for the *mistshimus*."

Two Blankets turned back to Lieutenant Sheridan. "The men and women of the Bent Creek Clan will comply with this request of the U. S. Government to wear covers at the waist."

Lieutenant Sheridan looked like he was having a bad day. "Please ask the chief—"

"The *Tyee*," Two Blankets said. "The Chinook have no chief. He is called *Tyee* Running Blade."

"Ahem. Please ask the *Tyee* Running Blade if he would have the women of his people cover their breasts, as well."

"For the same reason?"

"Yes, the sight of so many uncovered breasts disturbs our people."

"*Tyee* Running Blade," she said in Chinook Jargon, "the Sheridan wants the women to cover their *tatoosh*."

"Their *tatoosh*, but only the women?"

"This is how they dress. They cover the *tatoosh*," here she indicated her breasts, "and the *tenino*," and here she pointed to the place between her legs. "They even have special clothes they wear to bed."

"I will command it, but he will owe me in return."

"The *Tyee* says he can command this particular request from Lieutenant Sheridan, but you will owe him in return."

"Fine then. Let us be on with our business."

"*Tyee*, he agrees to your bargain."

The *Tyee* turned to his people and spoke in Chinook. "Not only does *tenino* and the *wootlat* bother the whitemans but also the *tatoosh*, as well. Dig into your packs and find something to cover your *tatoosh*. Apparently, they can look at a man's nipples but not a woman's. Maybe they like men's nipples."

There was laughter through the clan as they searched for things to cover the women's breasts, giggling as various articles were tried. One crone strapped two wooden bowls over her sagging breasts and cackled a laugh.

The clan began to open their packs, and Two Blankets could see the problem before it happened. Soon everyone would have unpacked to find *tatoosh, tenino,* and *wootlet* coverings. She looked at Lieutenant Sheridan, and his frustration was beginning to show, as well. The captain had joined their group as well, wondering what the delay was.

"Excuse me, Lieutenant Sheridan. If they unpack their bags, we may be here all day. I have a suggestion."

"And that is, Mrs. Johnston?"

"Can the great U. S. Government pay for blankets? Possibly the steamboat or a trader on board has enough blankets. That would solve the problem."

Lieutenant Sheridan thought a moment, looked to the Captain who nodded. "If the *Tyee* agrees, we will provide a blanket for each person."

"*Tyee*, I am sorry if I spoke out of turn, but I suggested, that if they would provide blankets, we could clothe ourselves. I hope that was a good bargain."

"I accept the Sheridan's offer of blankets," he said to Two Blankets in Chinook Jargon. To the clan, he said, "Repack your belongings. We will have blankets to cover our *wootlets, teninos,* and *tatoosh*. And the soldiers will be safe from looking at them."

"Lieutenant Sheridan, the *Tyee* accepts your offer. We may proceed."

Lieutenant Sheridan conferred with the Captain, who signaled for his second in command. The request was in process. "*Tyee*, I have a list here of all the people we are to transport, some eighty-four, plus children. But there are less than forty on the beach here."

"When the *Tyee* of the Bent Creek Clan makes a bargain and signs his mark, as you required, he keeps it to the letter. Every person will be accounted for. The rest have gone on ahead to Warm Springs."

Two Blankets explained this to the Lieutenant, and a look of relief passed over his face. It was only momentary, but she saw it and was sure the *Tyee*, as good a trader as he was, saw it as well.

The discussion was interrupted as the blankets were brought ashore and the clan moved as one to claim the design they each wanted. There was some confusion as they tried different ways of tying them on, but Two Blankets could see they were happy, and it would get done.

The *Tyee* said, "Let me see your list, and we will call the names, and they can board."

The Lieutenant glad of any progress produced his list and read each name. "Fox Tail."

The *Tyee* turned and said, "Fox Tail, board the whiteman's canoe with your belongings."

Fox Tail shouldered two heavy packs, his bow and arrows, and boarded the steamboat, his blanket covering both his *wootlet* and his *tatoosh*. He gave a little wiggle when he passed the nearest soldier.

Each name was called and either boarded or the *Tyee* indicated they had already gone on ahead.

Finally, they reached the name of Fire Stick.

"He died," said the *Tyee*.

"Dead," said Lieutenant Sheridan and marked his list. "How did he die?"

"A hunting accident," said the *Tyee*.

"Ah, a hunting accident. How did that come about?"

"He was hunting a wolverine that had gone mad. He wounded the wolverine, but when he went into the brush to kill it, it turned on him and tore into his shoulder. The wound festered and blackened from the wolverine's bite, and we could not save him. We raised his body in the Sacred Grove as a greatly honored warrior."

The *Tyee's* gaze was hard as flint as he spoke and Two Blankets translated.

Lieutenant Sheridan made notes on his list, *Fire Stick killed by an insane wolverine.* "That's it then. Sergeant, have your men inspect the village for any of the savages that might be hiding."

The sergeant ordered his men out, and they began searching every area.

"Mrs. Johnston, what happened here? Every building is burned."

"Not every building. Mr. Marshall Johnston's buildings are not burned. He is in Salem getting a deed for the clan's land as we speak. The clan only burned their own longhouses, which I believe was their right by treaty."

"That bastard," he said. Realizing it was Mrs. Johnston he was speaking with he said, "My pardon, Mrs. Johnston."

"You needn't apologize for speaking a truth, Lieutenant. That is a belief of the Chinook that the whitemans might learn."

"I would have to agree with that. Still, it is an eerie sight." They both gazed upon the remains of the *Tyee's* longhouse, the bones reaching for the sky and the strange smoke shrouded *totem*.

The men reported back and marched onto the steamboat. The *Tyee* walked up the gangplank followed by Second Lieutenant Phil Sheridan. The gangplanks were pulled back, and the steamer backed out into the current and steamed upriver, leaving Two Blankets alone, truly alone for the first time in her life. Even when she had made her escape attempt, she was not actually alone for she was being pursued. She was solitary here with the *totem* wreathed in curling smoke.

ALONE, AND THEN NOT ALONE

CHAPTER 6
JUNE 23 TO JUNE 26, 1856

TWO BLANKETS WALKED half-aimless back toward what remained of the *Tyee's* longhouse. Her mind, always so used to communal life and the next task to be performed, to give herself and the tribe the best shot at survival for the coming summer or winter, had nothing to grab onto. It seemed like it had happened so suddenly, though she knew that it had not. The Bent Creek Clan, and she with it, had been preparing for this day for a few days shy of a year so it was not a surprise that this day had come at last. Her reaction to the event was surprising. The fact that she had not actually contemplated this particular part of it, at all, was surprising.

She stood before the *totem* entrance to what had once been the hub of communal life here, for a time beyond her ability to contemplate. It was all well and good to say this longhouse had served for three hundred years, but such a calculation was beyond her mind's ability to grasp. Six years she had been here, a mere droplet in the *Nch'i-wána* to be carried downriver, but that did not make it any less real or any easier for her to bear.

The smoke still rose from the coals and ashes, though not as it had. A tendril swirled out of the "mouth" entrance in the *totem* to twist about the figures above as if each were tasting the smoke. Some of the rafters still held, and it appeared they would not burn, but there in that deep pile of ash in the center, where the fire pit had been, she had eaten hundreds of meals or passed the time in amiable work. On the right side, nearer the back, beneath one of the surviving roof posts, was Standing Bear's sleeping area. Nearby, was the sleeping area of Fire Stick where all had waited those days for his spirit to extricate itself from his shell of a body and rise through the smoke vent. Near the rear of the longhouse, at the head of the elder's sitting area, the *Tyee* Running Blade of the Bent Creek Clan had sat and stood. Always watching, forever calculating what would be best for his clan, it had seemed like he would stand forever. Now, he stood there no more. Only the *totem* stood for all the clan, still watchful, still protecting. If she knew Marshall Johnston at all well, it would not long survive his arrival to this devastation.

The thought of Marshall Johnston increased her awareness of how constricting this whiteman's clothing was. She tore her gaze from the hypnotic vision of the *totem* and the memories it masked and turned for Marshall's longhouse. She would rid herself of these clothes, then decide what she must do.

She removed the bonnet as she walked and shook her hair down from the pins that held it. Enough forethought remained in her barely reachable conscious mind that she did not lose any of the pins.

Am I thinking ahead about the pins or just being practical?

She shook her head, already feeling a little freer. *In either case, it is wrong to waste them. The Bent Creek Clan does not waste a resource.*

She walked past the midden pile, struck by the idea that this old pile would no longer take the waste of the clan. If it grew, year by year, it would be from the garbage of the whitemans, a people who were almost entirely strange to her. She crossed the small stream, already diminishing with the summer. No snowmelt fed it, and soon it would dry up to half its current size, and then half again until it was a trickle she could walk across in some locations without getting her moccasins wet. It was not that small yet, and Two Blankets splashed across it. A glance toward the animal pen showed all there were behaving normally. She brushed aside the door flap and entered Marshall Johnston's longhouse.

She stripped off her whiteman's clothes and folded them carefully in the box Marshall had provided her. Looking about, she grabbed up a knife and sheath and strapped it on. The village would be different for the next few days with no one in it. Throwing on her cape, she took a haunch of venison, some *camas* flour, a mixing bowl, and an empty whiskey bottle for water. All this she packed into a buckskin bag. She could not sleep or work in this longhouse alone. There was no understanding of the why of it, only that she could not.

Walking back toward the remains of the main village, she stopped at the creek, filled the whiskey bottle, and corked it. She approached the old cooking fire pit, warier now. Her senses were alive and feeding her information. She could no longer depend on anyone else. For the next few days she would have to depend upon her own senses and sensibility.

She dropped her pack at the fire pit and roamed to the edge of the wood for kindling and the smaller sticks she would need for a fire. She laid it carefully in the old fire pit, then went to the *Tyee*'s longhouse. Saying a prayer to the spirits, she poked along the edge until she found what she was looking for—the remnant of a framing post buried in ash. Blowing off the ash she saw that it still glowed in places. It wasn't a large piece, maybe two U. S. government feet in length, so she pulled it out of the pit of the ash with two sticks used as tongs. Once on the unburnt ground, she picked it up with the tongs and transported it to her carefully laid fire. She blew on the coal, and a small flame responded to her call. Soon she had a blaze going. She built it up a little larger then walked back up to the forest to gather more branches.

It would be necessary to keep it going all night, not for the heat, for the evenings were comfortable, but to keep any predators away that might be interested in exploring the now-deserted village. Years of continuous occupation had generally trained the local critters of the larger variety to cast a cautious eye toward any two-legged critters, but now, it was hard to tell. Two Blankets did not want to wake in the middle of the night staring into the eyes of a critter that might see her as a meal.

She dumped one armload of branches and went back for another. Two loads of wood were enough for the day. She would get more later. Spitting the venison haunch on a long sapling, she set it over the fire to roast slowly.

Two Blankets made a careful appraisal of her situation. From her vantage point, Marshall's Landing was clearly visible upriver. The other landing place for the village was also visible from her position by the fire. Two Blankets realized she had been thinking like prey.

A tiny voice seemed to whisper in her ear, *How does the fox hunt the little white mouse?*

She needed to think like a predator. If she could see the landings from where she sat by the fire, that meant any who might land there could also see her position. Once the venison was finished cooking, she would have to move her fire. Especially at night, one could see it all the way across the *Nch'i-wána.* Someone on a passing steamboat could see the fire and the village and come to investigate.

Now, you are thinking, the voice chittered. Two Blankets tipped her head to that side. *The village has been burning for two days and the smoke rising all day.*

Surely that would attract the curious at best, looters at the worst. This was a difficult concept for her to grasp, but she had seen enough of whiteman's behavior to predict at least a curious investigation. Finding no one there, there was no telling how far the behavior would go. At the very least she knew Johnston's Landing was vulnerable, and she might be attacked.

You need to be able to fight and hide. Hiding is best, White Mouse said.

She needed another weapon and a place to hide if necessary. Roaming the village, she saw any number of things left behind. Here was a small moccasin from a child of five or six summers. Broken pots and worn-out baskets were scattered about. What had been deemed useless and not burned in the fires was left to the weather and predators. Near the hut where the children practiced their bow and arrow work, she found several short arrows. These were either only pointed on one end and fletched rather poorly or clad in simple rough flint. Still, she gathered several. Poking from a pile of debris she spotted the end of a child's practice bow. She pulled it out, hoping it had been unburned by the fire and was rewarded. It was whole, if unstrung.

Well, she could solve that. Crossing the creek back to Johnston's Landing she entered the longhouse. From her sewing supplies, she fished out a long piece of gut. She had planned on splitting it into thinner sections for sewing, but as it stood, it was close to perfect. Another buckskin sack she filled with two more bottles for water, the gut bowstring, and a sleeping fur. She thought for a moment, then took a flint and steel from the store supplies and a length of rope. That was all she could think of at the time. No doubt, if she needed something later, she would lament it later.

She headed back to the fire pit and turned the haunch on its spit, then set about stringing the bow. With only a cursory knowledge, it took her awhile. It had been years since she and her brother had practiced or played with bow and arrows. That was indeed a lifetime ago. Finally, the bow was taut. It was small, but she was small as well. It would have to do.

Turning the venison again, she saw that the sun was on the descent. Setting off for the verge of the forest again, with the second of her bags, she sought a place where she could practice and still keep an eye on the village. There was a little spot where the cliffside dropped near the forest and village and bent away from the river. Her fire would not be visible here, though she would be in more danger from four-legged predators. Two Blankets decided avoiding two-legged *cultus* whitemans was worth the risk.

She hid her bag a hundred paces back into the woods, then came back to the clearing to practice her bow and arrow work. Aiming at a tree fifteen paces away, she drew the string back taut, and let the arrow fly. She missed it by her own height. The arrows were poorly fletched and unbalanced. Moving closer, she found she could hit the target tree if she were ten paces or closer. That was knowledge. Not good news, but she knew. Against a determined foe, she would get one shot off.

She cleared a small area for a fire pit against the bare rock of the cliff side, then went to the fire pit to bring her fire over. A burning branch or good coal was all she needed, and she brought a branch back and started her fire in the new place. She fed it a bit then went back to transfer the venison and the rest of her belongings. Finally, she kicked out the fire in the pit and brought back the branches, allowing some to trail and partially brush out her footprints.

A piece of partly-burned venison gave her something to gnaw on, and water would do for now.

Food is best. Need good place to hide. Places to escape to. White Mouse dug her claws into Two Blankets shoulder.

Two Blankets shrugged her shoulder. It felt almost like something was there clinging on.

You no like me on shoulder? I climb on head.

Two Blankets tore off another large hunk of venison from the haunch then tied a rope end around the larger portion and threw it over a branch on the edge of the forest. It wouldn't keep a raccoon away, nor a fox or cat, but ground scavengers wouldn't get to it. She lay down against the cliff, took out her skinning knife and pulled the sleeping fur about her. The fire was coals now, but she daren't build it higher.

"Keep watch, White Mouse, will you?" she said. "I need to sleep."

I will watch for you, White Mouse squeaked.

Sometime after midnight, Two Blankets felt a stirring on her shoulder. She opened her eyes cautious and aware. Across from her, with just the remaining glow of the fire between, stood a gray wolf with green eyes. Neither of them moved, though Two Blankets's grip on the skinning knife tightened. She did not feel threatened.

Apparently, the wolf did not either, for he just stood there looking.

Is he just curious? Or is he sizing me up for a meal?

Slowly she drew out the piece of venison she had torn off and tossed it past the wolf. The wolf's lids blinked once over those huge green eyes, and he pounced on the venison and trotted off into the wood. It took a while for Two Blankets's heart to stop beating so hard and her breath to settle back to normal. She rolled up in her furs and fell back to sleep.

In the morning, she wondered if it had been a genuine visitation or just a dream. Examination of the area showed his prints clearly, so it was no dream. She had let the fire die down during the night and decided against starting a new one. Blowing this one up into a new fire would be simple, and starting one from flint and steel would be difficult, but the risk was just not worth it.

She rolled up her fur, packed up everything into the buckskin bag, and hid it back in the forest with her other bag. The meat she lowered down and moved it back as well. If she lost it to tree-borne predators, so be it. She only had a couple of days to go before Marshall came back. She could last that long without food at all.

Checking her first campsite revealed little she could do to make it more obscure. An average person finding it might very well think it as old as the other fires. A tracker would know different and would be able to follow her path into the woods. There was nothing she could do about that.

She walked back through the village, keeping an eye on the river. There were no canoes or boats headed toward the village at present.

I just need to keep a wary eye out. As long as I am not caught unawares, I have a good chance of hiding in the woods, woods I know, and they do not.

This was assuming there was a "they," but that was the safest assumption she could make. She washed in the creek and made her morning toilet. Feeling like an animal, she carefully covered it up. At Johnston's Landing, she fed the forty-odd chickens and collected the eggs. She recorded the count in Marshall's ledger, then she fed the other animals and milked the two cows, who were in pain and complained to her the entire time.

"I am sorry, dear cows. I have neglected you," she said. She didn't drink milk herself and couldn't understand why anyone would want to either, so she left the buckets in the pig pen for them to drink. The pigs left off their food and began eagerly drinking the milk.

A small suspicious voice in her ear said, *Anyone who sees the animals will know they have been cared for.*

"I can't just let them suffer. I am not that cruel."

She decided the best place for her to camp was the clearing she had shared with Standing Bear. The next two hours she spent moving her bags and venison up the creek and thence up the little rabbit trail to the small open space. It was hidden here, and her path would be masked by the stream. It was unlikely even a tracker would find this spot. She spread her sleeping fur and slept a little. It would be easier to keep watch this night and sleep during the day.

Late in the day, she slipped out and snuck back down to the village.

The small voice warned, *Keep watch. Look out.* The mouse-like voice wasn't at all clear, but Two Blankets was getting used to hearing it. So far, the warnings held solid. She would continue to listen. As she approached the verge where the streamside foliage opened onto the village, some sound made her duck back.

"I'm telling you, Virgil, someone's been taking care of them animals. The eggs is all gathered, and the cows milked. Pig's bellies is round as a pumpkin with milk. If there's anything I know, it's pigs."

Two men were peering up into the foliage surrounding her, apparently looking for something or someone. The one who had just spoken had sandy hair pressed down by a slouch hat. He was on the short side for a whiteman, just three fingers taller than she was, and his slumped posture made him appear even smaller. In his middle thirties, he spat through broken teeth and wiped his scraggly beard with his shirtsleeve.

The second man, Virgil, was taller in comparison, though not unreasonably so, perhaps a good handspan taller, and possessed an erect posture and a searching gaze. His dark eyes looked out past thick, black eyebrows into the surrounding brush.

"And just where do you say we look, Hank? We done searched the whole damn village. Ain't nobody there. So, you saying we should search up this stream? Forest is so close there a man could shoot your eyeball out 'fore you ever even seen him."

"Well, I don't want nobody to shoot my eyeball out," Hank said. "I was just saying, is all."

"Keep your musket handy," Virgil said. "Let's go back to the store and invest-i-gate. I been here once 'fore. We'll drink a little of Johnston's whiskey and act like we was waiting for him. He don't show for a couple days, we load up everything we can carry and hightail it out of here. If he's out hunting and he does show, we either kill him or just be good customers."

"That's fine with me. This place gives me cold sweats."

"You getting the ghost creeps, Hank? Ain't much of a man gets the ghost creeps in the daytime."

"I'm just telling you how I feel, Virgil. You don't have to get all personal and insulting."

"Get some whiskey in your belly. You'll feel a lot better."

The voices receded down the stream and toward Marshall's longhouse. Two Blankets stayed where she was, tucked behind the broken stump of a tree. She was glad she had moved and hidden her camp. They were unlikely to venture far up the creek, and she would be relatively safe if she were careful.

Good idea. Stay safe, White Mouse whispered.

"Yes, White Mouse, good idea." Still, she didn't like them roaming the village. There was little she could do now, so she backed up quietly and made her way up the creek, always walking in the water so as to leave no trail, until she reached her little path to her hiding place. She glanced around. So far there was no clear sign of her exit here, but a few more trips and the trail would become more evident. With care not to disarrange any sand or rocks on the bank, she stepped onto the dried moss verge of the stream bank, then stepped with care again onto the rabbit trail.

There was nothing to do but eat and sleep, and so she did both, waking after dark. She could occasionally hear the cows bawling in pain. They needed to be milked, or their udders would swell painfully.

White Mouse chittered, *Not safe to go. Pain in cow not worth it.*

Two Blankets patted her shoulder, "I know, White Mouse. I know."

Good. You no go.

Two Blankets thought on this problem. To emerge from her hiding place would definitely put her at risk. Yet the pain in the cows was evident and would only get worse. Finally, she gathered up her bow and arrows and slipped out of the little hollow. At the edge of the forest, she could faintly hear two voices coming from Marshall Johnston's longhouse. She could not hear any words, but the tone of the conversation sounded like two drunken men.

Good. If they stay there, I will be all right.

She walked along the forest edge to her left, downriver toward the main village. Off to the backside of the *Tyee's* longhouse, she found enough ash burned a whitish gray to coat her entire body. With charcoal, she drew upon her face and breasts jagged marks like lightning.

I no like this. This dangerous for you, sweet one. Dangerous for me, White Mouse said.

"I know, White Mouse." She petted the area on her shoulder that seemed to feel the scratchiest. "I know." She slipped back toward Marshall's longhouse as quiet as the night. She had to wait until the men passed out from drink. Especially the dark haired one. He was the dangerous one.

She dozed for a couple hours but woke to the voices again. They were in front of the longhouse. "Hank, take your musket. You got the first watch. Ain't likely you'll see anybody coming up here at night, but let's be careful, anyways. Wake me up in about four hours."

"I don't like it out here. This whole place is like a graveyard and that damn *totem* staring down on us. There's evil here, Virgil, I'm telling you."

"If you're gonna puke 'cause you got the collywobbles, I'd just as soon you was out here. Just sit on this stump here out front. Prop up your musket and keep an eye out." Virgil went back inside, and Hank settled into his spot.

Two Blankets slid as quiet as a mouse toward the corral. Measuring the moon against the sky, she waited another four fingers. She could just see Hank on his stump slumped over his musket. She picked the buckets up from the pig pen and took them to the cow corral. They were obviously in pain. She stroked them and tried to quiet them, but she knew only milking them would help. As quickly as she was able, she milked the two cows, and they did quiet down. She looked back over to Johnston's Landing, and Hank was still sleeping. She put one of the buckets in with the pigs and fed them. They were sleeping, but the food would be there for them tomorrow. Next, she came to the chickens and scattered the grain. She thought about the eggs.

No. No. No. Don't do that, White Mouse said.

"I'm sorry White Mouse." Two Blankets smiled. "I have to." She gathered up the eggs and put them into a fold in her cape which she carried across the stream with the bucket of milk. Hank was still snoring. His musket had fallen to the ground. Two Blankets scattered most of the eggs in front of Hank and some in front of the door flap. She left the bucket of milk in front of the doorway. Picking up his musket she carried it toward the *Tyee's* longhouse. Every ten to fifteen paces she dropped an egg leaving a path all the way to the *totem* at the *Tyee's* longhouse. She dropped the last two eggs just inside the doorway and threw the musket into the longhouse where it settled into the ashes. Slipping to the verge of the forest, she snuck back to the edge of the creek side. Tucked back into the brush, she settled down to wait.

This is bad idea, White Mouse said, *really bad.*

"Shh, White Mouse. It will be all right."

About three hours later, as the sky was beginning to gray, she heard voices coming from Marshall's Landing.

"Holy Christ, Hank. You been asleep this whole time?"

Hank stood up. "What do you mean?" He slipped on the eggs and sat down hard in the midst of them. Virgil stepped through the doorway and kicked the bucket of milk over.

"This is what I mean. You are sitting in eggs, and here's a bucket of milk. You been sleeping, goddammit."

"I might have dozed off for a bit, but I been watching."

"You call this watching, fer Christ sake? Where's your musket?"

"It was right here on my lap."

"You let someone sneak up here and surround you with eggs and take your musket?" Virgil said.

"I don't know what happened. I really don't."

"Well, let's follow the eggs, shall we?" The tone of disgust in Virgil's voice was apparent. "There's an egg over there toward the creek."

Hank got up and looked down. He was covered by broken eggs and shells and half a bucket of milk. They began following the egg trail toward the *totem.* At the *totem,* as the sky was lightening, both stood there discussing.

"Well, there's your gun you stupid son of a bitch, in the middle of all that ash. Go and get it."

"I ain't going through that mouth, I can say that. I tell you this place is full of ghosts." Hank stepped gingerly down into the ash. As the longhouse was dug in about three feet and it was full of ash, it was knee deep on Hank. The ash and dust swirled up over him. "It's still hot here." He waded out to the middle and fished the musket out of the ash. "Jesus, Virgil, it's clogged with ash and dirt."

"Of course, it is, you idiot. Let's get back to the Landing."

As they walked back to Johnston's Landing, Hank looked like a bedraggled man who had been egged and ashed by a mob. Virgil was obviously enraged. Hank was just—Hank.

Two Blankets eased back into the forest and up the stream. All she could do now was wait and hope that Marshall and his people would arrive and catch these two. She did not like Marshall, but these two emanated an evil that she could feel. She slipped up the stream and carefully walked her rabbit trail path to her hiding place. Lowering the venison haunch from the tree branch, she coiled the rope. She ate a little, curled up on her sleeping robe and drew her cape over her.

"Keep watch my friend, White Mouse."

I will watch out for you, friend.

She woke once during the night when she heard the cry of a cat hunting. It was a way off, and she went back to sleep. The excitement of the previous day had worn off, and now she was just plain tired.

The next day, June twenty-sixth, she awoke with a start. It was full on morning. She wondered if she dared sneak down to the village and see what was happening there. Desperately she wanted to, and just as desperately she was afraid to. She ate a little and realized that she had to. The two men at the Landing drew her, and she had to find out. Still, she had to be very careful.

She slipped from her hiding place, all her senses hyper-alert. True, no one could see her here but also true that she could not see anyone. She had slept in, so she didn't even know if someone had passed her hiding place and was already up the creek, waiting for her to come out. Or if the men were even still at Johnston's Landing. As she approached the clearing, she crept on her belly and peeked out. She heard two men's voices, one down by the dock and the other at the doorway of the longhouse. A wave of relief passed over her, and she exhaled the breath she had been holding.

"Hurry it up, Hank. Get that canoe packed and let's get out of here."

"I *am* hurrying. Come on let's go. I'm ready."

"Just going to get one last crate of whiskey and another bag."

Around the bend, in the distance downstream, came the now familiar huffing of the steamboat. Two Blankets could see the tips of the smokestacks pumping smoke into the still morning air.

"Now. Virgil. *Now.* The steamer's coming."

Virgil bolted out the doorway with a crate of whiskey clinking under his arm, a heavy canvas bag over one shoulder and his musket over the other. He threw the bag into the canoe and Hank began paddling before Virgil had even gotten in.

"Let me get aboard you fucking idiot." Hank paused in his paddling, and the canoe drifted back a few feet. Two Blankets could see that they had also loaded Marshall's canoe down with loot and tethered it to theirs. "All right, I'm in. Let's get out of here."

Both began paddling vigorously upstream away from the Landing.

Two Blankets felt safe now. She dashed to the doorway of the longhouse. The steamboat was quite visible, and she could see several men gathered on the foredeck pointing first at the village and then at the canoes. The steamer was a sternwheeler, which meant she could maneuver a lot closer to the bank, maybe even dock at the raft itself, and it was angling in to do just that.

She ducked inside and quickly pulled on her dress. If Marshall were aboard, he wouldn't want her to greet him and his men dressed only in a cape. It was the act of just a moment, and she opened the door flap to the longhouse and ran down to the dockside.

MARSHALL RETURNS

CHAPTER 7
JUNE 26 TO JUNE 27, 1856

MARSHALL JOHNSTON WAS at first excited for his part as the steamer came in sight of Marshall's Landing. On the foredeck, he had his crew with him, a master carpenter and his two apprentices, a millwright and his apprentice, a bullwhacker and his boy, and four laborers. Also accompanying him was Mr. Shales, who distinguished himself from the others with his city suit and waxed mustache.

Marshall waved his arms as he explained his plans. His back to the village, he continued gesturing for a full minute before he noticed his audience was not paying him any attention. They all stared at the village, or what was left of it. Marshall slowly turned, and his jaw dropped open. At first, he couldn't comprehend what he was looking at. Were they even in the right place? Well, yes, there was the *totem* rising from the wreck of the *Tyee*'s longhouse. But everything was gone, just *gone*. Every building he had depended on being there was just gone. He closed his eyes and forced them back open again. It was the same. Every single building was burnt to the ground.

Had something horrible happened? He looked upstream, and his storage building and animal building were still standing. No damage there. His own longhouse, Johnston's Landing, still stood. His dock was still standing, and there was his wife by the dock waiting for him.

"So, this is the property I loaned all this money to develop," said Mr.

Shales pulling his waxed mustache out to its full extent. "I think we may have to renegotiate."

"Shut the fuck up, Shales. Them two canoes. One of them is mine, and it's loaded down with my goods," Marshall said pointing. Unshouldering his Model M1841 Mississippi rifle, he began carefully loading it. The stern-wheeler *Jennie Clark* nosed into the Landing and made fast. Marshall lay down on the deck, sighting down the long barrel of the rifle on the distant men paddling furiously. Captain John C. Ainsworth joined them on the fore-deck. A whip-thin, narrow-faced man, he peered at the retreating canoes.

"Permission to shoot them thieves, Captain Ainsworth?" Marshall asked.

"Well, they're on a boat, and we are, too." Captain Ainsworth straightened his jacket. "I figure as captain I can make that decision. That's got to be a good three hundred yards. You hit the bastard, I'll buy the best bottle of whiskey you got and share it around."

"You'll never make that shot," said Mr. Shales. "You can hardly see them."

"I'll not only make it. I'll call it," Marshall said. "right shoulder blade on the man in the back. Five gold double-eagles say I make it."

"I'll take that bet," Shales said. There was considerable excitement as the men began taking sides on the bet.

"Quiet now," Marshall said, adjusting his sighting. The men on the canoe had quit paddling so fast, considering themselves out of range. All was silent except the light huffing of the steamboat. The gun cracked, and a moment later the paddler in the back of the canoe dropped his paddle and fell half out of the canoe. Marshall reloaded.

Captain Ainsworth cupped his hands to his mouth and shouted, "Surrender, and we won't have to kill you."

Marshall lay back down and sighted in on the second man, but he had thrown up his hands and said, "Don't shoot. Please don't kill me. I give up." His canoe was drifting back downriver.

"Bring your vessel about and paddle back to us. You don't want to even touch that rifle," Captain Ainsworth said.

"Yes, sir," Hank said. "I'm going to pick up my paddle now. Don't shoot."

"Damn," Marshall said easing back into a crouch. "I really wanted to shoot him, too." He got up. "Shales, I believe we got a hundred dollar bet to settle up?" He held out his hand. Shales opened his dandy's pocketbook and placed five gold coins in Marshall's hand.

"That was quite a shot, Mr. Johnston, quite a shot," Captain Ainsworth said. "I am impressed." The other men settled their bets.

By now, the canoe was nearing the dock, and Hank let it drift up against the bank and threw up his hands again. "Don't shoot me. It weren't my idea. Honest."

The men disembarked. "Get out of the canoe real slow like and lay down on the bank," Captain Ainsworth said. "Josephs, tie that canoe off and bring that other man down." Josephs, a burly steamboat man, hurried to comply.

"We was just going to wait here for Johnston to come back and—"

"Shut up," Marshall said and aimed a solid kick to Hank's ribs.

Hank doubled up in pain. "You didn't have to kick me."

Josephs had, meantime, brought Virgil to join Hank. Marshall inspected the back of Virgil's coat. "Right shoulder blade, just as I said." He pulled the coat half off. "Likely shattered it. Maybe he'll live, but he'll be crippled the rest of his miserable life."

The captain nudged the shuddering Hank with his boot. "Jaysus, he shat his pants. Sit up, you cowering thief."

"Yes, sir." Hank pushed himself into a sitting position.

"Josephs, tie his hands."

"Aye, Captain."

Two Blankets stepped forward. "Husband Marshall, I am glad you returned safely."

"Gentlemen, this here is my wife, Two Blankets." His back was still toward her as he examined the thieves. For the second time that day, one of his remarks was marked with open-mouthed astonishment. He turned to Two Blankets. "Holy Jaysus F. Christ. What you gone and done with your face and your body, too?"

Two Blankets was momentarily taken aback and looked down. "Oh, this. Well, when the men came—"

Hank looked up at her. He shook violently and tried to push himself away from her along the ground. "I told him there was ghosts hereabouts, but he wouldn't believe me. Said I had the ghost creeps. Said I had the collywobbles. Wouldn't believe me."

Marshall and the others looked from Virgil to Two Blankets to Hank.

Marshall got that crafty look. "Tell us the truth why you came here and what you were doing here and maybe, just maybe, we won't let the spirit touch you. You do know what will happen if I let her touch you, don't you?"

"I don't want to know. We came here, Virgil and me, thinking we'd see what the fire was all about. You could see it for a couple miles upriver, and you could see the smoke for miles beyond that. When we got here there weren't nobody here, so Virgil says, 'We'll just wait a bit and see if old Marshall comes back. If he does, maybe we'll kill him and take his goods, or maybe we'll just act real peaceable like we was just waiting for you.'"

"When was this?"

"We come down on the twenty-fourth. Village was all burned down. We didn't have nothing to do with that, honest we didn't. We was looking around, and Virgil said I had the ghost creeps. I was right to have them, too. And then, the ghost milked the cows and fed the pigs the milk. That was the first night."

Two Blankets edged closer to Hank, and he scooted back. "So, then what happened?" Marshall asked real soft. "Remember, to tell the truth."

Hank continued talking to Marshall, but his eyes were on Two Blankets. Suddenly he looked down. "Now, I done pissed myself."

"Just answer the question."

"Well, you didn't come back, and we drank some of your whiskey. We started planning how we'd steal your canoe too and take as much as we could the next day. We drank a little more, and Virgil told me to keep watch outside your longhouse. I stayed real alert. That there ghost must have witched me because the next thing I remember is waking up and falling down in the eggs."

"The eggs?" Marshall was beginning to smile.

"It ain't funny. Somehow the ghost witched me to sleep, then she spread eggs all over the ground and put a pail of milk and more eggs in front of the doorway. When Virgil come out, he yelled at me for falling asleep, only I was witched asleep, and I fell in the eggs. Then Virgil kicked the bucket. See, he was witched, too, and the milk went all over me. So, he yelled, and then we followed the egg trail back up to the *totem*, right up to the *totem*'s mouth. There was two eggs in its mouth, and my gun had been spirited clean into the middle of the burning ashes. So, Virgil made me go in there and get it. He was real mad, but I was right all along. The next day, we loaded up your canoe and ours, and when we saw the Jennie Clark coming, we took off."

"So, you did intend to steal my goods all along?"

"We did." Hank looked glum. "But we wouldn't have done it if we hadn't been witched."

"That sounds like a complete and sincere confession to me," said Captain Ainsworth.

"I stole the goods, and I was witched into it," Marshall parroted. "I'm thinking the judge will be laughing when he sentences this fool."

"Josephs," Captain Ainsworth said, "throw him in the river and let him get the crap washed out of his pants." Turning to Marshall, he said, "I'll thank you for holding these men until I come back downriver."

"Sure, I can do that."

Surveying the village, Captain Ainsworth said, "You got some hard decisions to make. Let's get your cargo unloaded, and I'll take that whiskey while the crew works."

Walking up to the Landing, Marshall fell back to Two Blankets's side. "You might want to go up the creek a bit and wash up. You look a sight." He slid away from her and rejoined Captain Ainsworth on their walk to the Landing longhouse.

Two Blankets walked up the stream until she could no longer see the clearing, hesitated, then walked a quarter of a mile further up. There were many men in this group working for Marshall. There was no point of giving any of them ideas. She stripped off her dress and looked down at her body. She had completely forgotten about her "warpaint." That would not make her look very civilized. It was short work to clean off, and soon she was walking back down the creek to Johnston's Landing. As she approached the longhouse, she saw Virgil sprawled against the wall, unconscious and Hank in his soaked clothes looking miserable. He glanced up and saw her.

Two Blankets made what she hoped was an evil face and Hank backed up against the wall. She cackled in an hysterical fashion, and he squirmed. Turning the corner, she could see Marshall's goods stacked on the bank. Two bullocks had just been unloaded, and the bullwhacker was walking them up to the corral. The millwright had the tarp off the Scott and Herndon portable steam-powered sawmill. She entered the longhouse.

The men were gathered about what passed for the bar, drinking. Half the bottle was done already, and it looked like the other half would not be long in the bottle.

"I have to say, Marshall," Captain Ainsworth said, "that was a magnificent shot. If I hadn't seen it, I wouldn't believe it." He lifted his glass. "Here's to Marshall and two fewer thieves on the river." He drained his glass. "As entertaining as this is, some of us have to work for a living. I will stop on the downriver run for my prisoners." He set the glass down with a thump and exited.

"Two Blankets, could you fix us something to eat? It's been a mighty hungry trip up from Portland," Marshall said.

"Yes, husband Marshall. Then I must rest a bit myself. It has been a trying two days dealing with those two men and worrying they might get away before you returned." She stirred the fire pit and found a coal still barely glowing and blew it alight. Adding kindling, she soon had a cheering fire going. In a large cast iron cauldron, she cut up potatoes and carrots and added what she could find of the remnants of venison. Four quarts of water and she pushed the big pot onto the edge of the fire. Then she retired back to her sleeping furs. She could still hear the men's discussion from the back of the longhouse, but most of the talk she just didn't care about.

Occasional wisps of conversation made it through her subconscious haze. Mr. Shales speaking, "We are going to have to renegotiate our arrangement," and Marshall's sotto voiced reply, "Later, Shales. When the men are gone. Christ."

Marshall to the master carpenter, "I ain't going to need you like we thought originally. I'll pay you and your apprentices a week's wages if you'll come back in the spring. There'll be more work for you than just some flooring and windows and partitions then. Agreed?"

The sawyer entered and took up his drink. "Looks like I got some catching up to do." He tossed back a shot. "That's fine whiskey, Marshall. So where will we be cutting first?"

Marshall rolled out his plan of the village and weighted it down with glasses. "We're going to want to bridge the stream down here in the village near the midden pile, and we're also going to need timbers and thick planks to build up the dock. I want you to start pushing up the stream on the village side. By next spring I want to have a road of sorts up to the plateau. About a quarter mile up, we'll have to jump the stream with another bridge."

"Why not just make the cut up this side of the stream and avoid that bridge?" the sawyer said, examining the plans.

"This map don't show it, but the terrain is too rough on this side."

The sawyer nodded. "So, you'll be needing my services and my apprentice?"

"With these changes, more than ever before. The bullwhacker—ah, speaking of the devil—grab yourself a whiskey and your helper, too."

"Don't mind if I do. This here is my son, Kenny."

"As I was saying, the bullwhacker can haul that saw nearly anywhere you want, Ike, and anytime you need it moved, you co-ord-din-ate with him. The rest of you fellers, I want a decent bridge across the stream, not just something we throw together. I want a smooth approach on both sides. It may not look like anything now, fact is it looks like shit, but this here Marshall's Landing is going to be a town. We want to be thinking town whenever we build anything here."

Two Blankets lifted her head from the sleeping furs and sat up. An hour or two must have passed. She got up and went to the stew pot. It was bubbling nicely, and she added a couple smaller logs to the fire. She stirred it and judged it done or done enough. There were not enough bowls, but with coffee cups, small pans, and bowls she had enough. She ladled out stew into the first three bowls and took them to the men at the table. That had the anticipated result. The rest of the men grabbed a bowl or cup and started serving themselves. Two Blankets went back to her sleeping furs.

In another hour or two, it was Marshall shaking her awake. "We're going to tour the village. I want some answers to what happened to my town."

Two Blankets got up and followed her husband outside. They walked back across the stream, and Marshall looked into his storehouse. Except for the stores that the men had stolen, all seemed in order. They walked up to the clearing in front of what used to be the *Tyee* Running Blade's longhouse. It was strange staring at that *totem* that seemed to be staring, uncaring, back at them.

"Holy, fucking Christ, it's all gone. Every bit of it." Marshall slowly pivoted clockwise taking in first the *totem* and the *Tyee*'s longhouse, then as he turned, the spot where Stinging Nettle's hut used to stand, the river, the fish drying house, and the fish racks. All was gone. Continuing his turn, his eyes took in the tanning longhouse, the meat drying and smoking house, two other longhouses, and finally Bone Rattler's longhouse. "All gone," he said again as if saying it would make it go back to the way it was.

He turned to Two Blankets, his eyes hard. "When did all this take place?"

"Honorable husband Marshall, it began on the day you left, June twenty-one, I believe you say. The clan first stripped all the cedar planks from the sides, front and back of Stinging Nettle's longhouse, there to the right and riverward of the *totem*. The long planks they cut into shorter ones. That night they burned the longhouse to the ground. In the morning, Stinging Nettle left in a canoe towing a raft of cedar behind them. It continued like that until the night of June twenty-two when they burned the *Tyee*'s longhouse. His big canoe departed towing a large raft of cedar on the twenty-three, the day the steamship *Belle* came to get the clan. Lieutenant-Phil-Sheridan was on the *Belle*. There was some discussion about clothing. Finally, all the tribe got on the *Belle* and left. That is what happened. I speak truly."

Marshall looked up at the *totem* and said, "You're laughing at me, ain't you. Damn you." Turning back to the bullwhacker he said, "First thing tomorrow, I want you to get a line around this thing and pull it down. Hear me?"

"You're the boss. Might take some doing, even a couple days if it ain't burned through, and it's rooted deep."

"I don't care how long it takes. I don't care how hard it is. I ain't going to have that thing smiling down at me like it's laughing the whole time." Turning to Two Blankets, he said, "I suppose you couldn't do anything about this?"

"Husband Marshall, I am *mistshimus*. What could I do?"

"What's this *mistshimus*?" Mr. Shales asked.

"I keep forgetting. You ain't been here long. A *mistshimus* is like a slave. The Chinook keep them."

"A slave? But we don't allow any slaves in the Oregon territories," Mr. Shales said.

"We don't allow no nigra slaves in Oregon. We got plenty of Indian ones."

"So, your wife is a—"

"I am a *mistshimus*, a slave. Marshall bought the right to marry me from the Bent Creek Clan when I was fourteen summers," Two Blankets said.

"It ain't as bad as it sounds, Shales," Marshall said.

"And you don't have a problem with this, Mrs. Johnston?" Shales asked.

Marshall looked to her. She knew she could destroy him, what was left of him at this moment, but she didn't have the option of returning to the clan, and it would not be truth. She turned to Mr. Shales, "It is true that I was *mistshimus* to the Bent Creek Clan. I was stolen from the Nez Perce when I was ten summers. But as far as how my bride price was arranged, I have no complaint. This is how it is done among the Chinook, and my status was elevated when I married Marshall. No other *mistshimus* was married. I was free to leave Marshall, at any time, if I was mistreated. He always treated me with the respect due to a *mistshimus* wife. I speak truth."

"Are you satisfied, Shales?" Marshall asked. "Two Blankets, could you not stop this in any way? Argue my case for me while I was gone? Keep them from burning everything? Anything?"

"My husband Marshall, I think we discussed this, and I did warn you. When you stopped caring about the clan, the clan stopped caring about you. I do not know if it would have made a difference, but in their mind, you were Bent Creek Clan no longer. The longhouses were their property until the twenty-five of June. They disposed of their property as they wanted. Even Lieutenant-Phil-Sheridan agreed they had this right by treaty."

Marshall slumped. "Well, nothing for it now. We must go with what we've got. We will discuss this, Shales, but for now, let's go back to the long-house and open another bottle."

Back in the longhouse, Marshall opened two bottles. Two Blankets thought he planned to get everybody drunk enough they would forget about how glorious Marshall's Landing was to be and accept the new plan. She didn't think Mr. Shales was that kind of man. This was a significant setback for Marshall, and everyone knew it. The workers did not care as long as they got paid. Shales was a different story.

Late in the afternoon, the *Jennie Clark* came steaming up, and they trans-ferred the prisoners. Captain Ainsworth agreed to make the report. It was a quick stop, and she was soon steaming off downriver. Two Blankets re-tired to her sleeping furs. The men separated out to their various temporary sleeping quarters, the bullwhacker and his apprentice to the barn, the labor-ers to the storehouse. The millwright, the carpenter, and their apprentices, as well as Mr. Shales, were to sleep in the Landing longhouse. Two Blankets did not care. Just having bodies in the camp made it feel more like the clan again. Apparently, the bullwhacker's boy milked the cows. She no longer heard them. She no longer heard anything. She was so exhausted all she could think of was sleep.

Late that night, Marshall slipped into the sleeping furs and rolled over, wrapping his arm around her, and fell asleep. She moved the heavy arm off her shoulder and slipped off to sleep again.

June twenty-seventh saw some activity in the camp. The bullwhacker had hitched his team up to the portable sawmill and hauled it across the stream and up to the forest verge. The millwright and his apprentice were already hard at work felling the first trees.

Mr. Shales was showing Marshall his new rifle when Two Blankets re-turned from her milking and egg collecting chores.

She started frying up the whole batch of eggs. She hadn't much more than that for the men besides milk today. She did find a big hunk of bacon which she cut into chunks and threw into the other frying pan. That was going to have to do it for the men for breakfast.

"It's a Springfield M1855, just came out this year," Mr. Shales said. "My father had some dealings with the Springfield Company in Massachusetts. He knew I'd be interested and acquired a prototype for me. It is just going into production now."

"Well, Mr. Shales, we do need some meat. There's an elk herd up on the plateau if you want to try your luck?"

"I do, indeed."

"Harry, take another feller and go up with Mr. Shales here. Go on up the creek a half-mile, maybe a little longer. You'll see a trail leading out of the canyon to the west. There's a pretty good-sized herd up there, usually about a mile to the west toward the forest."

"Yes, sir, Mr. Johnston. I'll take Big Ed with me. He's big and strong and a good shot, too."

Marshall turned to Mr. Shales. "Mind you, don't take the big bull elk, the herd leader. He's old and tough as an old boot. Take one of the younger males."

"I understand. I am no stranger to hunting, Mr. Johnston, believe me."

"I would come with you as a guide, but I got too much to do here. Remember, this ain't no trophy hunt. We need usable meat."

Two Blankets fished out a plate for Harry and Big Ed and dished up eggs and bacon. All she could offer to drink was milk, which they took gratefully.

Shales was already digging into his pack for suitable clothes. When he finally emerged fully dressed, Marshall thought he might as well have kept the suit on although the hunting outfit appeared to have been worn before. The brown tweed jacket and pants were a matched set. He had a dark derby hat pushed down squarely over his carefully greased-back hair, and his boots still squeaked. Strapped over this was his case for the paper cartridges and minie balls on his left side. A new belt knife was strapped to his waist on his right. He carried a wooden canteen hanging over his shoulder as well.

"Ready to go, Mr. Everton, Big Ed?"

Harry Everton, who had been waiting for the twenty minutes it had taken for Shales to get dressed, rolled his eyes toward Marshall. "Yes, sir, Mr. Shales. Let's get going before tomorrow catches us still standing here."

Shales caught the look. "I'll have you know, this is proper hunting attire in the better sorts of society."

"Just bring him back in one piece. I still need him," Marshall said to Harry.

"Yes, sir, Mr. Johnston. Mr. Shales, shall we depart on our excursion? After you, sir."

This was a busy day for Two Blankets. Somehow, everyone else seemed to have a helper or an apprentice, but she was expected to cook for the entire party. She went out into the area in front of the longhouse. If she built a fire pit here, she could cook outside. That was a start. She raked out a circular area a good eight U. S. government feet across and then lined the edge with river rock. From the *Tyee*'s fire pit she got several baking stones and placed these in her pit. The millwright—Ike was his name—had felled an oak and was debranching it. She asked, and he said he would bring her all the branches unfit for sawing. That took care of a place to cook and the primary fire. She gathered what kindling she could and laid the beginnings for a small fire.

It was a little early, but she milked the cows. She needed the milk. She also gathered what eggs she could find for tomorrow's breakfast. About midafternoon she heard a sharp crack of a rifle followed almost immediately by two more reports. So, surely, they would have meat for dinner. She decided to cook it just like the clan typically grilled salmon steaks and set about making up the spits. When these were completed, she took a break and thought what to do next. She had never been responsible for the cooking for a group of hungry warriors before. She had *camas* flour and decided to make up *camas* cakes. Biscuits would have been a possibility, too, but *camas* cakes she knew how to do in quantity. Once these were all done, all that was left to do was wait. Ike's apprentice had brought a pile of logs, big and small, with a smile.

"Thank you, good sir."

"Well, I notice you ain't got no help, so I figured I'd be advised to keep the cook happy." He laughed.

He was a young man of sixteen or so summers with an easy smile. "What is your name?" she asked.

"Name's Frank Millson, Ma'am," he said with another blushing smile.

"Thank you, Frank Millson. My name is Two Blankets." She returned his smile.

"I'd better get back to work. Ike is a good master, but he don't like to be kept waiting."

A couple of hours later, Two Blankets heard voices coming from up the creek. In the lead were Harry Everton and Big Ed carrying a young buck elk, fully dressed out, its legs tied over a pole. Following them at some distance was Mr. Shales who was bearing his rifle, the head of the old buck elk, and one haunch. He was limping a bit, and Two Blankets guessed he had blisters. When he reached the clearing, he ordered the millwright's apprentice over to help him, and promptly gave him the haunch and head to carry as well as his canteen.

"It was a successful hunt, Mr. Johnston," Shales said. "I stalked and brought down the biggest elk you have ever seen."

Marshall looked at the head. Harry Everton just shook his head. Two Blankets looked to the neck of the elk they carried and saw it had already been bled out. "Good job, Harry, Big Ed," Marshall said.

"What do you think of this head? Is it not fine? I'm going to have it stuffed for my office at the bank," Shales said.

"I thought we understood you weren't to take the herd leader, the big bull," Marshall said irritably.

"I know. But once I saw him, I couldn't resist."

"He gut shot the damn elk," Harry Everton said. "I said wait for a clean shot. Hell, if I'd had a stick, I could have thrown it and hit him with it. Couldn't have been more than thirty yards. Fortunately, we had Big Ed, and he actually made the kill shot. I got this here small bull at the same time, so we got meat to eat anyways."

"I say, mebbe we fix him a nice big steak off that great bull he killed. Say it's just for him," Marshall said.

TYEE MARSHALL JOHNSTON

CHAPTER 8
JUNE 27 TO JUNE 28, 1856

HARRY EVERTON BUTCHERED out the small bull elk and produced sixteen good sized steaks for the night's meal as well as several roasts and meat for stew. He then cut a pound and a half steak from the old bull elk just for Mr. Alton Shales.

"Think this is big enough for Mr. Shales?" he asked Two Blankets.

"I don't want to say anything bad about husband Marshall's business partners, but any bigger and he might not make it back to Portland this year. I suspect he'll be chewing on that for a good week." She smiled and set up a special heavy-duty skewer for Mr. Shale's steak, then went back to skewering the other steaks for the crew. "This will be quite a celebration."

Later that evening, she built up the fire and angled the steaks in to cook, just as she had salmon a hundred times before. The *camas* cakes went on her baking stone to cook lightly on one side before being turned to cook on the other side. Ike had cut some rounds for seats which he arranged a distance upwind from the fire. They were small enough to move. It always seemed that no matter which way the breeze was blowing it blew toward people when they gathered. She had some early summer greens from the garden as well as cattail stalks. The cattail stalks, she just peeled off the outer layers of leaves and cut up in lengths to boil in a big pot. The greens she steamed lightly. The steaks were done on one side, and she turned the skewers to cook the other side. All the food looked in readiness.

They had brought out the trundle table that Marshall used for a bar. She set a bucket of milk and as many plates and cups as she could find. Always before, when the clan ate, there were more than enough bowls, plates, and cups to go around. This way of cooking, when she was used to just cooking for Marshall and herself at the Landing, was different entirely. It was like she was preparing a meal for a small clan but all alone.

"Well, it will have to do," she said to herself. The men were starting to gather and wash up in the stream. She pulled the *camas* cakes off the baking stone and put them in one large bowl. The cattails, she just poured off the water and left them in the large pot on the end of the table. Greens in another smaller bowl, and the steaks she left on the skewers and leaned them against the table. All except Mr. Alton Shale's steak, which she served up on the one large enameled platter she had. This she placed at the head of the table, in a place of honor.

Of tableware, she only had a couple of serving spoons and three forks, but all the men carried some kind of knife. They could make do with that. As they came up to the table, she noticed that most of them treated her with a sort of respect.

Perhaps this is the respect due to husband Marshall. *He is a bit like the Tyee of this work clan. As long as he pays them, they will treat him and me with some respect, even if they don't feel it.*

She shook her head. The whitemans were strange, and she might never figure them out. She was reasonably sure that they would not treat her with such deference if she weren't married to their boss.

Marshall brought out four pints of whiskey to a small cheer from some of the men. He did know how to work them even if he had not done so well with the Bent Creek Clan.

It makes sense. They are his people after all. She did remember that the *Tyee* was well regarded as a trader among natives and whitemans alike. The *Tyee* always observed and never prejudged a man when he was trading. Marshall thought he was better than the Chinook and so was out-bargained.

Two Blankets saw that all the men, except Mr. Alton Shales, had brought a cup of some sort and a plate. Mr. Shales was dressed in his business suit, a clean shirt, and a tie. He pulled up an oak round and sat at the head of the table. The others filed past taking greens, cattails, and *camas* cakes, and held out their plates as she slid the elk steaks onto their plates. A couple took milk. Most took a generous dollop of whiskey before going over to sit on the rounds by the fire.

Mr. Alton Shales opened a small canvas case and removed a knife, fork, and spoon, no doubt made especially for travelers.

"Would you like some cattails and greens, Mr. Shales?"

"Thank you, Mrs. Johnston. Yes, I will try some. Cattails you say?"

"Yes. It is common for my people to eat them. And here is a *camas* cake. I hope you are hungry. The men cut that steak especially for you from the huge bull elk you shot."

"I am." He held up his glass to the other men. "It was an exhilarating hunt."

Marshall tapped the cattail pot with a wooden spoon. Gradually the men quieted down. "I just wanted to thank all you men for coming out here to help me start this great venture. I know it don't look like much, as I said before. But by the end of next summer, I plan on having the start of a real town here. Marshall's Landing ain't just going to be another backwater trading post. It's men with vision, like you fellers, that will make this happen, and men like you fellers will make Oregon a great place for people to come and live. Let's lift a cup to that." He held out his cup, and everyone raised in toast a metal or wooden cup and Mr. Shales a glass he had produced from somewhere. They all drank.

"Second, I want to thank Harry and Big Ed for getting that excellent elk you are about to eat."

"You going to go on all night talking," one of the crew said, "or we going to get to eat this elk afore it gets so old Harry and Big Ed wouldn't have had to shoot it? Could've waited for it to fall over with old age." The crew laughed.

Marshall smiled. "I'm getting hungry, too, Ike. Last, Mr. Alton Shales had a great hunt today, and so we have a special steak prepared for him from the great bull elk he killed. Let's lift a glass to Mr. Shales and then let's eat." He lifted his cup in Mr. Shale's direction. "To Mr. Shales and his great bull," and drank it off.

"To Mr. Shales and his great bull," the others repeated and tossed back their drinks.

Mr. Shales lifted his cup and attempted to match them tossing his drink down. Marshall's "Let's eat," covered his coughing.

Some of the men carved off a piece of their steaks and popped them civilly into their mouths to chew happily. Some just picked up the steak on a knife or in their hands and tore off a piece with their teeth. Two Blankets saw appreciative smiles on the faces. Also, no few of them kept half an eye on Mr. Alton Shales as he attempted to carve off a bite from his steak. Two Blankets saw it wasn't overcooked. The great bull was just so old and grizzled it might take Mr. Shales half the night to get a bite cut off and the other half to chew the bite. It was what the clan would call "the meat that lasts all winter" because it would be the last to be cooked. Finally, he got a piece cut and began chewing. He smiled and chewed. There was no way he was going to admit he was wrong.

When Marshall judged enough time had passed, and the celebration was in full swing, he took his special bottle of whiskey and sat down with Mr. Shales. He poured substantial drinks for them both and made a toast that Two Blankets couldn't hear. She did see Mr. Shales join in and drink the glass down as Marshall did. He was going to have a very sore head in the morning and a sour stomach. Marshall poured a second glass, and the negotiations began in earnest. Two Blankets could see that Marshall might have some advantage in place, timing, and drink, but Mr. Shales—for all his tenderfoot sensitivities— was still sharp when numbers and money were concerned. She suspected that Marshall knew this, as well. He just wanted any advantage he could get. Marshall unrolled his plans and stabbed his finger on various spots on the drawing. Mr. Shales nodded amiably and made some counter-argument. This discussion went back and forth for a good two hours. Mr. Shales was pulling on his mustache and twisting the waxed ends. Finally, he made his last offer. Even without hearing the words, Two Blankets knew from watching innumerable Bent Creek Clan trades, big and small, the look of a trader when he was closing in. She could tell that Marshall saw it, as well. They both stood and shook hands on the bargain. Marshall didn't look happy but neither did Mr. Shales.

Ah, it is as good a trade as possible when neither trader goes away happy.

She eased away from the crowd and went back to the longhouse. It had been a hard day and a hard week for her. Without whiteman's sleeping clothes and the crowd sleeping in Marshall's longhouse she just fell back into the sleeping furs in her clothes and slipped into a doze.

It had to be three hours later when Marshall lay down to sleep.

"That son of a bitch insisted on twenty-five percent of the whole project to continue funding me. Twenty-five percent, the bastard."

Two Blankets turned over. "Husband Marshall, if you had been in Portland at his bank it would have been much more. I do not know what 'twenty-five percent' is, but I do know trading. I could see that you used every advantage you had."

"I did do that. Bastard can hold his whiskey. He may be a tenderfoot, but he still can drink and barter. The dollar is in his bloodstream even when he's asleep."

"As I said, he wasn't happy either and tomorrow will wish he had waited until you came to him in his bank office. You are *Tyee* of your own clan now, *Tyee* Marshall Johnston. It was a good trade."

"Well, I hope so. Your *Tyee* Running Blade left me in a bad spot, the bastard. I got to admit though, that man, Indian or no, was the best trader I ever seen. I hate the s.o.b., but he was a master at the game. Didn't help him in the end, but burning the village was a genius move. Made me mad as hell, but I can't do nothing about it."

"You are *Tyee* now," Two Blankets said.

"One tired *Tyee*. I got to sleep now."

Two Blankets did not believe in half of what she'd said about Marshall, but she had set up her furs in his tent. She had to make the best of it. She would see who was indeed the *"Tyee"* in this relationship.

Up before the dawn the next day, she felt like she had slept a week. She stirred the outdoor cook fire back to life and added some smaller logs. She wouldn't need such a large fire for today's breakfast. Two buckets of milk from the cows and two dozen eggs from the chickens. Eggs, bacon, and biscuits would have to do the crew for breakfast.

Most of the crew was up in an hour, and she served them informally at the table. Marshall roused himself, and lastly, Mr. Shales came out of the longhouse looking like he had been dragged by a horse.

"We saved you some of your steak from last night for your breakfast," Harry Everton said, and the crew laughed.

Mr. Shales just sat down at the head of the table and accepted his eggs. The steak was there. He grimaced and pushed it aside.

Marshall picked up a cup at random from the table and poured him a whiskey. "Take a little hair of the dog that bit you. You'll feel better for it."

Mr. Shales took the cup, examined it critically and sipped at it. He made a face, but if taking this shot of courage made him one of the men, he would do it. He tossed down the drink and set the cup down hard on the table.

"Thank you, Mr. Johnston. That refreshed me. I will take the steamboat downriver and start the paperwork for your line of credit tomorrow. Terms will be as we agreed yesterday."

"That'll be fine, Mr. Shales. I'll be down in a couple weeks to sign all the papers. In the meantime, I assume any promissory notes I write to these fellers or to my suppliers will be honored by your bank?"

"Definitely. We don't want to slow down the work on our town here."

Marshall looked up and toward the *Tyee*'s longhouse. "Well, as the new *Tyee* of this here village, I'm going to make my first pronouncement. That there *totem* is coming down. Samuel, let's get to it."

"I'd like to take it slow on that *totem*. Like I said, we don't know how deep it's buried," the bullwhacker said.

"Well, I'm saying let's do it now," Marshall said.

"Yes, sir, Mr. Johnston. I'll get my team." He got up and went to harness his team.

"I would take care with the *totem*, husband Marshall," Two Blankets said.

Marshall turned on her. "What, are we going to anger the spirits of your ancestors?"

"They are not my ancestors, husband Marshall. There are spirits, yes. But I was thinking more about the wasps. I have seen wasps coming out of the *totem* near the top."

"You done your duty then, warning your husband about a few bees," Marshall said to Two Blankets. "We ain't afraid of a few bees, are we fellers?"

Most agreed they weren't, but a few looked wary.

The whole crew, including Mr. Shales, accompanied Samuel, the bull-whacker, as he drove his team across the creek and down toward the *Tyee's* longhouse. He had a chain attached to the oxen's harness. The *totem* pole was a good four feet in diameter at the bottom where the old entrance to the longhouse stood. It tapered a bit as it rose up taller than the peak of the longhouse. At the very top was carved a creature with wings outstretched. They tossed a loop of smaller chain around the winged *totem* near the top and worked it down until it was secure about three feet down just below the upper part of the smoke-covered creature. Samuel hooked both ends of that chain to a hook and attached that to the massive single chain leading to the oxen's harness.

"That chain going to hold?" Marshall asked.

The bullwhacker said, "Should. I've hauled logs from the woods with it that were that size."

"Let's get her down then. I'm sick of looking at it."

The bullwhacker called out to his team, "Git up." The chain began to draw tight. Something about this entire exercise made Two Blankets un-comfortable, and she drew back fifty paces or so. The *totem*, once so brightly painted and the pride of the clan, seemed to glare down at these whitemans. Although it was smoke covered and partly burned, still it held a power. She caught a glimpse of gray-brown on the forest verge and glanced in that di-rection. For a moment, she saw the green-eyed wolf, and then she was gone, disappeared back into the woods.

The chain was taut, and the *totem* creaked under the pull. It was begin-ning to lean slightly toward the pulling oxen, but it just wouldn't give.

"Let's give this damn thing a push, men," Marshall said. "Show it who's boss around here."

He walked over to the *totem* and put his shoulder to it. The other men followed suit.

"Git, up now," the bullwhacker called to his team.

"Push, dammit, push." Even Mr. Shales had got into the act, though his push was only one handed. One man slipped and fell the three feet down into the ash pit that had been the floor of the longhouse.

The *totem* creaked more loudly.

"Git up," called the bullwhacker.

"One, two, three, *heave,*" said Marshall.

The *totem* leaned more toward the bullwhacker. There was a loud creak and then a very much more deafening crack as the *totem* broke about five feet up at a weak point. The top section fell explosively to the ground and shattered into several pieces. Shards of wood and great splinters kicked back into Marshall and the pushing crew, one piece large enough to knock a man back into the ash pit. Several were hit by large splinters which penetrated clothing and drew blood.

Marshall straightened up and wiped the blood from his forehead. "Well, that goddamned thing is down at last. Fought us to the end it did."

He didn't at first notice the swarm of wasps streaming from the hollow core of the *totem* on the ground. The wasps, perhaps because they had been trapped in the *totem* by the fire, were disoriented. It didn't take them long to find the cause of the disturbance to their home. The swarm first balled up over the broken *totem*, then found targets. Once it took notice of the men, it arrowed and drove straight for them. Mr. Shales was stung first by an advancing wasp.

"Ow, that hurt. Ow, dammit. Oh, Goddamn," and he started to run toward the river pursued by a ball of twenty or thirty wasps.

The bullwhacker's boy, Kenny, had already unhooked the team and was driving them away. Samuel followed. "Hold 'em, boy. Git up there. Hold 'em to a steady pace." A small swarm pursued him which he batted at with his hat.

It was a frenzy of men swatting and trying to get out of each other's way. A couple fell back into the ash pit and rolled in the ashes. They may have been the fortunate ones. The ashes seemed to discourage the stinging insects, and they sought other targets.

"Stand perfectly still," said Marshall. "Stand still, dammit." He modeled his command and stood as still as possible, his arm held up over his face. Some of the wasps hovered about him, and a few stung him.

The men were pushing past one another to get away from the angry insects. This frantic activity seemed to attract the wasps. If they had done as Marshall suggested, they might have escaped with a few stings apiece. Once panic had set in, there was no stopping it. As they fled from behind what remained of the *totem*, they ran, some for the creek and some for the river. Two Blankets was pretty sure most just ran. Each running man was pursued by an angry ball of wasps which seemed to take turns stinging their target and spurring him on. She backed away slowly. None seemed to notice her.

Twenty minutes later, they gathered back in front of Johnson's Landing. Marshall got out a couple pints of whiskey and these circulated among the miserable group. Marshall got away with a half-dozen painful stings. Harry Everton and Big Ed had fallen together into the ash pit. They also had only a few stings, although Big Ed took a large splinter in the arm. The bullwhacker, Samuel, and his boy also escaped with minimal damage. Mr. Shales's face already swelled up puffy and red with stings to his lips and eyelids. Two Blankets attempted to apply a cooling mud to his forehead, but he waved her off.

"It really will help with the swelling and the pain, Mr. Shales," she said.

"I'm not taking any old wives' cure for bee stings, especially from an Indian woman."

Two Blankets moved on to Ike, who had already applied tobacco to the worst welts. She put the mud on over the tobacco. "I never knew tobacco could help with stings, Mr. Ike."

"Oh, yeah. My Da taught me that, but I hear mud is good, too. Thank you, Mrs. Johnston." Ike noticed Mr. Shales squirming on his log round. "Looks like Shales took some down his pants, too."

Two Blankets glanced at Mr. Shales, who of a sudden stood up and passed out straight back over the log round. They helped him into the longhouse and over to the sleeping furs. Marshall stripped off his suit, cutting part of it away with his knife. Mr. Shales had a series of stings starting on his face, running down his chest and onto his genitals which were already beginning to swell.

"Well, I bet that's the biggest he's ever seen his balls. They look like a couple of grapefruits."

Two Blankets didn't know what grapefruits were, but his genitals were swollen to an impressive size.

"Slap some mud on there," Marshall said. Two Blankets just handed him the bowl of mud. Marshall slathered it on all the stung areas, covering almost all of Mr. Shales' face, down his chest and stomach to his privates. "Don't you die on me, Shales. We got a deal."

Mr. Shales was pale, Two Blankets saw, but his pulse still beat regularly at his throat. After about twenty minutes he opened his eyes a slit. That was all he could manage with the mud on his eyelids.

"Where am I?" he asked. He felt the breeze upon his half-naked body and ventured to look down, then looked up at the worried faces. He flushed when he saw Two Blankets. "This isn't proper." His hands covered his male private parts.

"Step back a little, Two Blankets. Mr. Shales is a bit shy." Two Blankets complied. "Though as big as you are down there right now Shales, I'd think you'd want some bragging rights."

"It's not proper," Mr. Shales said. He lay back. "Did I pass out?"

"Gave us a fright, you did. I don't think you're going to catch that down-river boat today. Better to catch the *Belle* tomorrow for Portland. Here's a bit of covering for you." He lay a piece of light cloth over Mr. Shales. "Get a bit of rest, there."

"I will." He closed his eyes with a grimace and tried to find some comfort.

They withdrew from the longhouse to the trundle table. Marshall stopped and got some papers out of his "important papers box."

"He going to live?" asked Harry Everton.

"I wish I didn't need him, the goddamn little pissant, but he'll live to make more people miserable."

"I don't like him, either, but it would be a hell of a way to die. I had a cousin, got stung once and turned white as a new sheet, then fell over. In half an hour he was dead."

Marshall turned to the others. "Half-pay today if you can't work. Full pay if you can work the rest of the day. Your choice." The men looked at the sun. Half the day was gone already with all the excitement. Everyone decided a full day's pay for a few stings and half day's work was pretty good and moved off onto their various tasks.

He motioned to the carpenter and made out promissory notes for his services for the week and his two apprentices. They shook hands, and the carpenter went to gather his gear and tools for the trip downriver. Marshall poured himself a whiskey, downed it and poured another. "Just another day in the life of Johnston's Landing," he said and sipped on his drink.

The whine and screech of the portable saw told him that work was proceeding on the lumber. He knew without looking that the bullwhacker would be up there too, cutting down the next tree. Looking down the creek, he could see his four laborers under the supervising eye of Harry Everton, leveling the approaches to his bridge over the creek. All was proceeding as it should, at least for the next little while. He sighed and took another swallow of whiskey.

Late that afternoon, the *Jennie Clark* nosed into the landing. As Marshall rose to go and greet her, he was surprised to see Mr. Alton Shales emerge from the longhouse. His face was still swollen, but he had managed to wash most of the mud off. He was dressed "properly" in his hunting suit since they had cut his other suit up to treat his welts. As for his luggage, he was dragging his portmanteau, and Marshall ran to grab that up.

"Are you sure you can manage this trip, Mr. Shales? You took quite a lot of stings," Marshall said.

"Just another day on the frontier, Mr. Johnston. I must get back to the bank and get that paperwork started, so we can build our town."

Marshall didn't like the way Shales kept saying "our town," but he held it in. "I respect your courage. I'm not sure I'd be walking if I had balls like pumpkins."

"I won't lie. It hurts a bit. But any man who can't stand a little pain doesn't belong out here on the frontier. Look to your people, Mr. Johnston, all back to work. Just a few wasp stings, and they are all back to work like nothing happened."

Marshall Johnston thought it better not to mention that it had taken the offer of a full day's pay for a half day's work to get them moving. "True enough, Mr. Shales. They're good men." He motioned to Harry Everton.

"Harry, go into the longhouse and fetch out Mr. Shales's great bullhead and his rifle."

Harry jogged up to the longhouse and met them back at the *Jennie Clark.* Captain Ainsworth was there. He lifted his eyebrows as he saw Mr. Shales condition. "No time for a drink this trip downriver I'm afraid, Mr. Johnston. Mr. Shales seems a little worse for the wear today?"

"He took a few wasp stings when we brought down that there *totem,*" Marshall said and gestured toward the remains of the *totem.* "More than a few, actually. He's a funny man. One minute he's acting the worst kind of fancy pants tenderfoot you ever saw, the next he acts kind of brave. I can't quite figure him out yet."

"Hmmm. By the by, them thieves seen the magistrate already. With the confession, their fate was sealed. Magistrate gave the one you shot five years and the other three. It was pretty obvious who was the brains. He is going to live, barring complications, but you was right. Shoulder blade was shattered. Magistrate also awarded you all their gear including their rifles. So not a bad day for you."

"Thanks for that news, John."

Mr. Ainsworth visibly stiffened at the familiarity. "I'll bring their gear up next trip. Now, I have to get steaming."

Mr. Ainsworth and Marshall shook hands, and the boarding plank was drawn back onboard. The engine started turning the sternwheel, and she backed away from the landing, turned smartly, and headed downriver with two piercing whistles.

The rest of the day went routinely for Two Blankets. She aired out the sleeping furs, which smelled of Mr. Shales's fear sweat. She found he had left his clothes discarded by the sleeping pallet. Looking them over, she decided to keep them. The fabric was beautifully woven, and she thought of several things she could make of them.

That evening, after the meal and the clean-up, she dropped onto the sleeping furs exhausted. She fell asleep immediately to confused dreams of the village life, her try at an escape when she was only ten summers old and just captured, her marriage to Marshall, her love of Standing Bear. A vision of the gray wolf startled her awake. Marshall had not come to bed. She heard a yowling outside, like a wild animal, but she knew it was a man. She slipped into the doorway and looked out to the east, toward the place of the *Tyee's* longhouse where until today the *totem* had stood guard over the *Tyee's* longhouse and all those who entered there.

She drew closer, crossing the stream and passing the midden pile.

Marshall was there, illumined by the crescent waning moon. The moon was only four days from a new moon, but it was enough to see his shirted figure, shaking his raised fist skyward. Drifting back on the slight breeze she could just catch some of what he yelled at the heavens.

"You bastard. *Tyee* Running Blade... Best trader on the Columbia they said... Well, I beat you, you son of a bitch. I am *Tyee* of the village now, Running Blade. What do you think of that? I got it all, and you got Warm Springs. History will remember Marshall Johnston and Johnston's Landing and forget all about *Tyee* Running Blade of the Bent Creek Clan. They'll forget all about the Chinook and what great traders they were, but they will remember *me*. You hear me Running Blade. They'll remember me, *Tyee* Marshall Johnston of Johnston's Landing."

I wonder, she smiled a bit slyly, *standing in the light of the moon, which of us shall be the Tyee of our relationship.*

No, no, whispered White Mouse. *This is folly. Hide.*

Gray Wolf growled at her side, *There are times to stalk the shadows where you are not seen, Little Sister, but these are not such times. You are strong, Two Blankets. You may not be powerful enough to tear his throat out, but you might hamstring him.*

Two Blankets curled her fist in the wolf's thick ruff, musing on Gray Wolf's statement.

"Hamstring him?"

Dash in and slash his ankles. When he drops to his knees, knock him onto his back.

Two Blankets was beginning to like this story. "And then?"

Gray Wolf looked up at her, the fierce sense of the hunt in her eyes. *Then you stand on his chest and howl at the moon.*

THE TIDES
OF LIFE

CHAPTER 9
JULY, 1856 TO APRIL, 1857

FOR TWO BLANKETS, life rose and fell like the foam upon the tides in a somewhat regular rhythm. True, there were a few high points, like a king tide rushing in and flooding low-lying areas. There were low periods as well where nothing seemed to go right, but in general, her life was a rhythmic cycle of rise early before the dawn, care for the animals, cook breakfast for the crew, clean up, cook supper for the crew, clean up and go to bed tired so she could face another day.

Accustomed as she was to the rhythm of the life of the Bent Creek Clan, this was a getting back to normal experience for her. She knew what to expect from day to day. Also, her life was tied to the pace of Marshall's life, although not directly. Marshall was rising early these days to supervise his crews and plan for the expansion of Johnston's Landing. The expansion was not without its problems. One of his laborers broke his arm and had to be dismissed in September. Marshall had to make several trips into Portland either to purchase more supplies for the work or to get more laborers. Fall was advancing, and he had set targets to reach before the winter set in.

In November, while Two Blankets was feeding the vast flock of chickens she had and collecting the fifty or so eggs she needed each day just to feed the crew, she heard a loud screech from up the creek where the sawmill was working. It started as an increase in the ordinary whine of a cut and rapidly built into a crescendo. This she was used to. Sometimes the mill hit a particularly hard section in the timber and noise of the cutting increased. This time, however, the sound built and built and then abruptly ceased in an explosion of metal on metal.

Marshall was out of the longhouse at a run toward the creek, drawing his shirt on as he loped toward the noise. He hopped and pulled on his second boot and, not bothering to tie them, ran around the bend in the creek. Several of the other crewmen were not far behind. Two Blankets went on gathering eggs. This would be a king tide event, not enough to stop the building of Johnston's Landing but possibly sufficient to anger Marshall. There was nothing to do for it but let her little canoe of sticks and leaves rise with the tide.

An hour later, she saw the team of oxen dragging the mill from the area where Ike, the sawyer, had been cutting lumber. Smoke still rose in wisps from its smokestack, and Marshall was engaged in active discussion with Ike. Other crew members pushed to assist the mill over the rough ground.

"I'll have to take it apart to see the extent of the damage, but I can say for a certainty that a main bearing is blown," the millwright said. "I'll know more this afternoon. Tomorrow, I'll take the *Belle* into Portland to see about getting parts. Worst case, I think, I can be back in a week if I have to have the parts fabricated. Likely, I will. Ain't a lot of these Scott and Herndon sawmills around. She's a sweet piece of equipment. Let's just hope nothing broke that I can't have fabricated in Portland."

"Damn," Marshall said. "I may come in with you and round up three, four more laborers. All right, get on it."

When Marshall reentered the longhouse, he shot Two Blankets an angry look. Most of the time he was so busy, often until late in the evening going over his accounts, that he paid little attention to her. That was the positive effect of the building project. But when he was angry, and she could see that in his scowl, she knew it would likely fall on her at some point. There was no managing that part of Marshall's life. Bad trades, unplanned delays, accidents to the crew, or worse yet, breakdowns that damaged equipment—all were likely to send him into a short-tempered rage. Generally, these periods were short in duration, but she was still the target.

"You got that meal cooked yet?" he asked. "Christ, do I got to do every-thing around here?" He poured himself a whiskey. "Hurry up with breakfast. Sun's been up an hour already."

"Yes, husband Marshall." She had learned this was no time to challenge him. "Just a little longer."

Marshall took a drink of whiskey. Two Blankets knew that frustration, anger, and drink did not mix well in her husband. No one was in the long-house at the moment and none expected. She was serving meals outside as long as the weather held. "Come over here. I'm going to be gone a few days, and I want a taste of you."

"Yes, husband Marshall."

She crept over to him and started to kneel before him to open his trousers, but he grabbed her beneath one armpit, spun her around and shoved her face down over the back of a wooden chair. The push knocked the breath from her and bruised her ribs, but she quickly braced herself for what she knew was coming. Marshall flipped her dress up over her back and fumbled with the buttons on his trousers. Soon he was pumping against her backside. In truth, Two Blankets preferred sex with him this way as she didn't have to look at him. Also, he was of small stature down there, and she felt it very little beyond the first rough entry. In just a few minutes he was done and withdrew, pulling up his trousers. He left her there and went back to his papers.

"Better get that breakfast served for the crew," he said as if nothing else had happened.

For the most part, the crew seemed to accept Two Blankets and treat-ed her with respect, but a couple of the new laborers were of a different sort. Two Blankets did not know whether it was because they were new and hadn't mixed in well with the rest of the crew or if they were just differ-ent. One was a small, shrewish man named Isaiah Thomas who was given to quoting the Bible and speaking in terms of prophecy. He also cast lewd glances toward Two Blankets, often in full view of the others.

"And, why shouldn't I look at her however I like?" he said upon being challenged by Samuel, the bullwhacker.

"It just ain't right," Samuel said. "She being Mr. Johnston's wife and all. Ain't you always quoting scripture about this sort of thing?"

"Scripture is for white people. Never mentions no Indians."

"I don't expect you'd ever have the nerve to do anything about it, Isaiah," said Small Willie MacKenzie. In contrast to his name, Small Willie was a huge man, fully six feet two and two hundred twenty pounds. He was dark-complected with straight black hair to his shoulders and had the look of a man who got what he wanted. Apparently, his father, Big William, was an even bigger man. "I wouldn't have no trouble dipping into that quim. No trouble at all."

Two Blankets always felt uncomfortable around these two men, though she wasn't sure why. To take a woman by force was virtually unheard of among the Chinook and the *Nimi'ipuu* as well. The *mistshimus* were expected to comply with a titled person's demands, but even a title born wouldn't force the issue.

Marshall left with the millwright on the afternoon steamboat, exhorting them all to keep working while he was gone. He had paid the crew before departing, so all were in good spirits. Several had bought pint bottles of whiskey or the larger clay bottles of ale from Two Blankets before retiring to their respective sleeping places to enjoy the drink and their fellows' company. She washed up the final dishes and banked the fire down to preserve the coals for the morning. She didn't feel threatened particularly, and in truth, Marshall had left her alone with the crew several times before, but something made her feel wary.

She lay down on the sleeping furs and closed her eyes. For one distinct moment, she saw the green eyes of Gray Wolf looking at her. When she opened her eyes, there was no one and nothing there, of course, just the empty longhouse and the chill late fall wind coming up outside. Still, she believed in trusting the spirits even if she did not know what they were saying, or even if they were really there and not just her imagination. She got up and picked up a carving knife from her cooking supplies. It had a sharp point to it and an eight-inch blade. Then she retired to her furs and, placing the knife beneath the wolf skin, fell into a disturbed sleep, comforted to be as prepared as she could be.

Somewhere in her dreams White Mouse and Gray Wolf discussed her current situation.

She should run. Run and hide, White Mouse said glancing nervously over her shoulder.

No. She must fight, Gray Wolf said.

This dialog was mixed in with a series of images of her capture and beatings by the Bent Creek Clan. The last view she had was of *mistshimus Nika* alive and her last words, "Live for me."

Some sound brought her out of sleep. A sound or a breeze coming from the doorway as the door flap was opened. Whatever it was, she knew she was not alone. A large, dark shape was near the door. Whoever it was came creeping on silent feet toward her sleeping pallet. When it passed the slight glimmer from the banked fire, she saw from the corner of her eye that he was a big man—massive. There was only one man that big on the crew, Small Willie. Some detached part of her mind wondered how often substantial men could move catlike and quiet.

When he reached the edge of her pallet, he spoke. "Don't make a sound, and I won't hurt you." He dropped his trousers to his ankles and knelt over her.

Two Blankets was frozen for a minute in fear, and a separate part of herself analyzed what she should do. True, she had the knife, but if she were to pull it now, he would likely take it away from her. She backed away from him against the longhouse wall. He pulled the sleeping fur off her and saw that she was sleeping naked.

"Ah, I see. You've been waiting for me." He reached down and between her legs forcing them apart with one massive hand. He probed her with a finger and then two and lifted the fingers to his lips. "Oh, so my sweet." Kneeling between her legs and grasping her wrists with one hand, he said, "Now, we will see how much you like me."

Two Blankets realized that perhaps she had waited too long and was trapped in his grasp. At that moment, the bullwhacker's boy, Kenny, lifted the door flap. Two Blankets cried out, just a small "help" escaped her lips before Small Willie rose up on his knees and dropped the hand enclosing her wrists to cover her mouth.

"Git on out of here boy. You want a piece of this, you wait your turn."

Kenny was pale white in the coal glow, but he stood his ground, fists clenched. "You get off her, right now."

"First of all, what's a puny runt like you going to do about it? And second, who is to say she didn't want it after I'm done?" Small Willie went back to his business, kneeing her legs apart.

Kenny approached Small Willie recklessly with no real fighting chance or instinct. He was about five foot six and a solid one hundred thirty pounds. Grabbing Small Willie's left arm, he pulled. "I said get off her."

Small Willie backhanded him across the face, knocking him to the ground.

Two Blankets found the hilt of the knife under her and drawing it back beside her head, drove it to the hilt into Small Willie's left shoulder. His hand dropped away from her mouth.

"I say who mates with me and who does not."

He just knelt there, a look of surprise on his face. Not even pain at first, just plain surprise. He looked down at the knife and began to reach for the hilt with his right hand. He looked at Two Blankets, incomprehension spreading across his face. The blood began to flow. Then he toppled like a great oak felled in the forest. The crack as the trunk broke was not there, but the teetering fall was. Two Blankets slipped aside so that he did not fall completely on top of her, but her legs were still trapped. Then Kenny was there, pushing Small Willie onto his back and freeing Two Blankets.

He looked upon her in the dim light, and it was evident to Two Blankets that he was smitten by her. The slope of her breast limned in the ruddy glow so near he could almost touch it. He looked away. "I'm sorry, Mrs. Johnston. You are just so beautiful, I couldn't help myself. I hope you don't think I would—"

"I know you would never do such a thing. Get your father, would you?"

"Yes, ma'am. I'll get him right away." Kenny ran out of the longhouse.

Two Blankets slipped into her whiteman's dress and built up the fire. Small Willie was rolling on the sleeping pallet now groaning in pain. "You stabbed me, you bitch. You fucking *stabbed* me."

Draft from the open-door flap momentarily flared up the fire, drawing her attention. It was Samuel, followed closely behind by Isaiah Thomas.

Taking in the groaning form of Small Willie with the knife still protruding from his shoulder, as well as the fact that his trousers were around his ankles, and glancing at Two Blankets, Samuel said to her, "What has happened here?"

"He tried to force me and—" Two Blankets began.

"She invited me to her bed, and then she stabbed me," Small Willie said overriding her.

"That's right," Isaiah Thomas said. "She wanted him. Then she stabbed him."

"Mrs. Johnston, what happened?" Samuel asked again.

"I will speak truly. He tried to force me to mate with him. Kenny came in and tried to stop him, and he hit Kenny across the face, knocking him to the ground. I stabbed him. Then I sent Kenny to get you. This is truth."

"She *lies*," Isaiah Thomas said. "All the savages lie."

"All of us heard what Small Willie said before. Kenny?"

"It's like Mrs. Johnston said. I saw Small Willie leave the barn where we been sleeping. He'd been talking about Mrs. Johnston and not nice talk, neither. I followed. When I come in, he was on her with his pants down, holding her wrists. I tried to stop him, honest I did, but he knocked me down. Then she stabbed him."

Samuel pondered but only for a bit. "Seems pretty clear what occurred here. Isaiah, take this bastard out of here to the shed behind the pig barn. You can doctor him there."

Isaiah moved to the sleeping pallet and put all his strength under Small Willie. Without Small Willie's help, he could never even have lifted him to a sitting position, but eventually, Small Willie was standing up. "Pull my damn pants up Isaiah, you idiot. I can't walk like this." Isaiah bent down and fumbled with the big man's pants. His pants half-buttoned, they walked out into the cold.

"That was pretty quick thinking, Mrs. Johnston, having that knife by you," Samuel said lifting an eyebrow.

"I do not know why I took it, truly. I just felt something was wrong."

"Good thing you did. I'll ask Mr. Everton and Big Ed if they'll sleep in here and keep watch over you just in case. I don't expect Small Willie to try anything tonight, but he's a mean one. You never know. Harry and Big Ed would never hurt you like that, I don't think."

"Thank you, Samuel. They will be fine."

When Marshall arrived two days later, on the *Jennie*, Small Willie emerged from the shed, his shoulder bandaged with dirty rags. He made a half-hearted case for himself, but after hearing the evidence from Kenny and Samuel, Marshall made his decision. "Get your gear and get on the *Jennie*. I don't want to see you here again."

"That ain't fair, Marshall," Isaiah said, "you taking an Indian's word against a white man."

"That *Indian* is my *wife*. One thing she don't do is lie. You get your gear too and get out, Isaiah Thomas."

"I ain't leaving without my pay."

"You been working these last two days?" Marshall asked noting Isaiah's reddened eyes and filthy clothes.

"I been tending to Small Willie here."

"Then you ain't been working for me. Get your gear and get out."

Captain John C. Ainsworth of the *Jennie Clark* took the two grumbling passengers on board. "You seem to have an attraction to men who have shoulder problems," he said. "Shot, broken, and stabbed."

Marshall laughed. "Seems like."

"You pressing any charges?"

"No. No judge or jury would ever convict a white man for attempted rape on an Indian woman. They'd likely fine me for wasting the court's time."

"Fair enough," Captain Ainsworth said.

For Two Blankets, that was the most exciting thing to happen that fall and winter. The four new men seemed to fall into the rhythm of the rest of the crew reasonably well, and she knew that stories about her occasionally were told around the campfire at night. She noticed an attitude of respect from the men. She tried to treat all of them fairly and kindly. They, in turn, were starting to bond together as a crew, as men working in close proximity could do, and that bond included an awareness and admiration from them that she didn't take any guff.

Big Ed expressed it best one cold January night when the men were drinking in the longhouse. "Sure, she's an Indian. Can't deny that. But any of us been here awhile know there's Indians you can trust and Indians you can't. Mrs. Johnston is one you can trust." The men, for the most part, agreed with him. "Other thing I can tell you. She ain't no slut. Next guy tries something like Small Willie might wind up with a real small willie, if you know what I mean." The crew laughed.

As the year turned and they started to approach spring, work redoubled on the road and the dock. There was already a very serviceable bridge across the creek, and the road graded up to it nicely. Marshall next wanted to extend the dock out from the raft that had been used so far. Though this wasn't tideland and subject to extremely high and low waters, it was subject to seasonal lows and highs that could be almost as great as those of a coastal town. Marshall finally settled on a floating dock that could be chained to the bank. As the river lowered in late summer the dock would be extended farther into the river. This arrangement also held the advantage of not requiring pilings to be driven into the river bottom. It took the crew a month to complete but was an admirable achievement when done, wide enough for a wagon to offload cargo from a steamship and railed in red with a series of white balusters.

"Looks more like a beautiful staircase in a high house than a damn dock," the millwright said.

"It's the first thing people going to see here and the last when they leave. I don't want it to look like every other fallen-down dock on this river." Marshall said.

"Well, you certainly got your wish there."

Two Blankets often wondered how the Bent Creek Clan was faring this winter. The treaty said all would be prepared for them to resume life on the Warm Springs reservation, but that was life as the whitemans knew it, not as the Bent Creek Clan lived it. At the very least, their routines of fishing and hunting, of the drying meat and fish for the winter and the collecting of the plants that they so depended on, would have been disrupted. They were in an entirely new area. They did not know the movements of the prey animals there, nor the locations for the dozens of plants they typically collected at specific times of the year.

Yes, and that was the best-case scenario. The whitemans knew one way of living. The Bent Creek Clan knew an entirely different way. But the whitemans would expect the clan to live in the whiteman way. They were supposed to become farmers when they had not been farmers for thousands of years. They would be expected to live in single-family houses if such houses had even been built. The clan was used to communal living. They would be expected to grow potatoes when they were used to collecting and cooking camas root. Two Blankets always thought that the Chinook would make the transition but suspected that this winter, in particular, would be very hard.

Marshall was much involved in his plans for Johnston's landing. Although he worked most days all day, and often well into the night, and had to make frequent trips into Portland, he did find time to become increasingly agitated with Two Blankets for not providing him with a child. They had been married almost three years, and she had managed through herbs she used and keeping most of their sexual encounters to the days immediately preceding or following her moon cycle. Of late, their sex had taken on an angry and violent nature which sometimes frightened Two Blankets. It was also becoming harder to be sure Marshall got his daily seeds because of his trips downriver as well as the communal nature of their eating arrangements with the crew.

In March of 1857, Two Blankets counted the seeds she had left. She had only the amount necessary to last through April. She could not bear the thought of catching a child from Marshall. It would not be the child's fault, and she had no objection to a pregnancy, even from Marshall. It was that a child she knew was Marshall's would tie her to him for life.

PORTAGE

CHAPTER 10
APRIL, 1857

TWO BLANKETS WAS out of options. She had seeds for Marshall for only one more month and no way to replace them. The thought of catching and raising his child was unbearable to her. It seemed that her only option was to go to Warm Springs, not to live—that she knew she could not ever do—but maybe she could win a child that way. A child she could live with.

The chickens gave up their eggs as she pursued this idea to its end. She tossed out their grain and the chickens greedily crowded in as the thoughts and possibilities crowded her mind. Warm milk flowed in squirts into the pail and swirled, the cream slowly rising to the surface, rich and light-yellow. The pigs she fed with corn and wheat meal, some withered camas bulbs, and a pail of the milk.

The chickens were happy. The cows were happy and the pigs, as well. Everyone in Johnston's Landing seemed to be active and happy. Everyone except for Two Blankets. It was time to make a change in that.

After they had finished breakfast, Marshall dispatched the men to their tasks. When they were alone, he said, "Come into the hut."

"Yes, husband Marshall."

Once inside, he pushed her face down against the counter and flipped up her dress. His trousers dropped, and he proceeded with the deed.

What a small thing this has become in my life.

The act itself was of little consequence. The consequence of a child as the outcome was vast and dreadful in her mind.

When he had finished, he pulled up his trousers and stepping to her side opened his sheaf of paperwork. He muttered as he figured.

Two Blankets stood up and straightened her dress.

"I'm going to have to go into Portland for mebbe a month," he said. "There is a lot to arrange for the building of Johnston's Landing. We got to get a big crew in here, and there's plenty of supplies to buy."

"If I may ask, what will you do with me for that month?"

"You'll remain here, of course," he said, his thoughts already moving on.

"You know what would happen if I am left alone here for a month, husband Marshall. Big Ed or Harry cannot sleep in the longhouse and watch over me all the time."

"No, they can't. They're going to be busy dawn to dusk."

Two Blankets poured him a whiskey which he drank all in a gulp, holding out his hand for a refill. "Well, I can't very well take an Indian to Portland as my wife, now can I?"

"I would only be a distraction from your important duties, husband Marshall. And here I will be a disruption."

"Damn right you're a disruption. Last time I left, you stabbed a man, and you are a distraction right now." Marshall scratched out his figures and started over. "You made me make a damn mistake." He bent his head over his work. "You come up with a solution, let me know."

Harry Everton entered the hut. "Mr. Johnston, you got a minute?"

Marshall looked up, "Sure, Harry."

The moment was now. "Pardon my interruption, Mr. Everton."

"What the hell do you want now?" Marshall asked.

"Just to be clear, *Tyee* husband Marshall. This problem is mine to solve as long as my work gets done?"

"That's what I said, wasn't it? You are a distraction and a disruption. More trouble than you're worth. Get away from me."

"As you say, *Tyee* husband Marshall. Thank you. Mr. Everton." She passed out of the longhouse.

You will make him very angry, said White Mouse, hiding in her hair.

He is a fool, said Grey Wolf. *We will hamstring him and tear out his throat.*

Two Blankets approached Samuel with her idea, and he accepted. Kenny was thrilled to do any kind of chore for Two Blankets. She ran him through her gathering and feeding chores for a couple days—especially Marshall's exacting egg count—and was satisfied.

Harry Everton said, "The men can damn well cook for themselves. I'll take over dispensing of the foodstuffs."

"Thank you, Mr. Everton."

"That's no problem, Mrs. Johnston. You always been good to us. But mind you, it ain't no easy trip up to the Deschutes. And I can't spare nobody to go up with you."

"You are a thoughtful man, Mr. Everton. I will be careful."

She began gathering supplies for her journey. They had to be minimal, but she could neglect nothing. Though only a journey of a few days, it was still needful to be careful. Also, she could not afford for Marshall to discover her plans before it was too late for him to change them. The only place she could think of to hide her preparations was in the small moon cycle hut. No man would dare enter that place. Food, traveling supplies, a flint and steel and tinder, some few gifts, clothes, both a whiteman's dress as well as Chinook clothing, the pile she hid in the hut was too large and had to be pared down and pared again. Finally, she had it down to the bare minimum and thought it would fit into the smallest canoe.

Meantime, Marshall was a whirlwind of activity. Only his plans were important to him, and he had detailed instructions for each crew member.

The day arrived, and the *Belle* took him on board.

"I'll be back in a month," he said to his crew. "You better damn well be working every day."

All nodded their agreement. "I'll keep them grinding, Mr. Johnston. Don't worry about the work here."

"I trust that's true, Everton." He turned to Two Blankets. "You solve your little problem?" The *Belle* began to pull away from the dock.

"Yes, husband Marshall. I am going to Warm Springs until you get back."

"What? You never said—"

"You said it was my problem to solve, husband Marshall. I have solved it."

Marshall paced the foredeck. "You cannot. I forbid—" The *Belle* blew a long whistle.

"I will see you in a month, husband Marshall."

Harry Everton said, "Mr. Johnston is going to be mighty angry when he returns."

"Yes, I know well, Mr. Everton. I will deal with it. I will be leaving at dawn tomorrow."

"You won't get no objections from me."

"Thank you, Mr. Everton."

Two Blankets glanced about the moon cycle hut in the semi-darkness before dawn. She picked up a stack of moon cycle pads and put them into her *parfleche*. As she withdrew her hand, she felt the handle of the knife she had placed there.

This is dangerous, said White Mouse from her shoulder.

"There are times for caution, times to hide, little one," Two Blankets said. "And you have served me well during those times. But this is not such a time."

She finished loading her canoe. Kenny ran up. Out of breath, he said, "I am glad you are not gone yet."

"Kenny, I am happy that you came to see me off. I hope you will not anger your master."

"Samuel will know where I am. I just wanted to say—"

"You will always be my friend, Kenny." She grasped his hand. "Take care, my friend, and if you do your duties, you will have done me a great favor."

"I will, I promise you."

"Thank you." She pushed off and dipped her paddle into the *Nch'i-wána*. She was finally off on her journey. She hoped her decision was the right one.

The sun was not yet risen, and the river calm in the area where she paddled. One look to the right at the turbulent current dragging down trees and debris reminded her of the dangers that lurked there. Always, she had to remain cognizant of the power of the *Nch'i-wána*. Yes, here it was calm, but only a half-mile to the east it was a rush and potential disaster.

She paused in her paddling and let the feeling of the day and the water pass over her. Her decision had been made. To her rear lay Johnston's Landing. There was no future there for her. Ahead lay an unknown. She did not know what lay there, but it was her only path.

Resuming her paddling, she paid more attention to her environment, to the flow of water, to the light breeze passing over her, and to the bank sliding slowly by. She planned to take two days paddling up to the Cascades and to try to reach them early enough to make the portage. She had a small amount of coin for the portage and hoped it would be enough.

White Mouse nuzzled her ear, and Two Blankets absently petted her. *Wary. You must be wary,* White Mouse said.

Two Blankets noticed a gray shadow keeping pace with her on the bank among the trees, Gray Wolf. *Be wary, so you are not caught unawares. Then rip their throats out.*

"I am fortunate to have you two watching out for me. Why, Gray Wolf, do you pad the banks?"

I do not like getting my feet wet. That would seem obvious.

Two Blankets pondered this statement for a moment. Gray Wolf was a spirit, but to her he was as real as the trees, the mountain, and the *Nch'i-wána.*

Toward evening she steered her canoe over to a small stream. She pulled it up and hid it in the overgrowth, then sought out a camping spot in the brush and trees behind. Fifty feet up the stream, a cedar had fallen across the water and left a small meadow behind, a place deprived of light and brush. Two Blankets removed her pack and set up camp. With flint and steel, she soon had a small fire going. She kept it low and invisible from the riverside. A little warmth, enough to heat some food and prepare some tea. Enough to warm her spirits as well and to let predators know they might just want to seek another meal. As the evening turned to night, she rolled up in her sleeping fur and looked up through the canopy of branches to the stars.

During the middle of the night, she felt the cramping and knew her cycle was about to begin. She fetched a pad from her pack and clamped her legs together over it. Tomorrow and the next three days were going to be hard days, she knew, but there was no avoiding it.

As the predawn lightened the sky, gray fog pushed up from the river accompanied by a light drizzle. Two Blankets looked hopefully toward her fire, but it was dead out. Rolling from her furs, she carefully folded her whiteman's clothes and put on her Chinook clothing. For this part of the journey, she had to wear a skirt of sorts, a deerskin wrap, and her red and white tablecloth poncho. She loaded her canoe and pushed it out into the river. Nothing to do now but keep paddling as she chewed on some dried salmon.

The fog lifted toward mid-morning, burning off from the sky first. For a time, she was paddling through a swirling soup. The banks of the *Nch'i-wá-na* rose from the dirty gray below until they stood out sharp against the cloudless blue sky above. Two Blankets began to hear the intermittent rush of the Cascades layered over the constant sound of the river. Another turn in the river and she could see the distant spray rising off the water. Within an hour, she reached the Cascades and the portage. She looked about and saw first a middle-aged Indian man, dressed in dirty and torn whiteman's clothes, with a bandana tied over his graying hair. He smiled at her, but it wasn't a comforting smile. It was the smile of a predator sizing up his prey and revealed yellowed teeth. This was one who had met the whiteman and succumbed to the pressure of his ways.

Holding her canoe in place some two or three arm spans from the bank she asked, "Can you portage my canoe and belongings past the Cascades?"

He replied in a language she did not understand though it sounded familiar.

"You are Cayuse? Do you speak the Chinook Jargon?"

"Yes, I am Cayuse. Speak some Chinook."

"What is your name then? I am Two Blankets."

"I am call Little Feather. I portage you for three dollar." Two Blankets thought about how much coin she had. "Three dollars is too much. I will pay one and one only. Where is your honor as a man and a native of this land?"

"My honor died at the Whitman's uprising with my natural born brother and at the Cascades fight. Come a little closer, and I will show you my manhood." He grasped himself suggestively.

His suggestion of a sexual liaison did not bother her. The Chinook were oft quite brazen about such things. Out of the corner of her eye, she saw a boy, perhaps twelve summers old edging up. "Don't do it, Miss. He just wants to get hold of you."

"I will come in, and we will negotiate," she said. She heard the guttural growl of Gray Wolf as she paddled in and Little Feather grasped the bow. Two Blankets climbed out.

"I too lost a good friend at the Cascades. His name was Fire Stick, so I know somewhat how you feel. But I do not understand why you would treat a woman so."

"You say you have not enough money. I merely offer trade."

"And if I say no?"

"Then maybe I take what I want." He pulled out a short-bladed knife.

Two Blankets stepped closer, which surprised him. "Maybe you will take this in trade." She lifted her skirt and pulled out the moon cycle pad which was spotted with blood. "Do not the Cayuse have the same taboo as the Chinook?"

Beneath his dark skin, Two Blankets could see him pale. He sheathed his knife and stepped back. Two Blankets stepped again in his direction.

"It is true I have little honor left," said Little Feather, "but I do respect the taboos."

"Are you sure you do not want to stick your *wootlat* into this taboo woman's *busi?*"

"No, I do not." He fell to his knees. "All taboo women before were in the moon cycle hut. That is why I make a mistake."

"I go to Warm Springs to visit Bone Rattler. Should she and I discuss you?"

"Bone Rattler, the ancient shamaness?"

"That is the person. Should we discuss your lack of respect when a woman says no?"

"No, no. You not need to do that. I portage you, and I do not charge you. I do not need any more bad luck."

The boy, a scrawny youth by the look of him just stood and stared, his mouth open in a silent "Wow!" They pulled the canoe up on the bank and unloaded it. It was clear to Two Blankets that all could not be carried in one portage.

"Can I help?" asked the boy.

"What is your name?" Two Blankets asked.

"Tom, miss. Tom Clement. I'm trying to get to The Dalles."

"Tom, if you help me, you can ride with me to The Dalles. Right now, we need you to guard what we cannot carry. Can you do that?"

The boy agreed and quickly they had the packs sorted into two piles. "Hide these back in the brush and guard them well." Two Blankets pointed back into the dense wood.

Little Feather and Two Blankets put on their packs and lifted the canoe, steadied it then began the trek.

"So, you lost a born brother at the Whitman's uprising, Little Feather?"

"I did, yes. It was Klokomas. He was executed by the whiteman for fighting them."

"That was a few years back wasn't it?"

"Yes. Back in 1850 when you were a young thing. But the problem began when I was as young as you were, back in 1837. When the Whitman family came, they promised a shipload of goods for the use of the land every year. A year later, when Umtippe, who owned the land, demanded payment, they refused."

Little Feather shifted his position and looked out over the river with sadness in his eyes before continuing. "The next year, he returned and demanded payment. Again, they refused saying the land was given to them. In 1841, Tiloukaikt, another Cayuse chief, grazed his horses near the Whitman's place, destroying their maize crop. Mr. Whitman told Tiloukaikt that he would never give him anything. Later he put poison out in his melon crop and spread poison meat out which our dogs ate and died." He stopped walking again. "Let us put this canoe down a minute," He eased the canoe down to the ground and sat down against it.

Two Blankets drank from the water skin and handed it to Little Feather.

"You can see. It went from bad to worse. When the whiteman's disease came and killed many of the Cayuse, we thought it was the Whitman's doing. Tiloukaikt said Mr. Whitman was a shaman."

"Ah," Two Blankets said, "is similar with the Chinook. If the shamaness cannot cure the people, sometimes her life is forfeit."

"Yes. That is how it was. Tiloukaikt struck Mr. Whitman down, and it turned into a bloodbath. The whitemans attacked and killed Cayuse who were not even involved in the war. Eventually, there was peace but only after the whitemans demanded we turn over the men responsible. Five went to explain and were hanged. One, Kimasumpkin, was not even there at the Whitman's place when they were killed. He just tried to help. The whitemans did not care. They hanged him anyway. Even though I killed more whitemans during the war than Klokomas, he went to be hanged, and I did not. That is my shame."

Slowly he got up and shouldered his end of the canoe, and they walked on in silence. Silence but for the occasional bird cry, the rustling of the breeze, and the rush of water down the *Nch'i-wána*.

When they reached the end of the portage and lay the canoe on its side with the packs beneath, Two Blankets said, "I trust you to guard my goods and canoe. That you feel shame tells me you still have honor. You have not been exiled by your people. You have exiled yourself, from shame." She turned about and began jogging back down the path.

Her side protested, and she had to slow to a quick walk. The cramps were still bad, but she kept walking. She finally reached the beginning of the portage and looked about. Tom was not to be seen. Two Blankets pushed through the brush to the hidden packs. They were still here.

"Tom. Tom Clements," she said.

Tom emerged from behind a tree, holding a large branch as a weapon. "Oh, it *is* you, Mrs. Blankets. I didn't know if someone was coming for your packs. Or if that Indian might be coming back."

"His name is Little Feather." She smiled at Tom. "And I am just Two Blankets. Let us get these packs up the portage before dark."

As they shouldered the packs and moved on up the trail, Tom said, "I was worried about you with that Indian. He's dangerous."

"Mostly he is just sad," Two Blankets said, "from events long ago."

"Why is he sad? He's just a dirty Indian. No offense. You are different."

"Sad because his tribe is mostly dead. Full of shame because he was involved in the Whitman's incident and his brother was executed for it."

"My Da told me about that. Whitman's Massacre he called it, where the Indians just killed all the Whitman people for no reason at all."

Two Blankets bit off her reply. "Why were you waiting at the portage?"

"I was down to Portland to visit my Grandma. Da gave me coin for the whole passage back to The Dalles, but—"

"You lost it?"

"Something like. Someone took it on my way up."

Two Blankets guessed, "A white man?"

"Weren't no Indians on board, so, yes."

"A little like the Whitman's incident. Every story has many sides to it."

"Never really thought of it that way. So, I've been waiting at the portage point, hoping to earn enough coin to get to The Dalles."

"I am heading past The Dalles. You can ride with me if you can paddle," Two Blankets said, easing the strain.

"I will take you up on that, Miss Blankets. I mean Two Blankets." He spat on his hand and held it out as solemn and proud as only a twelve-year-old boy can be.

Two Blankets did not know this custom, but she spat on her hand, and they shook on it. They reached the canoe and loaded it with a couple hours of daylight left. Two Blankets turned to Little Feather and got out her purse.

"No, no. I will not take your coin. You have made me think, and it is wrong to take coin from a woman in need."

"Please, Little Feather. A bargain is a bargain, as the Chinook say."

"Do they not also say *cultus potlatch?*" He smiled.

Two Blankets smiled, "Between friends they do."

"*Cultus potlatch*, then. Will you not camp here until tomorrow?"

"I think not, friend Little Feather. I would take my chances alone. I have not had such good luck with the whitemans. I am not one to give advice, but think on going back to your tribe. We are not a people to live alone like the whitemans."

Little Feather seemed to stand more erect with, if not pride in his bearing, less despondency. "I may try to find them. They are east with the Nez Perce."

A wave of old memory washed over her. "If you go and you come across Elk Clarksonson, tell him I am all right. That is the tribe I was kidnapped from."

"Ah, so you are a granddaughter of the Clark? I will remember."

They pushed off in her canoe with Tom perched on a pack in the front. He paddled like one who had grown up on the river. The two hours passed quickly, and shortly thereafter Two Blankets spotted a small creek. She steered the canoe in, and they made camp there, building up a small fire. Eating the dried salmon and tea she had brought, she leaned against a tree and watched the colors of the dusk rise along the canyon wall until they finally disappeared.

"Good night, Two Blankets."

"Good night, Tom. Tomorrow I will drop you off near The Dalles."

"A great-granddaughter of Lieutenant William Clark—Lewis and Clark— no one will ever believe I met you."

"All he did was lay with my great-grandmother. She had a son, named the Clark. It is not so surprising."

They neared the outskirts of The Dalles by midday. Two Blankets looked about. Even to her inexperienced eyes, she could see differences since the last time she had been up this way only six years ago. A small fort sat atop a knoll, partially surrounded by wooden outbuildings. Wooden houses spread out, and there was less timber now. Almost every tree had been cut to make the small town.

"I will let you off here," she said steering the canoe in to the bank.

"You don't want to go into the village?" asked Tom.

"It would not be safe for me, and I still must find portage around the Narrows and Celilo Falls."

Tom looked at her as if he did not understand. "Ah, now I understand. You ain't never been here in the spring?"

"No, I have not."

"Well, this time of year with the runoff we had this year, there ain't no falls. Current will be fast, but no falls."

"But I was here, and the water dropped straight down over twenty U. S. government feet, all the way across."

Tom, unaccustomed to being worldly, said, "You'll see. You might be able to tow your canoe up on a rope if you are careful. Stick to the shallows and watch out for deep holes. You are going to have a worse problem with the Narrows. Current be deep and fast there. And it's only seventy-five feet wide. I don't think you can make it alone. But I don't know what I can do to help. Be careful. "

"Thank you, I will be careful, Tom. Take care."

"I will. This been a memorable time. Great granddaughter of William Clark. Imagine that."

She gestured him closer, and he leaned over the canoe. Grasping him by the neck, she gave him a kiss, right on the lips. Releasing him, she drifted away. "Imagine that," she said smiling.

A few miles upstream, she saw what Tom had been speaking of. Where they had crossed the river and been forced to portage over the Narrows, was only swift water. There were spots of white water where the water swept around submerged stone, and huge gouts of spray where the river hit a rock and was forced upward.

The steamboat *Mary* came up behind her then sidled through the current to the north side to disgorge its passengers and freight. From there they would take their goods up the steep incline to the mule-driven portage railroad around the falls. A dozen or so men gathered on the side near the little dock. Something about them made the breath tighten in Two Blankets throat. She steered the canoe over to the Oregon side of the river and looked for a place to camp. At any rate, it was too late to start up the river. She eyed the river upstream again. It looked possible, but appearances could very easily be deceiving.

She saw an inlet and steered toward it. Gradually, it narrowed into a small stream. She got out and began tugging the canoe up the stream. About a hundred paces up was a grassy area, protected from the eyes and the greed of strangers.

Well, tomorrow will be soon enough for that challenge.

She made her small camp. She tied off the canoe securely and laid out her sleeping fur. Building up the little fire, she made tea and leaned back, just listening to the river. There was a peace that came with the flow of the river and the breeze. It was transient, she knew, but she would take it.

White Mouse curled up in her hair. *Such adventures,* she said. *It is scary, my, oh, my, how scary.*

Gray Wolf lay alongside her and put her head into Two Blankets lap. *You are learning your true nature, small human. I am at peace with that.*

Her cramps forced her to curl around Gray Wolf. That was true, but at the same time, she looked forward to tomorrow with a new clarity. She was beginning to feel alive again, dependent only on herself and her ingenuity.

After tea the next morning, Two Blankets loaded her canoe and looked upstream. She was unsettled not so much by what she could see as by what she could not see. She had been here before and knew of the drop and the swiftness of the current. Here the water only flowed smooth and fast.

As she paddled, she stayed near the right-hand bank where the water was shallow and the flow of the current easier to paddle against. Approaching the Narrows, she remembered the boulders beneath as the current increased. She was paddling hard and making little progress and ahead she could see she would not make any progress there. Suddenly, an eddy of current caught the bow of her canoe, and she was turned sideways, pulled further into the main channel. Torn downstream, she paddled hard and was happy only to lose thirty paces progress. She had not swamped the canoe.

She paddled over to the bank and slowly made back the thirty paces, searching the bank for a spot to pull in. A narrow beach jutted from the basalt and shale. Unloading the canoe, she tied a length of line to the bow. She settled for a bit of food before gathering her courage to attempt the passage. The canoe floated high in the water and light to the pull, in this flat water. As she advanced slowly along the bank, sometimes wading, sometimes climbing the crumbling cliff, she approached the churning water. She slipped and fell into the water in a deep spot and was forced to repeat her advance. There was just no beach or solid rock here, even under the water which now soaked her from head to foot. The drop in water was not so large—only about four feet. She would have to try from above.

Allowing the canoe to float free in a small eddy near the bank, Two

Blankets clambered up the bank until she stood knee deep in water above the canoe. She began hauling on the rope, and at first, the canoe responded smooth and easy.

Mayhap, this is not going to be so difficult after all.

She wrapped the line once around her hips and pulled the canoe up the wet incline. The drag increased. She pulled, slipped the slack line around her hips and pulled again. The carved cedar bow of the canoe was almost within reach, but she could not reach it. Water was beginning to slosh into the stern. No matter what she did, she could not raise it any farther. She was stuck with the stern half underwater, and the bow pointed toward the sky and toward her.

She shivered and looked to the sky as she rested and thought. Shaking her head, she looked again. It was mid-afternoon, and she did not know what she was going to do.

"Hey there! Miss Blankets."

Two Blankets looked upslope toward the call. It was Tom Clement bounding down the incline like a goat. Farther up the incline a mule waited with a second boy dismounting.

Tom arrived with a scattering of rock. "You need help, Miss Blankets?"

"What—what are you doing up here, Tom?"

"I told my Da about you. He said, even though you was an Indian, I still owed you for your help. Said it was the way people should treat each other like they was equal," Tom said. "Joseph, get down here."

"Well, I declare. You have come at the right time. I have got myself stuck here."

The second boy clattered down. He looked at Two Blankets with suspicion. "This the Indian girl that helped you, Tom?"

"This here is Two Blankets. My little brother Joseph."

"Don't see why you had to get mixed up with the likes of her."

"Da said, Indian or no, she helped me. Said I should come up here to see she made it through. Now, get down here, be polite, and grab onto that rope. And don't fall in the river."

Together they lifted the canoe up. Two Blankets was surprised at how heavy it was until all the water drained out. Then, with one heave, they popped the canoe up onto the rock where they stood, floating high and almost dry.

"We'll bring your gear up, Miss Blankets."

"You don't have to, but thank you."

"It isn't a problem," he said. "Come on, Joseph."

Two Blankets could barely hear them over the rush of the water.

"You let that kiss you?"

"Shut up. She was nice. Get her gear, and we'll tie it onto the mule."

Joseph stared at his brother, "You ain't my Da."

Tom waited him out, "What would Da say?"

His brother waited a moment, "All right. I'm moving, ain't I?" He walked downstream to Two Blankets's gear and began hauling it up to the portage path.

Tom turned to Two Blankets. "You're going to need a portage. Let's get this canoe up to the path." They floated the canoe down to where her gear was. Together the three of them hauled the canoe out of the water and up the shale bank.

Tom inspected the mule. "That's a good diamond hitch, Joseph. Da would be proud of you. You lead the mule, and we'll take the canoe."

Two Blankets lifted the rear of the canoe and put it over her head. Once they got it in position, it was easy if they took it slow.

This portage was three miles or so, and still, they had to be careful. The portage trail wandered away from the river for a piece then closed on it as the hillside on their right steepened. Soon they were picking their way across a narrow path alongside the edge of a seventy-five-foot gap. Two Blankets stepped along this part of the path with care.

As they paced the trail, Two Blankets remembered the last time she had portaged along this portion of the *Nch'i-wána*, a day much like this one, though later in the summer. A day when the Stinging Nettle's *mistshimus* and Two Blankets's only friend, *Nika*, babbled on about this and that. She was there, then she was over the edge, held only by a leather cord tying the two together. Then Stinging Nettle had cut her loose. It saved the canoe, but the look in *Nika*'s eyes as she dropped the fifty feet to lie broken on the rocks below still haunted Two Blankets. The rocks *Nika* fell onto couldn't even be seen—only the violence of the river.

At the end of this section, both Two Blankets and Tom lowered the canoe with relief. "I hate that section," Tom said, "but you handled your end just as good as a man."

Two Blankets smiled down at Tom. He was only twelve summers, mahap thirteen. "I take that as a compliment, Tom."

"It will be easier to paddle the canoe the three miles or so to the next portage. No point in repacking the mule."

They lowered the canoe the forty or so feet down the embankment to the water. Tom looked up at his brother. "Joseph, get down here."

Joseph woke from his daydream and slowly clambered down. "What?"

"If Miss Two Blankets don't mind, you can paddle this next section." He cast his inquiring look to her.

"Get in front, Joseph."

"I'll lead the mule and meet you at the next portage. That's a short one," Tom said and climbed back up to the mule.

Two Blankets climbed into the back of the canoe, and they started paddling. "I will need you to keep a sharp eye out for rocks, Joseph."

Enlivened by her confidence, he straightened his back and searched the water ahead. Two Blankets could see just as well from the rear, but the added responsibility etched a new confidence on the young boy's face.

From boys are young warriors made. This she knew from her own experience.

At the next portage point, they hauled the canoe up the bank and sat down beneath the shade of a cedar.

"I'm tired," Joseph said, "and hungry."

"Don't complain," Tom handed him the canteen. "We didn't bring food. Drink some water."

"I have food," Two Blankets said. "Dried salmon and *camas* cakes." She opened her pack and began dividing up the food.

"Miss Two Blankets, you don't have to give away your food," Tom protested. Even Joseph agreed with his brother.

"You do the work of men, you deserve to eat like men," she smiled.

This portage was only a mile, and although the river was still violent with water sucking down over hidden rocks and spume rising high into the air, it was soon passed. A second mile and the river widened where the falls were. Two Blankets just stood there looking. Slowly, she set her end of the canoe down.

"But where are the falls? Ciello Falls? I remember them. The water dropped some thirty U.S. Government feet. Right there and all the way across."

"U.S. Government feet? There is no such thing."

"I have it on good authority there is. It is a form of measurement. Your own government said how big such feet are."

"Ah, ha. U.S. Government feet. We just call them feet. As to your other question, the water is so deep with the runoff this time of year, there ain't no falls, just a huge rush of water," Tom said.

"That is amazing."

"Ain't it, though?" Tom squinted at the sun. "We better get going. It'll be nightfall before we get home otherwise."

At the top of the falls, they repacked her canoe. "Thank you, boys. Or young warriors, I should say, after what you did for me." Joseph still looked at her, his face scrunched up under shaggy brown hair. "This is for you, Joseph," and handed him forty cents, "and for you Tom, sixty."

"You didn't need to do this, Miss Blankets. That's a man's wage."

"I did, and it is just Two Blankets. Thank you. If you two warriors ever get to Johnston's Landing, I will be there." She shook each young man's hand, and they shook hers back as serious as the men they were.

"Thank you, Miss Two Blankets," Tom said.

"I was wrong about you," Joseph said.

Then she got into her canoe and began paddling upriver on the next stage of her journey.

A short distance upriver, Two Blankets pulled over to the bank and made her camp for the night. She still had a couple hours of daylight left, so as soon as she had her furs laid out and a small fire laid, ready to be lit, she walked upstream to view the Deschutes outpouring into the *Nch'i-wána*. While no

Nch'i-wána, it was still formidable. The spring floods poured white, and Two
Blankets knew instinctively that she would be dragging the canoe by line
on the morrow. She didn't even know how far Warm Springs was up the
Deschutes, only that it was navigable by canoe. From the looks of the water
pouring down, she guessed two or three days.

*I am here. I am not at Johnston's Landing. I am alive. For that, I will be thankful.
Tomorrow I will go as far as I can. The next day will follow.*

She went back to her camp and took out her flint and steel. In short
order, she had her fire going, at first just a flicker of flame, then licking up
the larger branches to a true fire. Once her tea was steeped in the small pot
with a few hot rocks, she settled back to drink, eat some dried salmon, and
watch the night approach. Although she was afraid, even terrified of what
she had left behind, of what was to come, she also felt an aliveness that she
could almost touch.

Gray Wolf padded over and lay down with her big head upon her paws.
*You are learning, small one. For all of today, you have not thought of the man who
betrays, of the cultus wootlat.*

"I am glad you are with me, Gray Wolf. You and little White Mouse are
my guides."

Gray Wolf lifted an eyebrow and looked at White Mouse. *She would not
even make a mouthful for me. You may keep her.* Gray Wolf closed her large
green eyes.

The next morning, Two Blankets set out afoot, dragging the canoe
through the shallows. The rapids at the mouth of the Deschutes were not
nearly so intimidating as those on the *Nch'i-wána,* but the canoe kept hanging on rocks just below the surface and had to be freed. Three hours passed
before Two Blankets could climb in and begin her paddling upstream. Thus,
began her routine for the next two days. She paddled for an hour or two,
climbed out and dragged the canoe over a short rapids or occasionally a longer one, and paddled again. At one point on the first day's journey, she felt
sure she was crossing her path years ago when she had tried to outrun Wolf
Scent, the Chinook tracker, and Great Bear. She thought she could see the
spot on the east bank where she had climbed out of the canyon and camped.

Had she really only been ten years old? What had happened to that fire inside her that said, "I am *Nimi'ipuu.* I am not Chinook."

She knew, of course. It had been beaten out of her, and the *Tyee* Running
Blade had threatened her death should she try it again. Now, she was going
to him to solicit a favor, to beg a child. And what would it be like to see
Stinging Nettle? And Bone Rattler? The sense of a community teared her up.
This whiteman's way of living alone was no way for her. And what of Standing Bear? She knew, without doubt, that she loved him. Part of her hoped he
loved her too, but the stronger part hoped he had found someone else, had
moved on. And yet—and yet—she must still ask him if he would try to give
her a child. If he were married, she would have to convince his wife as well.
If worst came to worst, maybe she could ask Fox Tail, but she knew it would
not serve. Only a child by Standing Bear would give her enough strength to
leave the Chinook and go back to Marshall.

WARM SPRINGS

CHAPTER 11
APRIL, 1857

THE PADDLING HAD become routine over the last few hours. Two Blankets had been through every stage on her way here, from frustration and fear on the *Nch'i-wána*, to strained patience on the beginning of the Deschutes at the rapids, to resolution upon the paddle upriver to get here. At first, she had thought a lot about the meaning of why she was coming and fear that it would all come to naught. Now, she simply paddled, camping in the late evening and up the next day early to paddle once again. She had forgotten about actually arriving.

As she rounded a bend in the Deschutes, she glanced up. She stopped paddling, drifting with the current. There, just there, ahead of her was her destination, Warm Springs Reservation. It all seemed almost unreal. There were people about, some Chinook, she was sure, and some from other tribes. On the bank on the right side was a small dock, and she pulled up. The sun was lowering in the sky, lengthening the shadows. She pulled up and tied the canoe off. Stiffly, she climbed out.

One thing she noticed immediately was that everyone she could see, male or female, wore a covering over their *wootlat* or *busi*. After so many years among the Chinook where they wore only jewelry, or sometimes a grass skirt, that was a shock. The two men on the dock she didn't know, but they were not unfriendly, merely curious.

She straightened her red-and-white tablecloth cloak. It seemed so shabby compared to these men's clothing. "I am Two Blankets. You are *Tenino* tribe?"

The men nodded. One man approached. He said in Chinook Jargon, "We are. I am Old Father. This Crow Beak. He called that because his voice is like crow. You don't look Chinook, but you speak Chinook. You seek *Tyee* Running Blade?"

"Yes. I am Chinook, but I was stolen from the *Nimi'ipuu.*"

"Well, welcome. For *Tenino,* this Warm Springs is home. A small home, but we lived here before. For Chinook, they have a hard time, but is hard for all. *Tyee* Running Blade up that way," he pointed the way. "You can leave canoe here. It will be safe."

"Thank you, Old Father and Crow Beak." As she stepped up on the bank, she noticed the lack of trees immediately. It was like the plain above the village, above Johnston's Landing, rocky ground near the river and then grass as far as the eye could see. Looking farther, she saw the straight street with every building lined up facing the street.

On the higher ground, as the land sloped up away from the river, lay the whiteman's buildings. Several houses were complete, but they seemed to be whiteman's houses. All of these were separate from the residences for the natives. A small church with its steeple poked up into the sky above, its walls whitewashed, and she noticed what appeared to be the Indian Agent's home. A whiteman sat on his porch watching her and smoking his pipe. A mill was under active construction.

The native buildings were on the lower ground, on the riverside. Here she saw many buildings that were only partially complete, with people living beneath tarpaulin covers. A few of the native houses were finished, but two in a strange way. Though each was of unpainted wood and had the door and one window fronting on the dirt road that was not what made them unusual. What made them odd was that wide cedar boards connected them into one building, very familiar boards, from her own village. Two Blankets smiled, remembering the stripping of Johnston's Landing. This must be the "longhouse" of the *Tyee* as well as the great house of the Warm Springs Chinook.

Two Blankets approached the entrance, a skin covered hole in the cedar wall. The Bent Creek Clan still tried to live in the old ways wherever they could. Smoke drifted up from the chimneys of the two end houses as well as from a hole in the roof of the connecting section. She pushed aside the skin and entered, taking care to step down the two feet where the earth had been excavated.

For the moment, it was like stepping from Johnston's Landing into a different world entirely. Immediately, she noticed the neat piles of clothes on a shelf to the side of the door. One glance around the room and she saw that the Chinook still held to the old ways, at least here inside the *Tyee*'s "longhouse." At the far-left end, she saw the *Tyee* sitting in his usual place, though in this case, he was up at floor level of the one cabin. Bears-Many-Children sat to his left, her baby nursing upon one of her full *tatoosh*. About her hips, she wore only her usual beads, and her shoulders were bare.

Four dozen pairs of eyes noticed her entrance and silently watched her. She untied the buckskin covering and folded it up, placing it with a gesture of joining back to the tribe upon the shelf. It was warm within, and she removed her red and white over-tunic, folded it and placed it on the shelf as well. It was odd that with *tatoosh* and *busi* exposed, she felt like she had joined back to the tribe once again. It felt like home. She knew her own original tribe, the *Nimi'ipuu,* covered themselves, but this was her adopted tribe, and it felt natural and freeing to walk again among them. When the eyes saw she would join them in custom and manner, they returned to their business, though Two Blankets could hear the hushed gossiping.

She advanced slowly toward the *Tyee* and sat at an appropriate distance from him. Only ten months had passed since Two Blankets had last seen him, but the difference was remarkable. Before, he had been an older man but stood tall despite the weight of his decisions. This man before her was sadly broken, stooped under the suffering of his clan. Still, there was wisdom in his eyes.

"*Mistshimus*, I was not sure I would see you again."

"*Tyee* Running Blade, it is good to seem to be part of the clan again, though sadness brings me here."

"So, you do not come to join us in our exile?"

"Though it would bring me joy to do so, it would bring heartbreak and misfortune, as well." The enormity of what she was about to ask threatened to overwhelm her.

"Come and sit next to me, and we will talk."

Two Blankets rose and approached, sitting to his right.

"You always bring problems, *mistshimus* Two Blankets."

"I am aware of that, *Tyee* Running Blade. I am sorry for it. If there were any other way, I would not trouble you."

"Yet, you have never brought a problem that was purely your own making. And since the first day when you stood proud before me as a ten-year-old, you have had honor. I do owe you a gift for your services with the Lieutenant Sheridan when you helped with the boarding. So, tell your story. We will see what we can make of it."

"I did not help as a bargain with you. That was a *cultus potlatch.*"

"Even so. As *Tyee*, it is my honor at stake."

"You know why I cannot join you here at Warm Springs, though I long to. My love for Standing Bear would force me to violate the taboo—"

"And then I would have to kill you."

"It is not fear of that that makes me obey. It is my respect for the Bent Creek Clan." She looked down, forced her hands to stillness. She had only one chance at this.

"Often honor is more difficult to bear than fear, even fear of death."

"It is. And my husband, Marshall Johnston, is not a true warrior and no true man. I cannot bear the thought of catching a child with him. I can bear his anger, his tantrums, even his *cultus wootlat* poking at me, but the thought of a child by him breaks me."

"I can feel myself aging as we speak."

Shame washed her. "I am sorry for that. I know if I were a woman among the Chinook, whose husband could not give her a child, I could ask a man to provide me with the seed for a child. If everyone agreed to it, of course."

The *Tyee* blew out a breath. "I think I see where this is going."

"If Standing Bear could give me his seed, I would not bother you again with this. If it is against custom, or if you or he just said no, I would not bother you, either. But this is the only way I see that I can bear living with husband Marshall Johnston."

"It is not for me to deny this request, *mistshimus* Two Blankets. Though there is no precedent for it, there is no taboo that I know of that forbids it."

Two Blankets exhaled a breath she didn't even know she was holding. "Thank you, *Tyee*—"

Tyee Running Blade held up his hand. "But you will have to address this question to Stinging Nettle and Bone Rattler as well. There will be preparation. Standing Bear is married now to a *Wasco* woman. She is with child. You will have to get both their permissions, their voluntary permissions. I will not have her hurt."

"I would not deceive her or hurt her, *Tyee*."

"Leave me now. After one of your questions, I am feeling quite tired."

As she withdrew, she saw Stinging Nettle motion to her across the fire. Bone Rattler, the ancient shamaness and dreamweaver sat with her.

"Sit with us, Two Blankets, and share a cup of tea," Stinging Nettle said. She poured from a stone pot into a wooden cup. The pungent odor of raspberry wafted from the cup. "It is the last of the raspberry. I don't know where we will get more, though blackberry seems to grow rampant here."

"Thank you, Stinging Nettle. Bone Rattler, my deepest respect to you."

Bone Rattler shook the staff clasped in her bony hand, causing the bones at the top to rattle. "Bah. I don't have enough years left for deep respect. Tell us, what brings you here?"

Two Blankets told of her predicament and her request of the *Tyee*.

"You know, I have no more of the seed for Marshall Johnston," Stinging Nettle said.

"Yes, I do know that. My hope was that I might get a child from Standing Bear and have somewhat to live for when I go back. It is a slim hope, I know." Two Blankets took a sip of the tea to cover the shaking of her hand.

Bone Rattler peered at her left shoulder. "What does your little mouse have to say?"

Two Blankets smiled and looked down. White Mouse peered out between strands of her hair. "Much as always. 'Hide. Be wary. Proceed cautiously.'"

Turning to the side, Bone Rattler began speaking in some animal language that Two Blankets did not understand. Bone Rattler turned back to Two Blankets and stared through piercing eyes. "There is another. I sense her, though I cannot see her."

"There is, ancient one."

"Bone Rattler and I will approach Standing Bear on the matter. He is married now to a *Wasco* woman." Stinging Nettle turned to Bone Rattler. "There is somewhat of a precedent, the widow's sister? Though Two Blankets is not Moon Song's sister. And Two Blankets is still *mistshimus.*"

"Pah. I have never held to this *mistshimus* business. We didn't have it in the clan I came from and hadn't since before I was born. It is a miserable and destructive custom. True, Two Blankets is not a sister, but all she wants is a seed. It will not deprive Moon Song any more than if Standing Bear spilled it on the ground."

The blush rose from Two Blankets throat as she listened to the two women talk. It shamed her to have her plight discussed this way.

"Two Blankets is a sister to all of us," Stinging Nettle said. "As long as you do not seek to take Standing Bear away from Moon Song?" Stinging Nettle looked deep into her eyes as if she could see the inner Two Blankets.

"You know I do not, Stinging Nettle. Though there is nothing I would rather have than Standing Bear for myself, he is that dear to me, I would not, I cannot." Tears flowed freely down her face. "I will not. I have made my choice."

Stinging Nettle took her into her arms. "I know, dear. I am sorry, but I had to be certain." She held Two Blankets until her sobs subsided. "Bone Rattler and I will discuss this, then we will know how best to proceed. We will have some boys bring your supplies up from your canoe, and you may bed down with me."

Two Blankets settled onto the sleeping shelf near the end of the longhouse opposite from the *Tyee*'s end. This was the area of the longhouse that Stinging Nettle and Bone Rattler had taken for their own. Herbs and potions were stacked everywhere, accessible according to a system only they seemed to know. Stinging Nettle's child slept at her feet, breathing in innocence.

Bone Rattler took her fitful rest nearby, and Stinging Nettle lay with her arm over Two Blankets's shoulder. Turning over, Two Blankets looked down the dim longhouse. Most of the tribe was here, perhaps seventy people, but instead of feeling cramped and pressed in, it felt like one organism to Two Blankets, a great huge family, snoring, wheezing, and occasionally farting. Two Blankets was comforted by this.

The next day, as Stinging Nettle and Bone Rattler went about their slightly surreptitious business, Two Blankets spent time catching up with friends and the giving of the many *cultus potlatch* gifts she had brought along. She found Fox Tail and Sweet-Pollen-Flower outside. Fox Tail was curing a hide and Sweet-Pollen-Flower ground *camas* paste. She saw that Fox Tail was dressed in women's clothes. Their baby hung nearby, strapped up snug in a cradleboard. Two Blankets saw his head was not being flattened.

Both smiled at her approach. Sweet-Pollen-Flower rose and kissed her in greeting. "Dear Two Blankets, please sit with us. You can see I am with child again," she said patting her rounded belly. Fox Tail may be a Two Spirits, but somehow she managed to get me with child." She laughed.

Fox Tail blushed embarrassment, but pride suffused her face as well.

"I have brought you *cultus potlatch* gifts, just small things, some beads for you and a metal scraper for Fox Tail." Both exclaimed over their gifts. It was difficult for Two Blankets to think of Fox Tail as a man now as she looked at Two Blankets with soft eyes and genuine thankfulness.

"I was wrong to think of you as *mistshimus*, Two Blankets. Until I became Two Spirits, I did not truly understand it. I know my position is not the same as yours. I am more accepted than a *mistshimus*. Maybe one day our positions will be equivalent."

So, her day went—presenting gifts, arguing that the gifts were *cultus potlatch*, not requiring reciprocity, warm regards, and friendship. Finally, on the following day, she caught up to Bone Rattler and Stinging Nettle, who were sitting on their heels outside the doorway to the *Tyee*'s longhouse.

"Greetings to you Bone Rattler and Stinging Nettle."

Bone Rattler looked up from the herbs she was grinding just as something poked Two Blankets on the shoulder.

She turned and almost jumped. Behind her was the tall whiteman she had seen before on the agent's porch.

"Who might you be?" he asked abruptly.

Gray Wolf stood beside her, her hair standing up along the ruff. Two Blankets curled her fingers into it, and an odd ferocity trickled into her. "I might ask the same of you, sir?"

What has gotten into me?

The man puffed up, his face reddened. "I am the agent for this reservation. This is *my* reservation."

Two Blankets had become somewhat of a judge of whiteman's character, though she still had difficulty telling the difference between one and another. This one wore a "Mr. Shales" suit, though by no means as tidy as Mr. Shales. His hair was a nondescript brown and hung to his shoulders, lanky and dirty. His collar was worn and blackened at the neck.

"You haven't answered my question."

Something in his attitude stiffened her back. "And you, sir, have not answered mine."

"I am Mr. Ami Dennison, appointed by the U.S. President to be agent for this reservation, my reservation."

Two Blankets took his hand, "I am Mrs. Two Blankets Johnston, wife of Mr. Marshall Johnston, of Johnston's Landing. I am Chinook, and I thought this was Chinook land. Am I mistaken?"

White Mouse scratched at her ear, *This is very rash.*

"Well, it is Chinook land, *Wasco,* and *Tenino* land. My job is to make sure there are no problems here."

"I am visiting with my friends, Bone Rattler and Stinging Nettle. There will be no problems."

Bone Rattler gave a sharp shake to her staff, clacking the bones at the top together.

Ami Dennison started and then stared at her. "Well, see that there aren't." He backed away.

Two Blankets sank back down on her heels. "I'm sorry. I don't know what came over me," she said, shaking her head.

Bone Rattler, her head twisted to the side, studied Two Blankets. "There is something different about you," she said more to herself than to anyone else. "Well, no matter. We will talk with Standing Bear and Moon Song. You will need to be cleansed. Come with me to the moon cycle hut, and we speak of the process." Bone Rattler disappeared into the longhouse and emerged a few minutes later with several packets of twisted paper. As they walked to the moon cycle hut, Bone Rattler questioned Two Blankets.

"When did you last have your courses?"

"They started when I was journeying up here, on the second day, and ended three days ago."

Bone Rattler made some internal calculations. "So, you are likely not fertile yet. Around ten days or so is the ideal time. When did you stop taking Stinging Nettle's herbs?"

"I did not take them at all last month," Two Blankets said, embarrassed. "I did not know you knew."

"It is women's business, girl. Stinging Nettle and I have few secrets. I know about the seeds she gave you for Marshall as well. It is a difficult choice, but I do not blame you."

"I still feel some shame," Two Blankets said under her breath.

"In hard times in the past, some women would sit on their babies and kill them. Those were harsh methods but may have been justified as opposed to not having enough food and having the child starve."

They approached the moon cycle hut. It was situated some distance away from the village proper with a small creek running beside it. Several women were bathing in the stream.

"The moon cycle hut looks just like it did in the village." Two Blankets noted the small longhouse shape, with low sides, only two planks of cedar high, the cedar planked front with its hide door flap, and the roof sealed with clay.

Bone Rattler chuckled, "There were many short cedar boards leftover when we came here. And some designs need no changing." Come here to start your cleansing tomorrow night." She opened the flap. "You will do a three-day cleanse. Take each of the three packets as a tea about two handspans of the moon apart. They will make you piss, retch, and shit."

"I understand. Thank you, Bone Rattler."

"They also taste horrible. But in the end, you will be clean, inside and out. While you are here, merge with your Spirit Guide and focus on your goal, the purity of your goal."

"I will, Bone Rattler." Two Blankets watched as Bone Rattler turned and walked away, using her bone staff as a cane. Her waist-length white hair whispered in the breeze which seemed never to stop on these plains. Two Blankets did not know what to do with herself on the following day. To date, every action had led directly to the next and the next. Now, she was in a waiting period, and that was difficult for her. Glancing down at the small creek and the bathing pool, she decided to relax and let events take their course.

Easy water. I will take the path of easy water.

At the edge of the pool, she stripped off her clothes and entered the pool. Though the day was sunny, and the sky blue and bright, the water was cold, and a shiver crept up Two Blankets's legs. She squatted down and let the shiver creep over her whole body. Still, the feeling that she should be doing something would not leave her alone.

A chitter from atop of her head disturbed her pondering. *I waited for you my whole life,* said White Mouse, pulling Two Blankets's hair over her tiny white body. *Be patient.*

"I am too deep in my worrying, little White Mouse," she said aloud. Petting the top of her head, she sank down to neck deep.

I am right as usual, White Mouse said, striking a proud pose.

A rustling in the bordering grass dragged her attention back to the bank. Gray Wolf paced the ground three times in a circle, then flopped down onto her back and squirmed, kicking out her legs.

I do not like to say it, little sister, but little White Mouse is correct—

White Mouse somersaulted on Two Blankets's head, catching herself from flipping off by grabbing onto Two Blankets's hair with tiny white paws.

—this time. Sometimes, all you can do is sleep in the sun.

The sight of her spirit guide acting so "dog-like," laying on her back, with her head thrown back and tongue lolling, set Two Blankets to tittering.

Gray Wolf let out a half-hearted growl and opened one eye to stare in Two Blankets's direction.

"I am sorry, Gray Wolf. Why do you not come over here?"

I do not want to get my feet wet, little sister.

"But you are in the vision realm. How can you—"

Gray Wolf closed her eyes. *Leave the vision world to me. You have visitors.*

Two Blankets looked down across the small pool, and she indeed had visitors. One was dressed minimally in Chinook fashion, with a cape, moccasins, and a short loincloth. The other was in her first months of pregnancy and dressed more modestly. She unwrapped the cloths that covered her lower half and folded them carefully on the bank. Her *tatoosh* and full belly were covered in a finely beaded white elk skin. This and her cape she removed and folded on top of her other clothes. Finally, she slipped out of her moccasins and stepped into the pool.

The conversations between the two seemed to refer to Two Blankets. The occasional gesture in her direction indicated so. The gestures seemed to show anger.

Gray Wolf raised her head and growled deep in her throat, *That one does not like you.*

Two Blankets tried to examine the girl surreptitiously. She looked to be about sixteen and was, despite or perhaps because of her swollen belly, incredibly beautiful. Two Blankets knew she was pretty enough herself, but this girl was... ravishing. She thought it was time to leave the pool and, hopefully, leave this dispute behind.

She climbed from the bathing pool and put on her clothes, including the red and white tablecloth cape. Titters from the two in the pool raised a blush along her throat. Two Blankets remembered when she had been so proud to receive that cape.

Interesting. That color is unusual on your throat.

Now the coloring lifted to her cheeks. "I feel shame, Gray Wolf. I don't know why."

People are so strange, Gray Wolf said as she stood up and shook the grass from her coat, though there was no grass, and sneezed.

"Perhaps, it is because I have only been thinking of myself, of what I need. I have not been thinking of how my actions might affect others." She tied on her moccasins and with one final look at the two girls, walked away.

Two Blankets managed the next day, although her thoughts were troubled. She had been thinking so much about her problem with Marshall and the tribe and Standing Bear, she had not delved into who else might be impacted. Now, her situation seemed to be only magnified and made much more difficult.

The sun was just setting over the western hills. This bothered her somehow. Though she had grown up in country that was frequently like this, open and distant, that was many years ago. Now, she was used to the more confined canyon of the *Nch'i-wána*. It was comfortable to be enclosed, to not see such vistas.

Bone Rattler was waiting at the moon cycle hut. Alongside her waited the boy, Sees-What-No-One-Else-Sees. Now, perhaps five and a half summers old, he was still as excited as he was when Two Blankets had last seen him, waiting to board Bone Rattler's canoe as the tribe left the camp.

"You see, ancient one? You see?" The thrill of his vision overcame him. "She carries the White Mouse on her shoulder, and the Gray Wolf walks beside."

Bone Rattler cocked her head to examine Two Blankets. Two Blankets instinctively reached to her shoulder to confirm White Mouse. Gray Wolf leaned against her leg.

"You have the true vision, Sees-What-No-One-Else-Sees, something I can only barely sense." The boy smiled. She turned to Two Blankets. "You have the packets I gave you?"

"I do, Bone Rattler, and I thank you."

"I have done little. It is you who must first cleanse yourself and contemplate what you seek. Then you will have to seek out Standing Bear and Moon Song for their permission to do this thing. I do not know how that will work out. It is... complicated. But this you know."

"I do. I can only proceed as I must."

"When you have completed your cleansing, come back before the *Tyee*. There, you will have your answer, perhaps." Bone Rattler turned and limped slowly away, supported by Sees-What-No-One-Else-Sees, his pace making hers seem somehow natural.

Two Blankets drew the flap and entered the moon cycle hut. She immediately perceived that it was almost a duplicate to the old hut at Bent Creek, with a low ceiling and benches along the sides for sitting and resting. It was dim within, and she could almost imagine Bears-Many-Children moaning on her bench near the sweat lodge. She removed her clothing and stacked it neatly. She crawled through the flap into the darkness of the sweat lodge and sat stilling her mind, trying to focus. She knew how difficult this was. Many thoughts flitted through, too quick to catch and expel, distractions all. She knew from past experience that she must work through all these thoughts and feelings before reaching a state of quiet contemplation. She did not fight it as she once would have, choosing instead to have this be part of the process.

Patience, White Mouse said.

"I know, little mouse," she petted the sweat-soaked lanks of hair on her right shoulder. "You are ever there for me."

Yes, I am. White Mouse sat up proudly.

"Enough for the first sweat. Time to take the packet."

Two Blankets slid the flap open and crawled out. Next to the center-pole of the hut sat a stone bowl of water, a bowl she remembered from the old moon cycle hut, perhaps even a bowl that had sat in the hut for a hundred years or longer. She poured a cup of water over her head from a carved wooden cup and opened the first packet. Bitter to the taste this brew, she knew what it would do. She made a strong tea in a deep wooden bowl and waited for it to brew. When the malodorous brew had steeped to bitter perfection, she tipped the bowl up and drank it down in one gulp. She sat back on her heels and waited. Past the initial choking stage, the mixture percolated slowly down through her stomach and into her intestines.

Suddenly, she knew she had to get outside and pass this concoction. She hurried outside, barely noticing that it was now dark and squatted beside the hut. She pissed and her piss stank and burned. For a moment, a weakness passed over her as she wobbled to her feet. She brushed dirt over her spoor and staggered to the small pool next to the hut. She sank deep into it and emerged with the water sheeting off. Somehow, the stars seemed a little brighter, but perhaps that was just her imagination. Still, her perception appeared to be heightened as she walked back to the hut.

Glancing at the moon, she saw it was just rising over the sparse trees of the plains. She opened the door flap and went straight to the smaller sweat lodge. Her eyes, adjusted to the dark, took in her surroundings. It was a tiny hut with a fire glowing in the center, its smoke rising to the vent hole but still so familiar. She added another log to the fire and settled herself. Thoughts swirled in her head, and she let them. This stage would pass. Before, when she had sought her vision quest, she had fought for each stage. Now, she just relaxed into it, with a sure sense of inevitability that her focus would come. The sense of what she had come to Warm Springs for had been paramount in her mind for so long, it was an integral part of her. Indeed, her difficulty was making it a balanced piece of her life, rather than the driving force.

Passing through the flap into the outer hut, she noticed Gray Wolf laying by the doorway to the outside. She opened one eye.

"Why do you lay by the door, my friend?"

It is too hot in there. Gray Wolf closed the eye and settled herself to sleep. *I do not understand why you humans do this strange thing.*

"You are silly, my Wolf. It is to cleanse the body and the spirit."

Ah, so the prey will not smell you. That is worthwhile.

Two Blankets made the tea from the second packet. When it was brewed to sufficient strength, she drank it down. This time it had a taste of the bogs, something rotten and organic. Her reaction to the emetic was almost immediate, and she rushed out the doorway to throw up beside the hut. The taste of bile was bitter on the tongue, and she retched again. When, finally, she thought she had no more in her to throw up, she covered it and went to the pool to rinse off and wash out her mouth.

Upon reentering the hut, she saw a small, dark figure sitting there. Shorter than Two Blankets, about five-foot-tall with waist-length, glistening, raven-dark hair and a protruding belly.

"Moon Song, is it not?"

"Yes, and I know you, Two Blankets."

"Would you like some tea? I have been drinking the cleansing tea, but I have regular here."

Gray Wolf stood by Two Blankets side, her ears cocked forward and the fur on her ruff standing stiffly erect.

"No. Do not act like we are friends. We are not. I know why you have come here. Many are talking of it."

"I have come to make a request of you, it is true, but—"

The girl stood and advanced. Two Blankets saw again how incredibly beautiful she was. "You have come to steal my husband, my Standing Bear. Do you deny it?"

Beware, Gray Wolf said, *she is hostile.* A growl emanated from back in her throat.

"Yes, I deny it. It is true, I need his seed, but I would never take him. I could not."

"You have already stolen his heart." She advanced again, until she was standing directly before Two Blankets, her fists clenched, her words spat out like the cuttings from Marshall's saw. "I see how he acts, how he looks at you. You will never steal him, I say never."

White Mouse tumbled down Two Blankets hair and climbed back to her shoulder. *No, not hostile. She is afraid.*

Although Moon Song quivered with anger, Two Blankets also saw tears in her eyes. "No, I would never—" but the girl had already turned and left.

"You are right, White Mouse," Two Blankets sat down on the bench. "She is afraid, very afraid. How I will deal with this, I do not know."

Make her feel safe.

———

AFTER ANOTHER SESSION in the Sweat Lodge, she prepared the third and worst cup of tea and drank it down. She immediately passed out of the moon cycle hut and made her way to the trench some fifty paces away and squatted down. From experience, she knew that when this concoction hit it would be immediate and in this, she was not disappointed. It was revolting but necessary. When finished, she washed off in the pool and returned to the hut.

Thus, she passed the next two days until she felt both a physical weakness and a pure clarity at the same time. Though she felt faint, all her senses were awakened and hyper-aware. When she crawled from the hut, Bone Rattler and Stinging Nettle were there to greet her.

"Is there word from Standing Bear? Moon Song was here."

"You must go before the *Tyee* and see what he has to say. It is not so easy," Stinging Nettle said.

MOON SONG AND STANDING BEAR

CHAPTER 12
APRIL, 1857

TWO BLANKETS STOOD respectfully before the *Tyee* Running Blade, hands clasped before her, eyes downcast, wearing only her cape and moccasins. She was nervous, and there was nothing she could do to assist her situation or to prevent the possible demolition of her last hopes and dreams. She had done all she could think of to do. The dice were cast, and they were spinning.

"So, Two Blankets, come forward," the *Tyee* beckoned with a peremptory gesture. The kindness she'd experienced before was not present this morning.

Two Blankets stepped forward. "Yes, *Tyee*."

"You have been to the sweat lodge and fasted, contemplated upon what you request?"

"I have. *Tyee*. For three days I have cleansed myself and focused only upon that."

"And you have not changed your mind? You are fixed upon this course?"

"If you will permit it, then I am bound to attempt it, if it is possible."

"There is some precedent, though it is not exactly the same, in the Widowed Sister. Standing Bear could take you as *mistshimus* at any time, of course, but I cannot force him to. For what you wish, you will have to get permission from both Standing Bear and Moon Song. Do you understand?"

"I think I do, *Tyee*. If they refuse me, then I am refused. Both must accept my plea."

"If you are refused after three days of supplication, you must abandon your request and depart."

"I understand. It will be as you say."

"Excuse us, *Tyee* Running Blade." Sweet-Pollen-Flower stood to speak.

"You have something relevant to speak regarding this discussion?"

"We do, if we may speak of it."

The *Tyee* nodded for her to continue.

"Two Blankets has long been a member of this clan. It was in part, the fault of my own Fox Tail that she was stolen and brought to us in the first place."

"There have been many times I have rued that day, Sweet-Pollen-Flower, though I do care for her," the *Tyee* said.

Two Blankets interjected, "I do not blame Fox Tail for that long-ago event. I hope you know that, Sweet-Pollen-Flower."

"We know, Two Blankets. Though my wife is Two Spirits, it is known that she can still seed a child," she patted her swollen belly. "If Moon Song and Standing Bear refuse Two Blankets, we would be pleased to offer Two Blankets the solace of the Widowed Sister and Fox Tail's services."

Tyee Running Blade turned to her mate, "You are in agreement, Fox Tail?"

Though Fox Tail's chest was broad and flat, she wore her hair in the women's fashion, and a skirt of woven reeds covered her from waist to knee. In all other ways, she was as female as Sweet-Pollen-Flower, from her long and lowered eyelashes to her demure countenance. "It is true, *Tyee* Running Blade. I will serve, and gladly. Two Blankets has done much for the Bent Creek Clan and us. If we can give back, we will be happy to do so."

The tears threatened to overwhelm Two Blankets, but she forced them back. "Thank you, my dear friends. It means much to me."

"I pronounce then, you have three days to persuade Standing Bear and Moon Song. If they refuse you, you may seek accommodation and the solace of the Widowed Sister with Fox Tail and Sweet-Pollen-Flower."

"I understand."

"Standing Bear and Moon Song."

"Yes, father," Standing Bear stepped forward with Moon Song.

"You will go to the Privacy Tent and reside there for three days. Accept

Two Blankets, and she may spend a week with you trying for a child. Then she will leave us. Refuse her for those three days, and your trial and hers will be over."

"Yes, father, we understand." Standing Bear turned to go.

"I refuse her now. She only wants to steal my husband."

"Go now. I have spoken."

"I am sorry, *Tyee* Running Blade. I did not mean to bring this upon you or the clan."

"Break your fast now, Two Blankets. It is not your fault or your responsibility. I do hope you do not bring me a problem like this again."

"On my honor, I will not. Before I begin, I would like to visit the place of the spirits and Fire Stick's canoe, if I may?"

"Of course, Two Blankets. You are first among *mistshimus*. Sometimes I wish we were not so rule-bound. If we had not been, I could have adopted you into my family, but I could not, or I was not strong enough to challenge tradition. Go now, Two Blankets, and my wishes go with you."

After breaking her fast, Two Blankets began her short trudge up to the Sacred Grove. As she hiked up the hill behind the village, she could not see the raising place, the place where the dead were raised up in their canoes of final resting. All she could see was the slope of grass, to begin with. However, walking away from the village and its rough squalor and sense of hopelessness, she walked into a sense of peace and a greater perspective, a longer view on the world.

Soon she could see the tops of a small grove of trees poking above the summit of a hill. As the vista opened, there was a mixed deciduous and evergreen grove before her. About her was mostly just grass with the occasional pine tree, and more often a scrub oak or two, but here in this one place, overlooking the village, almost watching over it, was this small grove of trees atop the hill. This was a sacred place, a special place. There was no reason anyone could see for a grove of trees to exist here, yet here it grew.

Two Blankets did not think of it in this way, this objectively, of course. It was not in her character to examine and compare. It was in her nature to apprehend the visage and to accept it. She turned around and looked out over the canyon and the village and saw them in perspective, both visual and historical.

She turned back to the grove, eight or ten oak trees with one grown abnormally large and a few fir and pine trees. She saw at once, two canoes raised up. One was a small canoe, only five or six feet long, raised up on four posts and resting on two cross beams. This was the canoe of a child and represented the death, the first death, here at Warm Springs, a child who had died from a cause she could not guess, whether it was by accident or disease. It still must have brought sadness to the child's family and the clan as a whole.

The other was the canoe that she recognized immediately, the canoe of Fire Stick, with its several bullet holes that she remembered came from Lieutenant Phil Sheridan's troops as Fox Tail passed them with Fire Stick in his arms.

She bowed deeply to the north and south, to the east and west, and knelt before the canoe of Fire Stick. She dared not enter the grove proper. As a *mistshimus*, she did not know whether she would have permission, though she had entered the grove at Bent Creek before. There she had permission from Bone Rattler and the clan. Here she did not, and she did not need to. She was here not from curiosity, but to pay her respects. Such respect did not require proximity.

Her previous experience in Bent Creek was with the Sacred Grove in that place. She remembered that grove, and its ancient cedars, its draping moss, the sensation that only came from twenty lifetimes of reverence and respect. That grove had had a sense of perpetuity that seemed to go back in the past forever and seemed like it could go on forever. The newer canoes were brightly painted. The bones of the newly dead had a time to rest and gradually to sink into a peaceful repose. As one looked back into the grove, one could see the older corpses and their decomposing bodies and canoes. The sense was of a watchful presence that had been there as long as memory and would be there for as long as memory would continue.

This grove was new and fresh. Fire Stick was the first to watch over this grove and this village. His presence was courageous, but someone had to be first. He was alone as his canoe stood upon its frame facing the wind and weather. He had no support from the previously dead. Alone and forlorn, he looked out over the village and its future, hopeful, but with little cause for hope.

"It is sad, Fire Stick, that we should have met in such a hard way. That you should have stolen me from my family and that I should have hated you for so long. Finally, I came to think of you as friend, both you and Fox Tail, but by that time you were taken from us so quickly and so permanently. Before I had a chance to tell you. Let me just say goodbye to you. I do hope that you and the clan pass through this trial, but change is so rapid now there is no telling."

The Sacred Grove had no response. Two Blankets got up and trudged down to the Privacy Tent where Moon Flower and Standing Bear awaited.

———

TWO BLANKETS KNELT before the tent, or partial tent as the case was. It was actually the half-beginnings of a Warm Springs cottage, a floor and back wall only, covered in front by a pair of tarpaulins. Not a memorable place, but it was a place unlike others in the camp, it was private. She spread her cloak upon the ground before what one could call the doorway, an overlap in the tarpaulins, and scratched on the cloth. Then she waited.

There was no answer from within, no sign of life even, though she knew Moon Song and Standing Bear were there. Not that she had any indication that they were there, but it was inconceivable that they would not be. If the *Tyee* had said they would be there for three days, then three days it would be. She waited.

A handspan of the movement of the sun, and she scratched again. No response, and she sat back on her heels and waited once more. Two children ran by and stopped to view the tableau. Their chattering died to a low whispering, then they ran off. Thus, she passed the afternoon. She scratched again.

"Go away. There is nothing for you here," Moon Song's voice demanded.

"I am sorry, but I shall not. I am sorry, Moon Song, but this is my last chance. I will wait until you let me in to speak my needs to you and Standing Bear."

"You want to steal my husband. You shall not. I will not let you."

"I do not want to steal Standing Bear. I cannot. I cannot even remain here in Warm Springs."

There was no more response. As the afternoon waned on into the evening, every handspan of the sun's movement, she scratched again, but Moon Song and Standing Bear did not speak. A child brought her some roasted venison, *camas* cake, and a bottle of water. She ate quietly and drank of the water. When she had finished, she got up and walked to the waste trench and relieved herself. She rinsed in the stream and returned to her wait.

To begin, she thought she might get an audience immediately, or she hoped so. Now, she knew it would be a battle of wills, and a battle she did not want. She had hoped for a different outcome and knew now she would face a more difficult time convincing Moon Song if she pushed her into a corner, but it seemed there was to be no other way. She scratched again, listened again and thought she could hear them talking in low voices within.

Finally, as the moon began to rise, she lay down on her cloak and pulled it up over her. The earth gave up her warmth quickly in this season and at this latitude. Light shivers passed over her body as the night wore on, and she curled up tighter. Out of the darkness, Gray Wolf padded over to her and lay down against her curled body. Two Blankets eased closer to her and placed her hand on her ruff, mindlessly running her fingers through the soft fur. Eventually, she passed into a light sleep.

When she woke, Gray Wolf was gone. White Mouse untangled herself from Two Blankets's hair and looked around, wary. Someone must have felt sorry for her because when she woke at her usual time, before dawn, she found a sleeping fur covering her. She got up and went to relieve herself and rinse. When she returned, she found a bowl of porridge and another bottle of water. She scratched on the tarpaulin and sat back on her heels to eat and drink and wait.

All that day she sat and waited. Broken only by another meal late in the day, it passed much the same as the previous one. People went about their business as usual, paying her no mind. She thought, no mind should be paid to her. Her task was only a small thing in the life of the clan, of interest only to a few. Perhaps some would even hope that she would fail and go away, but she could not abide that. Maybe it was not fair that Moon Song should have to share Standing Bear for a few days, should have to make that sacrifice. Yet, she had also made a sacrifice—maybe the hardest sacrifice—of clan, of her life within a supporting community, and most of all her own claim to Standing Bear's affection, such as she as a *mistshimus* had any right to make.

Before she lay down that night, she scratched on the tent and spoke just the one word, "Please."

Gray Wolf lay down next to her, watchful and wary.

Toward the setting of the moon, a pair of arms surrounded her and pulled her into the tent. "Thank you," she said, curling up into his arms.

"I could not bear it any longer." He stroked her hair. "My poor, sweet Two Blankets."

Moon Song sat back separate and angry. "You shall not take my husband. You shall not."

Gray Wolf sat at the door, her head just poking through the tent flap. This was a human thing going on here and not her domain, but Two Blankets was hers and must still be protected.

Tears flowed from Two Blankets's eyes. "Moon Song, I do not intend to. I cannot take him from you. Do you not understand? I cannot take him. I cannot have him."

"He loves you. You think I cannot tell this? He speaks of you, not all the time, but when he does there is a look in his eyes. He will never love me as he loves you." Now they were both weeping.

"I know this part is true. He does love me. As I love him. Though I was not sure of this before I came here, I suspect this will always be true. We will always love each other."

"This is what I mean. If you are here, he will never be mine." She whimpered and curled up, hurt.

She held out her arm where the *Tyee* had cut her. "Do you see this, Moon Song?" The scar glistened in the firelight from shoulder to wrist. "The *Tyee* cut me when he found we had affection for each other. I am *mistshimus*. We may love each other, but such love is forbidden between title born and *mistshimus*. Yes, we may have loved each other first, but I will never have him as you have him, as your warrior and husband. I cannot even live with the clan because I cannot stop loving him. So, I must give him up, and I must also give up the Bent Creek Clan and live with a whiteman who I despise. Otherwise, I would live here, with Stinging Nettle. Maybe, I would learn to be healer. I could live with the clan, be with all the people I care about. But if I did that, I could not keep from Standing Bear. I know I could not. I would destroy him, and the *Tyee* would kill me."

"*Kill* you? He would do that?"

"He would have to. He promised, and if he did, it would destroy Standing Bear and break the clan." Two Blankets broke from Standing Bear's embrace and crawled over to Moon Song. "It is why I say I cannot take him from you. And I would not take this," she stroked Moon Song's swollen belly.

"You would not? I was so afraid, Two Blankets. I did not know you were forbidden, though I should have. I thought he would leave me—and take you—and I would be left alone with my baby."

"I would not, Moon Song, and I could not. There is another reason, as well. If I were to stay with the clan and have a child with Standing Bear, the child would be *mistshimus*, a slave. I can bear it for myself. I would never bring a child into that position."

Moon Song looked to Standing Bear. "I do not know your customs so well. This is true, Standing Bear?"

"It is as she says. My father is of the old school. Time changes many things. It will not change this in him."

She looked down upon Two Blankets, who held to her, her face wet with tears, her hand still upon Moon Song's swollen belly.

"You are so beautiful, Moon Song, with your breasts full and your belly alive with a child within." She looked up into Moon Song's eyes. "I am so sorry to bring this decision upon you. It was wrong of me, and I was thinking only of myself. Not of you. I will go now, and you shall not hear from me again."

As she lifted to hands and knees and made as if to go, Moon Song's grip tightened about her shoulders, pulling her back to her breast.

"I have made my decision. We will give you what you wish."

"What? You will?" Two Blankets lifted her head.

"Do I not have a voice in this decision?" Standing Bear's voice was a little rough and prideful.

Moon Song raised her eyes to meet those of Standing Bear. There was a firmness in her gaze he had not ever noticed before. "No. You do not. This is a decision for women. It would be my shame if we refused her. Two Blankets, though *mistshimus*, has much standing in the clan. All know of it, and many know her deeds, her honor, and what she has given up for the clan. What she asks of us is reasonable."

"But I am the one who must perform this deed. I should have a voice."

"You shall not, Standing Bear. You are the rod and the seed, nothing more. Unsheathe that staff and do your duty, your duty to me and Two Blankets."

"I would not be the cause of discord," Two Blankets began to pull away. "I will go." Somehow, this event had become as much between Moon Song and Standing Bear as the fulfillment of her request.

"You will not go," Moon Song hugged her tight to her breast. "The decision has been made."

Gray Wolf, sensing the right human decision had been made, withdrew her head from the flap and padded off into the night.

This was something Two Blankets hadn't considered. She had never thought about how it would take place, only if it would.

She was still on her knees, her hips lifted. Her skirt lifted slowly and flipped onto her back. Standing Bear's knees pressed her feet apart, then a bit further and he knelt behind her. The tension was palpable, both the physical and the emotional. Moon Song's grip tightened holding her. It was a fearsome grip, but somehow comforting as well. A grip that said, "This is going to be painful in some way. For you or for me, but we will get through it together." Though Moon Song was young, this was a mother's grasp that held her. Behind her, she sensed the tension in Standing Bear, in his every muscle. He was angry to be dismissed so, yet as he pressed against her backside, his organ was stiff and ready. He wanted this, despite his protests. She could not see above her, but she knew Moon Song and Standing Bear were locked eye to eye.

Two Blankets thought she could not bear it, the suspension of time and thought, the tightness of Moon Song's arms as she held her, the locked stares of Moon Song and Standing Bear, the pressure of his shaft against her cleft. Despite herself, she lifted her hips to the thrust she knew was coming. It pained her to admit—no, it *shamed* her to admit to herself, and to Moon Song and Standing Bear—how much she wanted this now that it was upon her. Besides her supposed husband, Marshall Johnston, who she thought of as no husband at all, and the one experience with Fox Tail, Standing Bear was the only man to take her, the only man and warrior she wanted, the only man she *needed*. He was not hers to want, but now, that did not matter. She wanted to be able to just take him and his seed as she had proclaimed. She knew it would not be that simple.

When the thrust finally came, she lifted and pressed back against him. She was already lost. Standing Bear took her all at once, penetrating and filling her with one quick and deep thrust. She was wet for him. This, too, shamed her, but she could not help it. He pulled back until just the tip of him resided within and thrust again. She cried out this time, pressed against his shaft and groin taking him deep within her. She gripped Moon Song's shoulders as she did so. Again, his shaft drove into her. Again, she cried out. Moon Song's grip upon her never lessened.

Standing Bear's thrust upon thrust continued to shake her, like a trembling last leaf in that final windstorm that will tear it from the tree. This was no light spring wind but rather the first great storm of winter. The leaf clung desperately to the bare branch, but it was known from the start that it would fail. Its grasp, though summer long, was transitory, the storm too great. This was not at all like the sex that satisfied Marshall's needs. Nor was it the gentle, yet passionate, lovemaking she had known before with Standing Bear. This was some other, some violent cleaving, wrenching thing that had now taken both of them, even taken Moon Song, as well, into its grasp. There was no release now for any of the three except for the spending of Standing Bear's seed.

His breathing was coming coarse and harsh now. His hands gripped her hips pulling her to his twisting, plunging thrusts. Three more times he penetrated her until he cried out and fell upon her back sobbing.

"Moon Song, Two Blankets. I hope I did not hurt either of you. I did not want this, but I admit that I needed it."

Moon Song stroked Two Blankets's hair away from her wet and teary face. Tears were running from her own eyes as well. "Shhh, Two Blankets. Shhh." She rocked her gently like Two Blankets was a baby in her arms. "Shhh."

The balm of Moon Song's acceptance soothed Two Blankets. "You have given me more than I asked for, Moon Song. More than I could have thought of asking for."

Moon Song just held her, as she curled into her embrace with Standing Bear laying against her back, his arms around them both. Her wetness and his seed slicked her thighs as it leaked from her, but acceptance enveloped her. Standing Bear drew the sleeping fur over them, and they settled into a peaceful sleep. There was a momentary peace upon her that she had never known before in her life.

They slept in that way for a couple of hours. Two Blankets felt Moon Song stir, and she rolled off her, onto her back. "Husband," Moon Song's voice came through her fuzzy perception.

"Moon Song." He lifted onto his elbow.

"Take her again."

"Are you sure?"

"When this is finished, you will owe me, warrior Standing Bear."

Two Blankets sat up and removed her clothes, and when she lay back down, she was surprised to find Moon Song's body behind her. Her head lay upon Moon Song's swollen belly, Moon Song's legs wrapped about her. She may have accepted the love Standing Bear and Two Blankets felt, but she was not releasing her hold upon the two of them. She would be a part of this. For some reason, Two Blankets felt the rightness of this sharing. She, after all, was the intruder here.

This time, when he took her, it was not as fierce, not as needful. They were face to face, something she could not have borne two hours before.

Her knees lifted and he slipped into her. His movements were not so fierce, but still demanding. His tempo started slow but rapidly built until his climax. He did not attend to her own climax, nor did she expect him to. She had come here with the hope of seeding a child. A climax was not needful.

He fell back from her and lay down beside her, his hand clasped across her body in Moon Song's own, his eyes looking into Moon Song's own liquid pools. Two Blankets could feel the love there where she was the intruder. Perhaps it was not as intense as the love she felt for Standing Bear, but it had a quality, a depth, that her own love might never eclipse. Somehow, since she had not come here to reignite Standing Bear's feelings for her, this comforted her. It also comforted her to be included in their love. It was, as well, disconcerting. Though she had not come for it, it hurt that Standing Bear had found a new, and perhaps, more mature love.

She fell asleep, half-castigating herself for the sensation and half plainly feeling sorry for herself.

Once more, after a suitable period of rest, Moon Song roused Standing Bear for another performance. Two Blankets took him in a half-sleep and drifted off when he had finished.

She woke, went out to relieve and clean herself and returned to the shelter. Food awaited her, and she broke her fast with a hunger that surprised her. Breakfast completed, she was allowed no time for contemplation.

"Remove your clothing and lay back on the furs," Moon Song's voice brooked no opposition. Complying, Moon Song turned to Standing Bear. "Again."

"Moon Song, three times I performed this act last night," he knelt before Two Blankets. "I am not sure I can." Though his organ was half-risen, it was not fully aroused. "Can we not rest a bit?"

The slap, when it came, surprised both Standing Bear and Two Blankets. Perhaps the true surprise came to Standing Bear's manhood, which sprung back from it and, when finished bouncing, stood proud and ready, despite the reddened area much the same size and shape as her hand.

Two Blankets looked to Standing Bear's eyes, which were angry, his body tensed. Moon Song reached across her legs as they were parted before him and grasped his cock, and not lightly.

"Is this a blade of grass bent before the prairie winds? Or is it the shaft of my warrior's spear, ever ready to plunge into the helpless deer before it?"

The anger in Standing Bear's face transformed into a smile of pride, the muscles in his tense back rippled to strength without fierceness. As Two Blankets watched, he took her firmly and as strong as the oak above the village, but his gaze never looked away from Moon Song. Somehow, she took pleasure in this. She would not take him away from Moon Song, but she would be allowed to have him, for this short period, at Moon Song's command. She allowed the sensation of him filling her to please her. Her body moved against him. She didn't care that Standing Bear loved Moon Song. For this short time, she would take him into her and please herself upon him.

This time, she did climax. As she did, she looked upon him and saw that his eyes still locked upon Moon Song's. She did not care. She had her own climax, and she was happy. Moments after, he spent his seed within her. She fell away from him, but Standing Bear fell toward Moon Song, his lips in a deep kiss upon hers, his arms about her. Two Blankets smiled. She was happy for herself, and she was pleased for Moon Song and Standing Bear as well.

Twice more Standing Bear serviced her need, though, toward the end of the last time, even Moon Song's adamant command was barely enough to prompt action. After the third time, they heard a scratching sound on the tent flap. Two Blankets rose from the sleeping furs to answer, leaving Standing Bear in a collapsed heap. She staggered to the tent flap and threw it open. The evening sunlight shone on the disarray of her hair. As she pushed it from her eyes, she squinted at the visitors.

White Mouse disentangled herself from Two Blankets's hair and peered out from behind her left ear.

Before her were Bone Rattler and Sees-What-No-One-Else-Sees.

"Bone Rattler, my greatest respect to you." Two Blankets smiled a sincere welcome. "And you have brought your young apprentice. Though this is not my shelter, I welcome you."

Bone Rattler tilted her head to the side as was her way when viewing more than the mortal realm. Her nose wrinkled and a wicked smile spread across her face. "I do not remember when I last smelled so much sex in a place."

"I blush to say it is true, ancient one."

"You should. It is a pleasant smell, like the earth in spring. Let us hope you are as fecund."

"I hope so, Bone—"

Sees-What-No-One-Else-Sees leaped forward. "You cannot see it, Bone Rattler?"

"No, child, the colors are fuzzy. I do not think I can."

"Right here," he placed his hand upon Two Blankets lower belly, "a spark, tiny, true, but as bright as day. There is another life here. A girl life, I think. You cannot see it?"

Two Blankets looked down at the small hand upon her bare belly. "Truly?"

White Mouse dangled from Two Blankets hair at her shoulders by her hind feet, *I have known since this morning. I have, I have.*

Gray Wolf gazed at White Mouse indignantly. *I do not know why humans take so long to understand such things. And why they make such a fuss when they* do.

"His eyes are sharper than mine, and his inner vision has no equal. If Sees-What-No-One-Else-Sees says you have a life within you, then I would say that you do."

"A child." Her voice was filled with wonder, the corners of her eyes moist with tears. "A child. My spirits agree, yet it is still difficult for me to believe."

"It was a lot of work, but we did it." Moon Song's arm hugged her.

"Work. If anyone did the work, it was me," Standing Bear said.

"Oh, Pah!" Bone Rattler gestured, demeaning Standing Bear's efforts. "The warrior always talks about how much work we demand, yet if we women don't want it, they are hurt. We should go and tell the *Tyee* you have been successful in your quest."

Two Blankets ducked back into the tarped area and donned her moccasins and cape. In a moment she was out before Bone Rattler.

Bone Rattler wrinkled her nose, "It is a good smell, the smell of new life, the smell of living, but you may want to bathe before presenting yourself to the *Tyee*."

Two Blankets ducked her head, sniffed, and raised it back with a scrunched-up face. "Oh, my, yes. I am embarrassed."

Moon Song grabbed her by the elbow, and they headed off for the bathing pool. Standing Bear sniffed, as well and said, "I do not understand. I don't smell anything."

Moon Song turned back, never ceasing her walk, "I can smell the sex on you from here. Come, husband. You do not need to show it off. Everyone knows you are the best."

Standing Bear shrugged and followed the group. Bathing was a necessity, and soon the whole group was striding in a companionable happiness toward the *Tyee*'s longhouse. They pushed open the flap, and Two Blankets entered first.

She stood stock still at the entrance, for the moment forgetting those that were behind her. She had been so happy, living in the present, living with the clan and all that comprised. Looking about, she saw that life going on, a life she was about to leave, probably forever. Though she thought she had been prepared for it, the actuality of the event washed her like a cold stream. At the left hand, she could see the *Tyee* and his two wives, first wife Swimming Salmon with her baby suckling upon her sagging breast and second wife Bears-Many-Children, laughing. Stinging Nettle was there with her babe as well, along with so many people she knew and liked, even loved, as a family.

The longhouse was filled with ninety or so people, all eating or in animated conversation. It was life that she admired in these people, and a life she was soon to give up. The wave of pain she felt made her partially turn away.

Bone Rattler poked her in the side with a gnarled finger. "Move on, girl."

"I am sorry. I just became aware how much all this, and all of you, mean to me."

"The spirits have a different fate for you. It will be difficult, your path. Not all are chosen for such a fate."

"I am just a girl, just a young woman—"

"Pah. Many things I do not know. I do know you are not just a girl. If you were just a girl, you would not be a daughter of the Clark. When you were abducted, we would have broken you, but we did not. You would not have earned a name, Two Blankets. I do not claim to know your fate, but I can say these old eyes see that you have one. Now, move on. My bones are tired."

"Yes, Grandmother. I know you are not my true grandmother, but you have been such to me."

"Move on, I said," and Bone Rattler pushed on past, followed by Standing Bear and Moon Song.

Two Blankets removed her cape and moccasins and left them piled neatly with her travel clothes on a shelf by the door. She began to walk to a place with the other *mistshimus* on her right near the rear of the building, but she noticed Bone Rattler speaking with the *Tyee*. The *Tyee* motioned for her to approach. Now, there was nothing to do but comply.

She approached hesitantly, and the *Tyee* gestured her forward to sit near and across from him. She sat back on her heels with her head bowed.

"Bone Rattler tells me you have been successful in your quest. You are with child?"

"*Tyee* Running Blade, so says Sees-What-No-One-Else-Sees."

"And what do your spirits say?" he frowned with a certain sternness on this last question.

"*Tyee*, I—"

"Do not deceive me, child. Though it is forbidden under pain of death, I doubt there is any *mistshimus* here who has not attempted the spirit quest. It is well known that some taboos cannot be well enforced. You, alone, have not hidden it so well."

"My spirits say it is so, as well."

"You are satisfied with your quest, then? I have fulfilled my end of the bargain, as agreed to?"

"I am, and it is a bargain well completed."

"You will not be coming back in a week or two with another request to make my life more difficult?" The stern countenance was frightening.

"*Tyee*, no, I promise I—"

Tyee Running Blade knelt up and leaning over grasped her by both shoulders pulling her to him, brushing her ear with his mouth, "I am pleased that you came and pleased with the outcome." A smile tickled the corners of his mouth as he sat back down. "It is good that you will not. Every time I see you, my life gets complicated."

"Yes, *Tyee* Running Blade."

"I will assign three paddlers and another canoe to run down the river with you tomorrow morning."

"Thank you, *Tyee*, but it is not necessary to—"

"You see, my life is made more difficult already."

"I am sorry, *Tyee*."

"Tonight, we will have a small *cultus potlatch* to celebrate."

When Two Blankets made to object, one look from the *Tyee* across the curved bone in his nose quelled her.

LOSS AND GAIN

CHAPTER 13
APRIL, 1857

TYEE RUNNING BLADE waved Two Blankets away. She rose to go back to her place with the other *mistshimus*, but Stinging Nettle caught her elbow as she walked past, drew her down beside her, and embraced her. "He can be frightening at times, our *Tyee*."

"Always, Stinging Nettle, but, even though he has said more than once he would kill me, he has ever shown me kindness as well. I love him and will miss him."

Stinging Nettle nodded, "Sit and have tea and eat with me." She plied Two Blankets with a wooden cup of tea and a carved bowl of venison and root vegetables.

As she ate and played with Squall, Stinging Nettle's babe, she felt the sense of belonging rising over her once again. Perhaps, she would not be able to have this every day, but she did have it now.

"It is frightening how fast he is growing."

"Yes, he will be a warrior like his father. If he cannot beat down his enemies with his weapon, he will scare them away with his voice." Stinging Nettle's voice was stern, but the pride she felt suffused it. "I have prepared several packets of herbs for your pregnancy and a large one of raspberry tea."

"Stinging Nettle, you know I cannot begin—"

"*Cultus,* Two Blankets. *Cultus.*" She smiled as she passed over the leaf-wrapped packets.

"Joyfully, I accept, Stinging Nettle." Though she could not reciprocate, she knew Stinging Nettle gave these small items from her heart. Though the Chinook might say *"cultus potlatch"* to indicate no reciprocal gift was required, these gifts were more of a *potlatch* from the heart. Tears stung the corners of her eyes. "I have been crying a lot since I have been here."

"Tears are good, Two Blankets. They water your spirit like the spring rains do the soil."

Fox Tail, seeing her free for the moment, came over. She hugged Two Blankets with affection. "I understand you will not be needing my services."

"No, Sees-What-No-One-Else-Sees says that I will not. We will never find out if I have improved over your 'first, worst *mamook* or your worst, first *mamook*.'"

"No, we will not," she laughed, but there was sadness there as well.

"I am sorry. I didn't mean to remind you of Fire Stick," she said, remembering that it was he who had made the remark in his usual sarcastic humor, he who had been Fox Tail's first true love and perhaps the cause of her Twin Spirits change, he who had died in the abortive raid on the whiteman's settlement.

"Now we are both crying," Fox Tail said with tears clinging to her eyelashes. "He was a strong warrior and a—"

"Burr up my Ass," both finished together.

Two Blankets looked at her. Her broad shoulders, narrow hips, and flat chest demanded she think male, but her every mannerism, posture, the long lashes, and soft looks said female. No one in the clan, including Sweet-Pollen-Flower, had a problem thinking of her as female. That was the role she occupied within the clan, and that was how Two Blankets thought of her as well.

"Sweet-Pollen-Flower and I wanted you to have this, *cultus,*" Fox Tail presented a beaver pelt. "I know that it is small, but we thought of you often when we looked at it."

The fur, when she unrolled it, was only a foot wide and somewhat longer. It was definitely a youngling. "Fox Tail, it is so beautiful, and," she rubbed the fur against her cheek, "so soft. The tanning is incredible, but I cannot accept such a gift."

"You must. It is *cultus*. And it is too small really to be useful. The blackish-brown color is unusual, as well. I cannot match it with another skin."

"I will take it in the kindness it was given, then."

The gift from Fox Tail and Sweet-Pollen-Flower opened the gift-giving gates. From children who brought her a scrap of 'special' cloth or a huge acorn to Bone Rattler's gift of the rattle of a full-grown rattlesnake. "For the spirit of your child," was all she said.

When Standing Bear approached her, she said, "You have already given me my heart's desire."

"I still have something else." He brought out a small pouch. "I do not know if you remember this, but—"

"Of course, I remember when you were beading this." It was a small pouch beaded with whiteman's beads and tiny shells. The design was non-traditional and featured a canoe portaged by tiny Chinook and above it a strange wagon on rails pulled by a single mule. "It was when you taught me about how long a mile was and about U.S. Government feet."

"And you said my beading could have been bettered by an eight-year-old."

"Yes, I did say that," she laughed, "but you deserved it for telling me about the U.S. Government feet. I have learned since that they are just called feet."

For a moment, they were just as they had been before the clan had moved, together, in a private world inhabited only by the two of them. Then Standing Bear got serious, "I would like you to have it and think of me sometimes, and please think kindly of Moon Song, as well. This has been hard for her."

Seeing the seriousness on Standing Bear's face, she made no argument. "I will accept your gift as a remembrance of our spirit journey together, which includes Moon Song, as well."

Then he kissed her, and it was not the kiss of a brother or a friend. It was short, but it was the kiss of a lover saying goodbye. He withdrew, his dark eyes locked on hers, then turned away and walked from the longhouse.

Two Blankets watched him go and saw him step over Gray Wolf, who was lying across the entry. White Mouse sat atop Two Blankets's head, observing everything and everyone. Two Blankets often did not understand either of her spirit animals, only that they watched over her.

Her mind drifted until she noticed Sees-What-No-One-Else-Sees before her. "Two Blankets. Two Blankets." He smiled with a smile that was not five and a half years old.

"Sees-What-No-One-Else-Sees, I am sorry I did not notice you."

"I know. You were thinking of Standing Bear and your baby."

"You are right, in a way. How would you know that?"

"I could tell from White Mouse," he smiled again. "She sees everything. I brought a stone, a special stone for your baby." He touched the small, dark-red, almost black, garnet to her stomach.

The stone was smooth on her belly, river-worn. White Mouse looked down at it and chittered, eyes bright. When she put her hand over it, she felt something, not a shock, but a magnetism between the stone and her egg of a child.

"I thank you, Sees-What-No-One-Else-Sees."

"Do not lose it. It is special." He was serious now. "Do not lose it."

"I will not. I will put it in here." She placed the small stone into Standing Bear's pouch.

"That is good." And then he was gone.

The evening and the event wore on and wound down. Gradually, individuals, couples, and families sought out their sleeping furs. Sweet-Pollen-Flower approached and asked, "Would you come and spend your last night with us?"

Two Blankets took her hand and allowed herself to be led to a set of furs along one wall. Fox Tail lay against the wall, then Sweet-Pollen-Flower tucked against him. Two Blankets lay down against her and Fox Tail drew a fur over all of them. She felt like she was in a seed pod with her fellow seeds or a womb with triplets. It was warm and comfortable. She was secure. She drifted and fell asleep, happy.

All rose in the longhouse before dawn, no matter the occasion of the night before or their condition. Several groaned as they got up to perform their morning ablutions and start the work of the day. The *Tyee* and the government did not allow any alcohol, so there were no hangovers.

After she had pissed and washed, Two Blankets dressed in her traveling clothes. Her simple cloak-and-moccasin garb would not do for travel into whiteman's country.

No one, in particular, waited at the landing to say goodbye to her. Waving goodbye was not the Chinook way. Nor was any extreme emotionality on parting. Everything had been spoken last night that might need to be spoken. Today was a day for work and continuance.

She searched for her *potlatch* gifts near where she had been sitting with Stinging Nettle. Everything was gone, from the little square of fabric to the beaded bag given her by Standing Bear.

"Better you should get going, Two Blankets." Stinging Nettle was breaking her fast.

"I was searching for the *potlatch* gifts."

"Drifting Smoke has taken them and stowed them in your canoe."

"Thank you. I cannot bring myself to say good-bye, Stinging Nettle."

"I cannot, either. Perhaps, that is why we do not have that custom."

Two Blankets turned to leave, and a few steps away, Bone Rattler met her at the doorway and beckoned her aside.

"Bone Rattler, you honor me."

"I don't have time for honors, Two Blankets."

"Yes, Bone Rattler. I listen."

"You were young when you came to us, young and full of piss, a fighter. There is a fact that you should keep in mind when you think of your fate. I am certain you know this. The *Nimi'ipuu* do not hide their heritage from the young, but you are a daughter of the Clark."

"I do know this fact, Bone Rattler."

"Keep it in mind when you think upon how you have been chosen. The original Clark was of the Lewis and Clark expedition. He had a son by a *Nimi'ipuu* woman, your great-grandmother. This is the warrior the *Nimi'ipuu* call the Clark, who still lives with them."

"This is true, ancient Grandmother."

"The Clark is your grandfather. Though you are *Nimi'ipuu* and Chinook, you are also whiteman. It is in your history, and somehow it seems to be in your fate, as well."

"I knew he was my grandfather. It is no secret, but I never thought of it in that way before."

"In some way, you are not destined to be only one thing. That is all I have to say. Do not forget."

"I will not, Bone Rattler. I promise."

"Get on with you then." Bone Rattler turned about to her own business.

At the landing, as the sun rose above the surrounding hills into a light blue sky, two canoes waited, hers and a larger one. Three paddlers waited as well, one of the paddlers being Drifting Smoke.

"Drifting Smoke, hello. I am glad to see you."

"Two Blankets. I am a little surprised you are glad since I was one of those who took you from your tribe."

"I am more Chinook now than *Nimi'ipuu*. I hold no resentment to you."

"I am pleased." The other canoe was loaded high, mostly with tanned hides and furs. "We will take the skins to trade in The Dalles. Bone-in-Nose and Flaming Arrow will come with us to help in your paddle downstream. Then we will portage the canoe coming back."

Two Blankets looked in the bottom of her canoe. A carved wooden box rested there, secured tightly in place.

"Your *potlatch* gifts. The box has been sealed with pitch for the journey."

Two Blankets knew how to handle a canoe, but she was no expert so took the bow spot. Drifting Smoke took the rear position. He handed her a paddle and pushed off. Bone-in-Nose and Flaming Arrow pushed off in the other, larger canoe.

AWAY FROM WARM SPRINGS

CHAPTER 14
APRIL, 1857

THIS WAS EASY water, running free with the high water of the spring melt. The hills were green with new grass, occasionally clothed in oak and fir. It was a countryside that spoke to the heart of her youth, although she had spent the last several years living in the more closed-in environs of the *Wimahl*, hemmed in by forests and the river, the wide expanse and ever-present wind riffling grass drew her. She suddenly wanted a horse, to be riding these prairies, cantering without a care and covering large amounts of ground in a hurry.

As it was, they were still covering ground quickly. It might be forty or sixty miles to the *Nch'i-wána*, depending on the twists and turns of the Deschutes, but they were hurrying there. Two Blankets didn't need to paddle. Drifting Smoke made small corrections, and the river rushed on.

"We do not need to worry about rocks in the river until we have almost reached the *Wimahl*. Then we will have a little fun."

"Fun?" she asked.

He only smiled at her question. "We will stop and eat first, then run the rapids."

As they ran the center of the river, where the current was the strongest, Two Blankets looked to the left and thought about the struggles she had experienced paddling upriver. Sometimes paddling in the slack water which she could see reflecting the blue sky above, sometimes pulling her canoe up over treacherous sections by line. She had made steady progress, but all of it was work. This was enjoyable. She could sit back and watch as the miles flew by. Finally, when the sun had passed its midpoint, Drifting Smoke steered the canoe to the bank on the west side where there was a pool of slack water. There was no beach, just a shallow pool protected by a barrier of larger rocks. They got out and clambered onto the rocks, the boats drifting below. Drifting Smoke climbed out with a *parfleche* of food.

"We will eat and rest a bit here."

They ate the dried venison and *camas* cakes, sitting on the flat-topped stone, and watched the river flow by.

"It is not such a bad place, Warm Springs," Drifting Smoke took another mouthful. "I do miss the Bent Creek, but this has its beauty."

"I cannot get used to the openness, the wideness of it," Flaming Arrow said. "It always makes me nervous."

"You are nervous whenever you leave the longhouse," Bone-in-Nose said. "It is just different. It doesn't feel like home to me either, but our children will call it home. Well, all but your children. You probably won't have any if you have to go outside."

A venison bone hit him, and they all laughed.

"Our time is waning. We have to make the best of it," Drifting Smoke said. Turning to Two Blankets, he asked, "Do you want to walk the portage? We are going to run it in the canoes. You would be safer to walk it."

Two Blankets looked out over the river and remembered the upriver hike, the white water, and the hidden rocks. "No, I will go with you."

Drifting Smoke got up and walked over to the canoe. "All right. Just hang on to your seat, and do not lose your paddle."

Bone-in-Nose opened his trousers. "I've got to piss really bad, then I will be ready to go. Flaming Arrow, you might want to walk. It is wide and white out there." He let go a stream.

"I am as ready as you are," Flaming Arrow climbed into the canoe. "Push us off."

Soon they were back in the current with Drifting Smoke and Two Blankets leading. At first the current just seemed to pick up a bit, then a bit more. The walls of the canyon closed in gradually. Now they were flying, or at least it felt like flying to Two Blankets. The water was white from bank to bank, and the canoe was dipping, pitching with each set of rocks. Two Blankets saw whirlpools that they avoided. All of a sudden, a large rock projected before them.

"Back paddle hard, right side," Drifting Smoke said. Their progress slowed, and they gradually worked to the left of the rock. "I forgot to ask. Can you swim?"

Two Blankets glanced back at Drifting Smoke. A huge smile covered his face, looking a little evil with the bone curving down from his nose. "Yes, I can swim. This is a good time to ask."

"I thought it was. Stop paddling."

She did, and they shot toward the gap left of the rock. Spray bounced into the air and into the canoe. The canoe tipped, pointed almost straight down into the cauldron of white. They raced through and into the next rapid. No time to think now. Drifting Smoke steered the canoe through with finesse and expertise. Two Blankets's eyes grew large, and a smile widened on her face.

"*Aiee,*" she heard Drifting Smoke cry out, "*aiee, aiee.*"

"*Hai, hai, ayahai,*" echoed from the other canoe, diluted and diffused by mist.

The water smoothed quickly and soon they were in a pool of almost still water. It still flowed at a pace but was undisturbed.

"So, do you wish that you had taken the portage path?" questioned Drifting Smoke, a little sarcasm coloring his voice.

"Drifting Smoke, I never imagined. Can we go back and do it again?"

He laughed. "We will beach the canoes there on the island and make camp, check the boats."

The island was reasonably large, and portions of it were swampy and covered with spring melt, but it rose some four hundred feet in small peaks to the east and west.

They paddled to the island and pulled up onto the bank just a few hundred yards beyond. The water stilled here, and Two Blankets could see grass waving just below the surface. They pulled out supplies and started to make camp. Drifting Smoke inspected first her canoe, which was a simple dugout, then the other, which had an extra plank added to give higher freeboard.

"You took damage here on the right side," he indicated the cracked plank.

Bone-in-Nose said, "Yeah, well, Flaming Arrow got a little scared there at that big stone. I had to get up and spank him with the paddle. Missed and cracked that board."

"Liar. You set up that hole wrong. I told you it was wrong."

Bone-in-Nose laughed, "Maybe that's what happened. It was fun, and I forget the details."

"Pitch that before we settle in for the night," Drifting Smoke said.

The next day they paddled downriver. Gradually, the sound of the water rushing over the falls increased until it was overwhelming.

"If this was in June or July, during the height of the flow, we might be able to run it. The falls here at Ciello are covered and smooth at that time." Drifting Smoke stopped, back-paddled, and looked over the scene. "You just cannot see from here." He paddled to the north bank and climbed out in a slack spot.

The others followed, and they scrambled up the bank and walked downriver a hundred yards for a better view. The water tumbled over what would be Ciello Falls later in the year, what Two Blankets knew would be a twenty-foot drop in some places. Now, however, it was a turbulent mass of water, filled with spray and whirlpools.

"I don't like it," Drifting Smoke said. "We might be able to run it, or—"

"I say, let's try it," Bone-in-Nose said.

"Or we, as likely, might overturn and lose everything. I think we better long-line the canoes down. It will be slower than running it, but we won't have to portage."

Drifting Smoke removed a coil of hand-woven rope of leather from the larger canoe and secured it to the bow. The other two took positions behind him as he eased the line out. As the line paid out, the canoe caught the current and the line tautened. The dugout bucked and fought the line, then rode the line more stably.

"Easy, easy. It's only a three-foot drop, but the hole below is filled with white water."

They eased the canoe closer to the edge, then the current took it. The line slipped through their fingers. The canoe went over the edge and was lost in the turbulent water below. For a moment, all Two Blankets could see was white water and spray. Then, the bow came up, buoyant and proud. The stern followed, and the canoe floated, stable and even.

"*Aiyee.* I've changed my mind about running this water," Bone-in-Nose said.

"There are a couple more bad spots." Drifting Smoke worked downriver along the bank, sometimes climbing up forty or fifty feet, occasionally sliding down to near the water level, always keeping the line taut. "Let's run her down past those next two or three cataracts, then we will come back for Two Blankets's canoe."

The remainder of the whitewater took another hour until Drifting Smoke secured the canoe to an overhanging tree. They returned for the second canoe and spent another hour duplicating the process. This canoe was lighter and was easier to control. When they reached the bigger canoe, all three warriors were sweating despite the cool April day.

"That was a bit of work," Flaming Arrow said. "I say let us take a break and eat now."

They ate dried venison and nibbled on *camas* cake. Two Blankets never tired of watching the *Nch'i-wána*. It was her life's blood in a way, her spirit's blood. The horseshoe bend of Ciello Falls was just a jumble of white water at this time of year. Beyond that, the canyon at this point widened with the vertical basalt cliffs jutting up, in some places only fifty feet and in others two hundred. The contrast in coloring from the deep gray of the basalt to the beige-orange shale at the base and above was startling and lonely to her mind. She was used to being enclosed by the deep green of tree-lined shores.

After eating, they got back into the canoes for the short three-mile paddle to the next rapids. Over this short distance, the walls of the canyon began to close in and steepen. They paddled over to near the south bank and ran the rapids. The violence of the river surprised Two Blankets, though it should not have. This was the Short Narrows, and the current was such that most of the rocks could be passed with a modicum of safety.

The river ran deep gray-green and quickened. "Hang on, Two Blankets,"

Drifting Smoke called, and then they were in it, and there was no time to think. It was white roiling water everywhere, and Drifting Smoke steered the canoe. Occasionally, he steered the small boat directly toward an area of turbulence, only to quickly navigate along its edge to a calmer area below. Several times, spray rode the air until she could not see anything but the white droplets. The little canoe seemed to bury itself nose down into the water but always rose, steady and even. Drifting Smoke was a master of the water, and Two Blankets finally gave up fearing each tumble downward, releasing her trust to Drifting Smoke.

The excitement of the event overtook her once she'd given up on her fear. If the canoe was going to go down, so be it. Until that happened, she was going to enjoy the ride. Then she realized, she really had no choice at this point.

As quickly as it had begun, they were gliding along, still moving fast but over smooth water.

"Whooee," Drifting Smoke said. "That was not as bad as I feared. Snowmelt must be early this year."

Two Blankets relaxed her hold on the sides of the canoe, letting the paddle rest in her lap, "You thought it might be worse? You have run this in worse conditions?"

Drifting Smoke laughed, "Well, I have. I thought we would make it."

She laughed with him, the laughter of fear released. "I enjoyed it, too, once I gave up being afraid."

He spun the canoe around and watched the bigger canoe come down. One last plunge and then the canoe disappeared and righted itself. The warrior shouts passed through the misty air.

"You made it all right?" Drifting Smoke asked.

"We took a little water, but all is good." Bone-in-Nose looked to the fore of the canoe. "Oh, that water is yellow. Maybe Flaming Arrow pissed himself."

Flaming Arrow took a swing at Bone-in-Nose with his paddle, which he ducked away from, laughing. "When he isn't pissing, Flaming Arrow is the best second paddler I have ever had."

"Those are not farts you smell coming from the rear of the canoe," Flaming Arrow laughed, as well.

"We'll paddle the few miles down to the Long Narrows. I think we will have to portage that. I don't want to test this river flow when it is only seventy-five feet wide."

They paddled into the edge of the current and let the canoes float, occasionally dipping a paddle in the river to correct course. It was an hour of peace sandwiched between whitewater and danger. The canyon walls steepened and closed in. Soon, Drifting Smoke steered the canoe over to the south bank and climbed out.

"We are going to have to portage from here. It is a steep lift up to the path, but between the four of us, no problems. It will take a couple of trips."

Flaming Arrow and Bone-in-Nose were already unloading their canoe. Drifting Smoke attached a line to the bow and another to the stern of theirs. Two Blankets pulled out the small box of her *potlatch* gifts and the *parfleche* of supplies and began hauling these up the steep slope. The climb was pretty much three feet up and one sliding down, but finally, she reached the portage path on top.

Drifting Smoke and the two others joined her with packets from the larger canoe. Drifting Smoke had the two lines from her canoe in hand as well. They began hauling on the two lines, she and Drifting Smoke on one, the two others on the other. It was strenuous but not very difficult.

Once it was on the path, they turned it over. "Flaming Arrow, stay here and continue with the cargo from the canoe. We'll portage down below the rapids, then leave Two Blankets to guard her canoe and jog back to get this one."

Flaming Arrow just signaled "Go" and descended to the canoe for another load. Drifting Smoke and Bone-in-Nose lifted the small canoe easily and marched off at a quick pace, followed by Two Blankets, loaded down with gear.

This was a long passage, about four miles. It wasn't difficult in rise and fall, or in the path, just long and tedious. They stopped and rested after about an hour, drank a little water. Drifting Smoke and the others were coated with sweat but not out of breath. Soon, they lifted the canoe again and moved off downriver. Two Blankets passed the point she now thought of as the *"Nika* place," the spot where her early friend had dropped off the cliff to lie broken on the rocks below.

She knew that she would never forget. "Live for me," *Nika,* Stinging Nettle's *mistshimus,* had said so many years ago. She had and would.

When they reached the end of the portage and put the canoe into the water, Drifting Smoke and the two others breathed heavily, their hands on their knees. A couple of minutes, maybe five, and they were up.

"Will you be all right here?" Drifting Smoke asked. "We are close to The Dalles, and there are some strange whitemans there, and native as well."

"There is a small stream, just downriver. I will pull the canoe up in there out of sight and wait."

"Good. We will be back by early afternoon, maybe three hours." He turned and began jogging back up the portage path.

Two Blankets loaded her gear into the canoe and paddled downriver. A few hundred yards and she turned the bow into what appeared at first to be a small inlet. This narrowed quickly into the exit of a stream. Grass covered the bottom and the sides of the stream. She grounded the canoe, got out, and began tugging the canoe up the narrow watercourse. A hundred yards and the small canyon widened somewhat into a grassy area where she had camped on her way upstream.

Two Blankets climbed out and set up her camp, collecting wood for a fire. Tonight, she decided, they would have a real meal. She lay back onto her sleeping fur and watched the birds, the fluttering leaves, and the sky. Two Blankets must have fallen asleep, for she was startled awake by the call of a jay. But it was a strange call, not entirely natural. She repeated the call back, and soon her three friends, heavily laden with packs of furs, entered her glade.

They dropped to the ground. "Whoever made up those packs wasn't thinking about a portage," Bone-in-Nose said.

"Too much of the soft life at Warm Springs," Flaming Arrow said. "You need to get out more."

"We still have one more trip with the canoe and the remaining cargo."

"Eat a little food then," Two Blankets said. "I have smoked salmon."

They took the salmon and drank from the stream. "We go now. It will be almost dark before we get back. We don't need to leave a guard?"

Two Blankets pulled out her knife and showed it. "I do not think anyone will find me here."

Flaming Arrow grunted acknowledgment, and they began jogging back down the stream. Soon, there was no sign they had ever been there.

Two Blankets broke open one of the packs of furs and laid out a sleeping place for each of the three warriors. She gathered up more wood and built up a little fire to protect against the already cooling day. She knew the warriors would be used to a cold camp but thought they would appreciate a few comforts. She put some stones into the fire to heat. When she judged enough time had elapsed, she took up the small stone pot and began heating water for tea. Opening her packet of food, she took out four smoked salmon steaks, skewered these and put them near the fire to heat. They would have to deal with warmed over *camas* cakes, but she did find some fresh young cattail roots and some very young watercress along the river edge of the stream.

She lost track of time and was just finishing her gathering when the canoe surprised her. The three warriors were laughing tiredly but with the spirit of a well completed day as they turned the canoe into the inlet. Two Blankets waved with her free hand and walked up the stream ahead of the canoe. The cattail roots and watercress, she dropped onto a wide platter of leaves she had woven in her extra time.

The men looked with surprise on their small camp and collapsed upon their furs. Two Blankets served up warmed salmon and *camas* cakes. The roots they picked up and peeled, and they snacked on bites of watercress. Hot tea amazed them, though the four of them had to share from only two cups.

"This has been a hard day, but it has been a day to remember," Drifting Smoke said.

"We don't get so much salmon at Warm Springs. Used to be it was salmon every day until I was tired of it. Now, I miss it," Flaming Arrow gnawed off another piece.

"Even this little piece of forest reminds me of home, or what used to be home. No real big trees this high up, but even this...."

"Homesick, Bone-in-Nose?" Flaming Arrow asked.

"Always, Flaming Arrow, always."

As they pushed the canoes back into the small stream and began paddling down it, Drifting Smoke said, "Bone-in-Nose and Flaming Arrow, unload the canoe and leave the furs with Great Bear at the clan trading place above The Dalles. Then follow us to the portage at the Cascades on the south side of the river. We'll camp there. It should be late when we get in, so we'll portage her canoe in the morning."

A handspan of the passing of the sun later, they rounded the bend and saw the native trading spot a short span to the east of the whiteman's village of The Dalles. The large canoe turned out of the current, and Flaming Arrow and Bone-in-Nose raced, whooping and yelling, toward the encampment.

"Not many traders there yet," mused Drifting Smoke. "Three more months and it will be filled with different tribes, though nothing like the old days."

"Will it get better, busier, do you think?"

"I don't think so. The People are waning, and the whitemans are like a swarm of flies on a corpse, on our corpse. It is amazing what can happen in one lifetime."

Two Blankets mused. At first, they seemed so few, so lonely and miserable. We helped them when we could. Then, turn around a few times, a few summers, and Marshall came, and the steamboat. Then, another steamboat and, now, four running the river. Now, they had two paddle-wheelers just between the Cascades and The Dalles, a day's paddle. They had two boats running every day, and the portage railroad as well. For twenty lifetimes, it had remained almost the same, then, all this change in a lifetime.

It was too much for her mind to comprehend and inevitably would lead her to thinking about Marshall and Johnston's Landing. She wasn't ready to give up on her time with the clan yet. One might accuse her of avoidance of reality. She did not care. In a couple more days, her comfortable place with the clan would be history, and her ongoing struggle with whiteman's ways and Marshall would begin. The next part of her plan would begin as well. She would have her two more days of slow easy paddling, friendship, and camaraderie with her clan mates.

About noon, Drifting Smoke steered the canoe out of the current, and they made their way to the south bank. It was a relief to get out of the dugout and stretch her legs for a bit. They ate of the travel rations and drank water from the river. It was only a short break, but like everything the clan did, it entirely enveloped her attention. The river was wide and smooth here even though it ran fast, and a tremendous amount of water passed her every minute. The sky was a thin blue and the ever-present wind light. Diving birds flew over the *Nch'i-wána*, then dropped suddenly to the surface. They would disappear for a minute or two, swimming underwater, then emerge flapping hard to gain altitude.

Without speaking, Drifting Smoke looked over at her, then got up and moved to the canoe. No language was necessary. Within minutes, they were back into the current and virtually flying downriver. Though the river seemed placid, within three hours, they had traveled the twenty miles to the portage. The whiteman's portage and mule-driven railway were on the north side, so they camped on the south. It would be better to avoid the whitemans and their boats and problems.

They pulled the canoe up and made camp and a small campfire. Drifting Smoke lay back and within minutes was asleep. Though it took Two Blankets longer, there was no immediate work to do. Like a hunting cat, when you are full, and there is no work to do, sleep availed itself.

Three hours later, they were awakened by shouts and a spray of water.

"Wake up sleepers," Flaming Arrow tossed a bow line to Drifting Smoke who pulled them onto the beach.

"Bone-in-Nose will watch over the furs until we get back."

"You must have paddled hard to get here so soon," Drifting Smoke said.

"A good day. We paddled like madmen."

They flopped down on the grassy slope, half out of breath. Drifting Smoke tossed them some dried venison which they took eagerly.

"We camp here for the night, then portage Two Blankets's canoe tomorrow. Choose among yourselves who will stay here and who will go."

The next morning, as the mists rose from the *Nch'i-wána* and the sun was still below the horizon, Flaming Arrow and Drifting Smoke lifted the small canoe onto their shoulders while Two Blankets carried her *parfleche* of supplies and the little box of *potlatch* gifts. Bone-in-Nose rolled over in his furs and waved a happy goodbye. Two Blankets bent over him and gave him a kiss.

"Thank you, friend Bone-in-Nose. I will not forget you."

He looked up, still half-asleep, "Nor I you, Two Blankets," and dropped his head back onto the furs.

At the quick-pace they walked, the two-mile portage was completed quickly. Two Blankets didn't want it to be finished. This would complete another stage in her life, a happy period where nothing mattered but for the gain to be made today, or the next day. Though demanding physically, it was simple and easy emotionally. Tomorrow, she would return to her life with Marshall. Though that did not frighten her, it was going to be a trial. She hoped she was up to it.

Drifting Smoke and Flaming Arrow twisted together and dropped the canoe into the water. She was back at the portage point where she had met Little Feather and Tom Clement. Tom was not here, of course. He would be with his father at The Dalles. But Little Feather was gone, too.

I wonder if he went back to the Cayuse? Or is he just another person I have met who I will never meet again?

"We must get back to The Dalles," Drifting Smoke said.

"Thank you so much, Drifting Smoke. And to you, too, Flaming Arrow. Without your help, I would not have made it. It is too lonely to try and do it like a whiteman."

"I do not know how they exist, separate and alone, without a clan, as they do. They must buy clan members, when they need one. There are so many, they can always find one to pay."

Two Blankets loaded her box and *parfleche* into the canoe. Then, on impulse, she turned and held Drifting Smoke firmly. He stood. The Chinook were not given to public displays of affection. Slowly, he lifted his arms and hugged her back.

"You will ever be my friend, Drifting Smoke. I will carry you in my heart."

She climbed into her canoe and began paddling. She didn't see Drifting

Smoke and Flaming Arrow turn back to the portage and begin jogging back up the path. She was alone now, a day's paddle from Johnston's Landing. Letting the canoe drift to the current, she felt the tears held back rise within her. For several moments, she allowed her emotions to overwhelm her. The beginning of her voyage, her portage up over the Cascades, and her meeting with Little Feather and Tom. Even the beginning of her adventure had required the help of others, the type of support a tribe member would provide, clan help. Every step of the way, she had assistance. Tom and Joseph had helped portage her over Ciello Falls and the Narrows. At Warm Springs, she had the whole clan to depend on. In the end, even Moon Song supported her. So many helped her. Now she must change her approach.

With Marshall and the others at Johnston's Landing, she must watch out for herself. It would be a kind of low-level war, a war of conflicts, to manage. She wiped her eyes and set herself and her aim for Johnston's Landing. Two Blankets could only hope that she would get there before Marshall returned.

She began paddling again.

No hope for it. This is the path I must follow.

She paddled on, and it became a sort of mantra for her. *No hope for it. This is the path I must follow.*

Eventually, the "mantra" passed, but not so her determination. As she paddled, she sorted the possible outcomes. If Marshall were already there, she would have to pursue her path one way. If he were not, then it would be simpler, at least at the beginning. She wouldn't have an initial confrontation. With either variation, her path from there would be the same.

I am overdoing this. Perhaps, because I don't want to face it.

She stilled her mind and paddled on.

MARSHALL'S RECEPTION

CHAPTER 15
APRIL TO MAY, 1857

TWO BLANKETS PULLED up at the dock at Johnston's Landing. Glancing about, she was surprised to see how much progress had taken place. The road through the village was graded evenly and the bridge across the river complete. Stacks of raw lumber of different types and colors were everywhere, as well as in place already on several buildings. She could hear the screech of the portable steam-powered saw over everything. Everywhere, she saw men industriously at work.

Two Blankets climbed out and grabbed her *parfleche* and *potlatch* box and headed for the moon cycle hut. Big Ed was crossing in front of Marshall's hut and waved. She kept her path, and he jogged to catch up

"Hallo, Two Blankets."

Two Blankets doubled over her box as if in pain.

"Big Ed. I must get to the moon cycle hut. Is Mr. Johnston here?"

"No, ma'am. He left for Portland three days ago. Will be back the day after tomorrow, all goes right. He was pretty pissed when he came back here and saw you gone."

"That will be my problem. Thank you, Big Ed. I will talk with him when he gets back, and I get out of the moon cycle hut."

They had arrived at the hut, and he bent down to open the flap, then realized where he was. Looking sheepish, he said, "I'm sorry, Mrs. Johnston. I didn't mean to intrude on—on—on women's business."

Two Blankets looked down, as if demure. "You have not entered the moon cycle hut, so you have not intruded, Big Ed."

She could see from the flush on his cheeks that he wanted to leave. "Thank you. If you need anything?" hoping she wouldn't, Two Blankets was sure.

"Only firewood," she looked to the place where now only a few scraps remained. "It seems that mine is all gone."

"I'll get to that right away, ma'am. Right away." Big Ed was already retreating to get her firewood, anything to leave the area.

Two Blankets entered the hut and put down her *parfleche* and *potlatch* box. The hut was dim and somewhat dusty, particles circling in the now disturbed air. There on the shelf was a little dried food and below it, enough makings for the start of a fire.

She laid a small bundle of tinder. She made a nest of the dry grass and got out flint and steel, and her char cloth from the little metal box in her *parfleche*. She heard the first pile of logs dumped outside.

I must have upset Big Ed more than I thought.

She folded the char cloth on top of her flint and struck the steel with her flint. Sparks flew but didn't take. Again, she struck, and the sparks landed on the char cloth. The spark formed a small glowing crescent on the char cloth. She blew on the sparks until one suddenly began smoldering and wisps of smoke issued forth. With care, she laid the char cloth into her nest of tinder. Soon, she had a flame, then a tiny fire going in the tinder. From there, she just added twigs and bark to the fire, careful to be sure each was aflame before adding another. At length, she added a few larger sticks to her fire.

Another thump of logs startled her, and she went out to bring them in. Big Ed had brought both small and larger pieces. He departed for more wood, and she brought in the smaller logs. Another trip for some larger ones. She would need enough wood for four or five days and two fires—the main one in the hut and the fire to heat the sweat lodge.

It is so much simpler when one hut serves a whole clan. The fire is always kept up, and everyone helps. Here, it is just me.

Two Blankets made the trip to Marshall's longhouse for moon cycle pads, a knife, a glass bottle from her stash, a bottle of water, some *camas* cakes, and dried salmon. In the chicken pen, she killed two chickens by grabbing each by the head and snapping her wrist. The first chicken ran about with its neck broken for a minute before it finally realized it was dead and fell over. It took two trips before she finished her tasks. Two Blankets fed the central fire then hung the chickens in the hut over a stone bowl. She slit each one along the neck artery starting just below the earlobe and let it drain into the bowl. It ran as red as her own. That was good. That done, she went back outside to the creek and hauled water to the hut. She poured the water into a waterproof basket. After several trips to the stream, she was done. The fire was going quite merrily now, and she pushed the several heating stones into the coals.

She went into the sweat lodge and repeated the fire building process. Feeding it small sticks, then bigger ones, she deliberately kept it low.

Out again into the main hut, Two Blankets stripped off her traveling clothes. There was no point in bloodying these, and she was more comfortable naked. She placed the rocks into the basket using two sticks to raise the hot stones. They sizzled a bit when they hit the water, and a little steam rose from the surface. She placed some more rocks into the coals of the fire. This was going to be a long process. There was no point in being in a hurry.

She stripped out the rocks from the basket and placed the rocks from the fire into it. The water heated more, and she put the wet stones back into the fire and added a couple more logs.

The chickens had drained of blood. Carefully, she poured the blood from the stone bowl into the glass bottle and corked it. She rinsed out the bowl and poured the residue out into the dirt outside.

There was little to do now, so she got some salmon from her *parfleche* and sat back to nibble. She rocked on her heels.

Green eyes watched her from Gray Wolf's spot near the doorway. *You are impatient.* Her eyes closed. *When you can do nothing, sleep.*

Two Blankets took the advice to heart. She laid down on the sleeping platform and closed her eyes. She woke in a half-hour and changed the rocks in the basket. She slept again. When she woke again and placed the rocks, enough steam rose from the basket, she judged it sufficient to scald the chickens.

Grasping the chicken by the feet, Two Blankets dipped it into the hot water and swirled it for a few seconds. She withdrew the chicken, then dunked it again and swirled it again. After two more repetitions, she tested a long wing feather. It plucked, but not easily. She dipped the chicken again and swirled it around a few more seconds. This time, when she pulled out the large wing feather, it came out easily.

Good, one done. Now the water was cooled, and she had to wait for the rocks to heat once again. The feathers of the first chicken came out effortlessly. This was a long process, and much easier with a big metal pot over an outdoor fire, but that was out of the question right now. It was almost as simple to pluck ten chickens as two.

"Ah, well, what else do I have to do?"

In another hour, the water was steaming once again, and Two Blankets repeated the procedure. Two chickens plucked.

She gutted the chickens, being extremely careful not to pierce the intestines or other organs. The two chickens, she spitted and placed near the fire to roast. The heart, liver and kidneys, she wrapped in damp leaves and set them aside for later cooking.

Sitting back on the shelf, Two Blankets looked around and thought. *There were feathers everywhere.* She would need to clean those up. The hut smelled of cooking and butchered chicken, and the sweet pervasive smell of blood. True, it was chicken blood, which actually smelled a bit different than human, but it was close enough.

Two Blankets glanced outside. It was now evening and the activity, so evident before, had diminished entirely. She put on her cape and padded to the bathing pool in the creek. This was a camp full of men, so she was wary and careful. She submerged herself and scrubbed her hands to rid herself of the chicken grease, then cleaned her hair with sand. She ducked down and rinsed off, then washed her body with sand and rinsed. Finally, she felt cleansed from her long downriver paddle. She headed back to the hut.

Removing her cape, she examined the chickens. She turned them on their spits and placed the internal organs within their insulating wet leaves on the edge of the coals. Lifting the flap to the sweat lodge, she crawled in. Dark within, with only the coals for light, it was musty smelling from a month's disuse. She added two more small logs to the fire, and after a few moments the fire flared up.

Two Blankets felt the warmth rise, not at sweating level, but the temperature was climbing. Soon she was sweating, and she rocked back on her heels into a sitting position and let the heat envelop her. It relaxed her and released something tight within herself. The coming confrontation with Marshall was inevitable. It would come when it came, and there was nothing she could do about it.

After a time, she rose and crawled out. Laying down on the sleeping shelf, she fell into a light sleep. Gray Wolf lay at the entrance. White Mouse curled into her hair.

It is a dangerous path you walk, Two Blankets, White Mouse said softly.

Let it pass. Your path is set, and you will be ready. Or not. Gray Wolf opened and closed one green eye.

She awoke once and removed the chickens and the organs from the fire. Then she climbed back onto her pallet, pulled the sleeping furs up, and slept.

The next morning, she woke early. No sign within determined the time, but Two Blankets knew it was before dawn. Marshall might be returning today, or at latest, tomorrow. She built up the fire from the almost dead coals and poured a bit of blood upon it from her bottle. The sweet stench rose with the smoke. Within the sweat lodge, she built those coals into a small fire as well. She wouldn't need it anytime soon, but appearances should remain the same.

Now, there was nothing to do but wait. Two Blankets thought she was pregnant based on what White Mouse said. Her touch with White Mouse was something she believed in, but sometimes the interpretation might be unsure. But Sees-What-No-One-Else-Sees was certain. He had been excited and pointed at a specific spot. He could not understand why no one else could see it. If she had to trust, she would trust in her spirits and in Sees-What-No-One-Else-Sees. If she was not pregnant, she was lost anyway.

She left the hut in the predawn and performed her morning ablutions, then returned and lay back down.

"As Gray Wolf says, 'When you can do nothing else, sleep,'" as she let sleep take her. It surprised her that sleep could overcome her nervousness so easily. Perhaps that meant she had accepted her path and all that implied.

She woke a couple hours later and tore off a piece of chicken. Gnawing on the chicken breast, she still thought of chicken as tasteless, but it was meat. Meat was nourishing.

The rest of the day and evening passed much the same. She had no required tasks, which was unusual in her life. The only task she had was to pretend to be on her courses. Normally, that would involve cramps and some pain. It was getting to where cramps would almost be a diversion from the boredom.

Almost. My memory is not that short. Only one more day.

As night came on, she took another sweat and rinse in the stream. She ate the organ meat from the chicken. At least, that had some taste to it.

She woke before the dawn and performed her morning rituals.

The steamboat with Marshall will be here today, or so Big Ed said. Nothing to do but prepare and wait.

She built the fires up in the sweat lodge and the hut. She poured a bit of blood on the fire in the hut and got a moon cycle pad ready.

"Almost without question, Marshall will be angry enough to confront me here," Two Blankets said. "Even after the last time, he will not be able to help himself."

If he does not, what then? What if he does not even care?

A bit after noon she heard the whistle of the steamboat as it rounded the bend. A few minutes later, it pulled up to the dock. Two Blankets heard the shouting, and the shifting of cargo onto the dock. Then, she heard the commanding call of Marshall's voice directing which boxes were to go to the storage, which to the trading post, and which might be stacked for later.

Two Blankets crawled into the sweat lodge and listened. If events proceeded according to ritual, there would be a bit of drinking and trading before the steamboat pulled out and Marshall came looking for her. She stayed in the sweat lodge until she heard the steamboat engage her wheel and whistle the beginning of her trip upriver.

She crawled out, threw her cape over her head and sat back on the sleeping shelf. She poured blood on the moon cycle pad and slipped it beneath her cloak. Two Blankets waited.

Will he come? Will it be now, or will he wait until he is so angry, he can wait no more? Or will he not come at all?

She did not have to wait long.

"Where is Two Blankets?" She heard his demanding shout.

"In the moon cycle hut," Big Ed's voice. "Two days now."

"Goddammit. I want her. I want my wife out here now."

"Your pardon, Mr. Johnston, but I ain't going in there."

"I ain't afraid of her or that gawddamn hut. Get out of my way."

Two Blankets fingered the knife she held. She had to hold fast.

The tarp door was ripped open. "Two Blankets, get out here."

"My husband, Marshall. I am glad you have returned."

"I said, get out here," his feet moved tentatively into the opening.

"Husband, Marshall. You know I cannot. It is taboo. I bleed."

Marshall Johnston stepped inside. "I don't give a good gawd damn about your foolish taboos. I want to talk with you."

Two Blankets stood. The sweat rolled off her brow. She lifted the knife with one hand until it gleamed in the firelight between them.

"We have discussed this, Marshall." The omission of the "husband" was obvious. "You have repeatedly tried to break the taboos of the clan."

Marshall eyed the knife. "Now, put that knife down. You don't scare me none," but his stance was less sure now.

"You need to fuck me so bad, you cannot wait a couple of days? Or maybe you like it bloody? You like this?" She lifted the newly blooded moon cycle pad.

"No, it ain't like that."

Two Blankets tossed the pad onto the fire between them. The red blood and whitish pad formed a sharp contrast as the fire started licking the edges.

"Get out of here," Two Blankets waved the knife at Marshall Johnston. "Get out before your blood joins my own on that fire."

"All right. I'm leaving. We'll discuss this later when you're in your right mind. Jaysus."

Two Blankets sat back down smiling. "That we will, husband Marshall. That we will."

———

TWO MORE DAYS of the same routine. Blood on the pads and on the fire. Burn the pads. Two Blankets had never been so bored before. It had not been so tedious when she had cramps to deal with, and sometimes when the clan had been here, she had company. There was an empathy and sense of community then. Now, she was alone and propagating a deception.

She thought about that. There was a necessity about it. Under other circumstances, she might have alternatives. As it was, she could see only this one. Well, she could always throw herself into the river and end it, but her drive for life was too strong for that. It had always been too strong from the early days when she had been first abducted. She had maintained her integrity. This time, it was her integrity that was at stake.

Did Marshall deserve integrity from her? She felt that he did not, though honesty came from within, no matter if the antagonist deserved it. It still confused her to some extent, but her course was set.

She emerged from the hut in the early evening hours. There was a glow to the light surrounding her, a heightened sense of the buildings, a stark contrast between light and dark.

Was it a true contrast? Or was it just that her senses were more alive, more perceptive? She headed to the Johnston trading post. He was working at the outside table, a whiskey bottle half-drunk on the table.

"Good evening, husband Marshall. I hope everything goes well with you."

"So, bitch, you have finally come out to join me and do your duties?"

"Husband Marshall, you know I do not control my courses. You know of the taboo and the moon cycle hut."

"That was why you had to leave for a month?"

"Husband Marshall, the last time you left me alone, your employee tried to rape me. This is a rough camp of tough men, and I have only you, Big Ed, and a few others to protect me. To protect your wife."

"Well, you are right about that. Though, I suspect, the way you handle a knife, you are not exactly helpless."

Two Blankets looked down and let a few moments pass. "I'm sorry about that husband. I was upset and frightened. You surprised me. I am sorry, truly I am. Forgive me?" Her voice was meek and demure.

"You are going to have to do me awful good to make up for a month," Marshall looked her over, his eyes glistening.

She edged up to him, "Should we start now? To make up for time lost?"

Marshall looked about, thought for a moment. "No work pressing. Now would be good."

Two Blankets took his hand, but he turned her and threw her over his shoulder. She giggled. His hand slipped up and grasped her firmly by the buttocks. "You are going to be awful good, Two Blankets, awful good."

He threw her down on the sleeping furs and within seconds had his trousers down. He pushed into her. Two Blankets tried to show no dislike of the act. Marshall worked his organ within her.

I must appear to enjoy this. For me. For Standing Bear. For my child. It is a deception, but it is necessary.

Fortunately for Two Blankets, Marshall did not last any longer than usual. Within a few minutes, he was done, and he fell onto his side panting.

She girded herself, "I hope that is not all you have for me tonight, after such a long absence, husband Marshall."

Marshall chuckled, "Give me a chance to rest up for a bit, and I will show you how much you have missed."

"Good. There has been much activity here since I was gone. In only a month. I am impressed."

"Since those damned Indians have left, we have made real progress with the road and the bridge. I don't know how your people ever lived in these shacks. I'm gonna build a real house where the *Tyee's* longhouse was with windows, a door, front porch, and all." He lay back and crossed his arms behind his head. "Two stories with a bar below and a real trading post. I got plans." Satisfaction suffused him.

A few minutes later, he took her again. His organ was small, almost tiny, which made it easier to bear physically. It did not make it any easier to bear emotionally, though.

Sometimes you must put up with discomfort temporarily, Gray Wolf said, *to gain what you want. You can do this, Two Blankets.*

I know I must, Gray Wolf. Thank you. It is only for a month, and for this month I must be convincing. I want to stab him. Instead, I must act like I like it.

So, you act. It is not that difficult. You do it for yourself, for Standing Bear, and the child. This is worthwhile.

Two Blankets wrapped her legs about Marshall's hips. For the child.

"For the child," she whispered.

"What's that, Two Blankets?"

"I want you to give me a child, husband Marshall."

He stopped pumping for a moment. "A child?"

"Yes, a child. Give me a child."

You did that very well, little one. I am proud of you.

"Hmphh," Marshall went back to his action.

Two Blankets knew she had to take caution regarding Marshall Johnston. Marshall was not a very intelligent person, in Two Blankets's opinion, but he was sly, and once he got an idea in his mind, he could worry it like a dog until something came of it. She knew if she were asked directly, she could not lie to him about Standing Bear. Not only could her integrity not bear it, but she would be unable to bear up under his digging. There was nothing for it except to go with her plan and keep him occupied.

Slipping into her whiteman's dress, she emerged from sleep into another gray predawn. Marshall was still sleeping, the red-gold hairs on his chest rising and falling with his deep breathing, one arm thrown up over his head. She stirred the damped down fire into life and added a couple of logs.

Two Blankets washed off in the stream—the dried-up seed of Marshall and the refuse of her morning ablutions. She gathered the eggs and milked the cows, then fed all the animals.

As the sun rose as a lighter gray spot in the mists above the river, she reentered Marshall's longhouse. Marshall groaned and rolled over. She took a flaming branch from the fire and went back out to the cooking fire. No one had cooked here for a week, perhaps since she had last cooked here. Laying down the branch, she built it up into a cooking-size fire in a few minutes. In a half-hour, she had her largest cast-iron pan loaded with bacon, drop biscuits cooking in another, and forty eggs mixed for scrambled eggs. So, she began her campaign to convince Marshall, and to a lesser extent, the rest of his crew of her acceptance of her position as Marshall's wife and the mistress of Johnston's Landing.

The crew drifted her way. Harry Everton, Marshall's supervisor stepped up. "Glad to see you back, Mrs. Johnston."

"Harry," she dished up a plate of food, "good to see you again too."

A man stepped up, plate in hand. "You are the carpenter, are you not? I am sorry. I do not remember your name, but I met you last year."

He was average height, had graying hair and a whip-like build, not an ounce of fat on his body. His light eyes measured her, seemed to measure everything they looked at. "Yes, ma'am. I am Henry Haroldson. These two here are my apprentices, Zebediah and Ezekiel Jones."

Two Blankets looked to the two young men behind him.

"Morning, ma'am," one said, she couldn't tell if it was Zebediah or Ezekiel. To her they both looked the same, tall for boys, close on to six feet with hair as red and frizzy as she had ever seen, and a face full of freckles, a face now blushing even brighter red.

"Morning, ma'am," the other said. Not as bright a blush, but as shy a smile.

"Morning to you both. How do you tell them apart?"

"I don't. I just shout Zeb, and whoever shows up, he's Zeb till his task is done."

"Well, I welcome you all."

Big Ed greeted her, "Morning, Mrs. Johnston."

Two Blankets smiled, "Big Ed, thank you again for helping me."

"No problem, Mrs. Johnston." He was deferential and polite as always. "You always been good to us." He took a plate, and she loaded it with eggs, bacon, and biscuit. His own mug, he filled with coffee.

"You ready for breakfast, Ike?"

"Yes, ma'am, I am."

And so, it went for Ike, the sawyer, Frank Milson, his helper, Samuel, the bullwhacker, and his boy, Kenny. Once through the regular crew, Two Blankets saw that there were another dozen new faces. It would take her a while to get to know the names and, more importantly, the personalities of each. For now, all were polite and non-resentful. Nothing like Small Willie MacKenzie and his pal Isaiah Thomas.

She hoped there were none such in this group. It was always difficult being the only woman among twenty working men. For the most part, her reputation of integrity, fair treatment of all the men, and the story of her ferocity with a knife had kept them all at a respectful distance. It didn't hurt that Frank Milson treated her with respect and Big Ed had taken up her cause. His size alone was enough to make anyone rethink his plans.

Marshall finally rolled out of the longhouse, stretched and yawned. He looked at his men eating and chatting, glanced at Two Blankets, and squinted his eyes.

"Break your fast, husband Marshall?"

Marshall just grunted, and she dished up his breakfast.

———

TWO BLANKETS ROAMED the Landing, taking in the bright sun, the blue sky, and the activity. Everywhere, there was activity—Samuel and his helper, Kenny, were up the creek with the portable sawmill, and Harry Everton seemed everywhere at once, shouting orders to some laborers stacking lumber, then jogging down to check on the carpenter and his crew. Henry Haroldson, his two apprentices, Zebediah and Ezekiel, and crew of four laborers worked energetically to install a second-floor beam on the site that had been the *Tyee's* longhouse.

She looked to the location of the former *Tyee's* longhouse. Nothing of the original remained. The longhouse that had housed a clan of the Chinook for many lifetimes was gone. As she spun in a complete circle, she saw the other longhouses were gone as well. The former houses of the shamaness, Bone Rattler, the healer, Stinging Nettle, the smokehouse, the drying and storage house for the skins, except for her own and the storehouse, all were leveled as if they had never existed.

The former home of the *Tyee* and the clan was now a framework of timber. The first floor was framed in with a stone foundation. Marshall was building to last, at least on this building. It was surprising what a carpenter, two apprentices, and three or four laborers could accomplish in two weeks. Of course, the sawyer had his order of lumber for nine months, so he had his timber supply ready to go. But still, the man was a whirlwind when he got going.

Over the next month or even six weeks, Two Blankets felt that many things were happening at once. Previously, it seemed, that her life had occurred one step at a time, with each step logically following from the one before. It was easy to tell what tomorrow would be. It would be an outgrowth of the events of today and yesterday. Now, each period of time brought surprises. She wasn't sure if this was an outgrowth of her condition, a new sensitivity to her world brought about by her condition, or if it were even true.

Each day, when I rise, I do not know what will happen today.

Gray Wolf rolled onto her back and kicked her legs into the air as if scratching fleas. *You are just now noticing this? The world is always this way.*

She noticed that there seemed to be a schism building up in the crew. The old crew was coherent and a pretty tight unit. Harry Everton had whipped them into something resembling unity. They worked rough and hard during the day. They partied hard during the night. For the most part, with the exception of hangovers, the next day they dragged themselves out for another day's work. These were generally a happy crew, given the crude nature of their work and persons. Henry Haroldson kept his own counsel. He kept his two apprentices on a short leash. They didn't drink or carouse with the rest.

The other ten or twelve laborers, depending on the week and time of day, were a separate group, whether by choice or because the others had been working together for nine months or longer. They seemed, to Two Blankets, to be of a cruder cut, rougher men who required more driving to get the job done. They were housed, of necessity, in the second storehouse.

"Goddammit." Harry Everton stormed over to their sleeping quarters. Two Blankets paused outside the first circle of men. "Get your asses out here."

Slowly, the men exited the storehouse and shambled into a sort of a line. One had a black eye. Another was favoring a leg. All looked the worse for a night's drinking.

"Everyone else is already working, been working for twenty minutes now. What the hell is your problem?"

"We're a little tired, boss. Felt like sleeping in on a Saturday." A few of the other men chuckled.

Harry Everton's face started to go red. "So, Gilly, you too tired to work today?" His voice was quiet but serious.

Gilly was emboldened, "I might be ready by lunchtime. I got me a real headache." A couple laughed, but most had caught Everton's mood and looked down at their feet.

"You just take the rest of the morning off, Gilly—"

Gilly looked left and right. "Aw, I don't need to—"

"To pack. You're on the boat out of here, soon as it comes in."

"I was just kidding."

"It weren't funny to me. You're fired. Any of the rest of you got any complaining to do?"

"No, sir," was the principal response.

"Rest of you are docked two hours' pay for wasting my time. Problem with that?"

"No, sir. That be fair. We wasn't ready."

"Get to it then. Gilly, pack your stuff and wait on the dock."

"But boss—"

"This is your third time. Two warnings are all you get."

Gilly turned away. "It just ain't fair. Small Willie was right. Y'all just a bunch of cunts. Not a man among you."

That evening Harry and Marshall sat drinking after the evening meal. "I had to fire Gilly today."

Marshall took a long draw on his bottle, "Yer the Supervisor, Harry."

"Had to make an example of one of the new men. Just happened to be

Gilly volunteered. Could have been any one of 'em, though. All a bunch of hard cases."

"Won't be so much problem with the rest, ya think?"

"Don't know."

"We don't want to lose the whole new crew."

"I want to mix up the two crews a little, maybe even mix their sleeping arrangements."

"That'll rile up the old crew. They're getting along good right now," Marshall took another drink.

"I know, but I think they can take it. We want one big crew, not two separate ones, always sniping at each other."

"Yer the supervisor. Just keep 'em working."

———

THE OTHER THING that surprised Two Blankets was Marshall. True, he was busy, excessively so, during the daytime and exhausted every evening. The potential objections and arguments she expected from him regarding her recent trip to Warm Springs were absent. In fact, she had some difficulty keeping him interested in her body.

Nevertheless, she kept at it. She didn't really care if he was interested as long as he did the deed. Every time he put his organ in her and grunted his way to satisfaction, she felt was one more time toward her eventual announcement of her pregnancy, one more substantiation of his fatherhood, one more brick in the wall that evidenced the impossibility it could be anyone else.

So, every two days, at a minimum, Two Blankets made sure that Marshall did his fathering job. Sometimes, it was twice in one day when she could manage it. A quick fuck at lunchtime, or a double before he went to sleep. Sometimes, she would surprise him when he was still asleep in the morning. She learned to be coquettish, to be appealing when she did not feel it.

In the end, it became easy. Marshall was just a man, and a simple one at that. When something he liked—and he did like it very much—offered itself, he took it. He did not think of reasons or futures, he just took.

You are getting quite good at hunting this kind of prey, Gray Wolf said one afternoon as Two Blankets lay, sweaty and sighing, after one such encounter.

"I am."

Take care. Overconfidence can make you the prey, instead.

———

ONE EVENING, HARRY and Marshall were having a drink and making plans for the week. "Here's an idea. What do you think about building the bunkhouse now? I know we weren't planning on it until later, but it might solve our problem."

Two Blankets thought Marshall would dismiss the idea out of hand, but she was surprised to see him think about it. The silence passed for some time as he pondered the idea. "We were planning on that for later in the summer, so it would only be a change in schedule. Do you think it would help, with the crew?"

"I think it would solve our major problem, the division of the crews."

"You've got a week. Take an apprentice from the carpenter and half the crew. Drive 'em hard."

The next morning Harry Everton ordered the second crew out before dawn. The crew of laborers looked confused as they gathered in front of their sleeping quarters. "You men ready to work today?"

Some grumbled a "Yes, sir." Some just looked sour.

"You ever wonder why the other crew seems to be ready to work each morning? How they seem more or less happy to do it?"

"'Cause they get the easy jobs, while we do the dirty work, begging your pardon, sir."

"That ain't it. Who do you think did the dirty work before you? They are happy, or as happy as they can be, 'cause they worked full time all winter long. What was you doing Jonesy, last January?"

All the men turned to Jonesy, a mousy man of middle age. "I was lying in an alley in Portland, trying not to freeze to death. Half the time I had to walk around all night just to stay warm."

"Right. How you follow orders this summer will determine if you stay on next winter. So, first thing, I want you to clear out and stack everything from your bunks right here."

They were angry as they removed their personal items.

"Bedding, too. Everything out. Stack it neat."

Straw filled pallets were stacked in a pile, blankets with their personal items. Every man watched their own stack with some jealousy and possessiveness. When that was done, they lined up again. Some of the other crew made crude jokes which were received with sarcastic comments from the second crew.

"Now, that shack, which you men have used as a bunkhouse, was only used to store raw hides before. You gotta decide if you're worth more than a raw hide?"

"Well, sure we are. But that was all there was."

"I want it tore down completely. Save the boards, 'cause you're going to build a new bunkhouse."

They grumbled as they set about their work. Two Blankets could see that they were not a happy crew. She did not see how this action would make them a happy crew either. But as the day progressed, she could see some change taking place. Maybe it was just the rhythm of the work, but by the end of the day, there were some talking about the new hut. Two Blankets was surprised to see most were not unhappy to bunk down in the open.

There was some joking and some claims over which bunk several would claim when they were done. One of the men from the other crew joined them and shared out a bottle. These whitemans were a strange lot. It was not like the Chinook at all. With the clan, all would have joined in joyously, or at least comradely in any joint project, even one that was a dirty job. The psyche of these men was almost not understandable. They seemed to want to be talked into what was good for them. In a few more days, she could see, they would be pulling together in this new work assigned to them.

Harry Everton talked with Marshall that evening. "I think mebbe this is going to work out, Mr. Johnston." He took a swig from the proffered whiskey bottle.

Marshall took the bottle back. "You read the situation right, Harry. That's why I got you as supervisor."

"Well, it ain't done yet. You gonna let the new crew pick their own bunks out first? Before the other crew?"

"I figure it's their right to. They built, or will have built, the damn bunkhouse." He wiped his mouth and passed the bottle back.

"That'll piss off the first crew. I know that."

"It'll give the other crew something to think about. They'll start thinking their own position ain't so secure. Keep 'em a bit nervous about next winter. Nervous crew is a hard-working crew."

And she was surprised to see that he was right, and more surprised to see how right. As the crew woke and worked each day, they seemed to pull together. There was good-natured argument over which bunks they would get. The other crew began at first by poking fun at the new crew and their living accommodations, then as the frame of the new bunkhouse began to take shape, a little jealousy that they would be second after all. In ones and twos, they began to come over to the second crew's campfire during the evening and share a bottle and a story or two. Two Blankets could see that the initial disdain had turned into a sort of envy, or if not envy in actuality, a kind of agitation, a desire to participate in something new. By the time the week was over, several of the original crew were working a few hours in the evening "Just to help out" they said.

Whatever their reasons, Two Blankets could see that the results were paying off, more than Harry or Marshall could envision.

"I'll be damned, Harry, if you weren't right." Marshall and Harry watched as the crews good-naturedly worked on the bunkhouse. It was long into their free time, but still, they worked.

"Well, I thought it might, Mr. Johnston, but I never 'spected anything like this."

"Go figure."

———

IN A WEEK or so, the bunkhouse was framed, sheathed, and roofed, though only holes were in place where the windows would eventually be. The men lined up with their gear to choose bunks. The first crew was unhappy at being relegated second place for a change but accepting of the fact. All of the bunks were more or less the same, if truth be told, other than being closer to the fire in winter or closer to the door in summer, but merely the choosing made some more sought after.

"Wonder of wonders," Two Blankets said to herself.

There is no explaining whitemans, said Gray Wolf.

"No, furry friend. No explaining them at all."

With so many things happening all at once, the expansion of the settlement, the problems of the new crews, the building of the bunkhouse and main building, her egg gathering and livestock feeding, and servicing of Marshall's needs, Two Blankets lost track of time.

One evening as they lay in the sleeping furs after one such servicing Marshall turned to her and said, "Two Blankets?"

Two Blankets was pulled from her musing by the seriousness of his tone. She was instantly aware. "Yes, husband Marshall?"

"I been thinking, don't you usually go to the women's hut about once every month."

She was confused by this question. "Yes, once every moon cycle. Just shy of a month."

"Well, I been counting. When I came back from my trip, was about a month ago." He counted weeks on his fingers. "Actually, was five weeks ago plus a day."

"Five weeks?" She counted. She had been so involved in her daily work, she had entirely forgotten her main mission this month. "It *has* been five weeks." She realized she needed to let him lead her into this discovery.

"Well, five weeks is more than a month, and a whole week longer than a lunar cycle. Moon cycle is only four weeks."

"That is true, husband Marshall."

Play it ignorant, warned White Mouse. *Let this be his wonderful discovery.*

Marshall leaned up onto his elbow, looked seriously into her face. "I don't know much about women's affairs, got enough serious work to do, but if you are due for the women's hut and you ain't had to go yet...."

"Yes, husband Marshall?"

"Mightn't that mean that you are..."

Two Blankets brought a thoughtful look to her face as if she were considering this concept. "Are you saying I might be with child, husband Marshall?"

He fell back onto the sleeping furs. "Yes. Gawds, I thought I would collapse trying to worm that out of you."

Take care, now. Take care, White Mouse said.

My head almost hurts. Is he that stupid? Gray Wolf sighed. *Every wolf bitch knows when she is with cub, and the male knows, as well.*

He is not that stupid. He is sly, and so I take care and let him think I am stupid, my friends.

"You think I am with child. I am going to have a baby." Her tone was innocent and tinged with delight. "This is wonderful news you give me. I have tried so hard and wanted it so much." There, the lie was out.

"I am glad we got that settled."

"I am going to have a baby. Oh, my husband, a baby."

Marshall got up and went to the table, poured himself a drink. "It's just a baby. Just the kind of work God made women for. Let's not get too carried away with this."

"Having a baby is a grand thing for the clan and for the family." She smiled "I am going to have a baby."